Please call Detective McLean.

Mariah was not surprised to find a pink message slip in her mail cubby. Did he feel any guilt about making accusations he could never prove? Or did he believe that he held no blame for the disruption left in his wake?

She stared with burning eyes at his name, then crumpled the slip in her fist. It would be a cold day in hell before she'd ever call him.

She was glad she'd come early, so she had time to compose herself before her first class poured into her room. She paused to look at a wall mural lovingly created by one of her former students.

Her students liked her. Remembered her. Trusted her.

Tracy Mitchell had trusted her. Had come to her for help. How could she let one of her students down because her own scars weren't fully healed?

Tracy had promise she would likely never fulfill. But it was there, and teachers were sometimes wrong about who would succeed or fail. The teenager did not deserve to be blackmailed, to have to feel that this, of all things, was her fault.

With a sigh, Mariah went to her desk and dug in her tote for her cell phone. Apparently despite the sunlight, it was really a cold day. A very, very cold day.

Somewhere.

Dear Reader,

This book continues the story begun in *His Partner's Wife* about three brothers who felt compelled to become cops because of their father's senseless murder. *The Word of a Child* touches on the damage done to lives by sexual abuse, but most of all it's about trust and the suspicions that undermine love. What if you suspect your husband or parent or child of having done something terrible? Do you accuse them and find out you were wrong to trust them? We all want to believe that our family will always back us, will always assume accusations are wrong, will always believe the best until proved otherwise.

So what if you not only fear the worst about someone you love, but you *never* learn the truth? What does it do to that person, and to you?

These, of course, are the kinds of questions that fascinate me as a writer. I love the consequences that spread like ripples, touching so many other people. Sometimes I secretly suspect we authors are always writing about ourselves, on some level: How would *I* react? What would *I* say? Feel?

Hey, who needs psychoanalysis? Just write a few books! But you notice that I cut myself a break and always allow my characters to discover the deep, priceless love that gives our lives meaning.

My hope is that you, too, will find not just escape but occasional self-discovery in the pages of my books.

Sincerely,

Janice Kay Johnson

The Word of a Child

Janice Kay Johnson

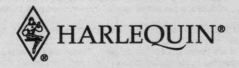

HARLEQUIN®

TORONTO • NEW YORK • LONDON
AMSTERDAM • PARIS • SYDNEY • HAMBURG
STOCKHOLM • ATHENS • TOKYO • MILAN • MADRID
PRAGUE • WARSAW • BUDAPEST • AUCKLAND

ISBN 0-373-71009-7

THE WORD OF A CHILD

With thanks to my wonderful editors at Superromance,
Laura Shin and Paula Eykelhof, who encourage me
to write the books that matter.

PROLOGUE

MARIAH STAVIG HAD NO reason to fear the unexpected knock on the door. Her husband and daughter were safely at home; she'd hung up the telephone from speaking to her mother not five minutes before. She felt only mild surprise and curiosity about who might be stopping by at seven-thirty in the evening.

Strangers, she discovered, had come calling in the form of a very large man in a dark suit and a pleasant-faced older woman, neither of whom she knew. Which were they selling, vacuum cleaners or religion?

"May I help you?" she asked.

"Are you Mariah Stavig?"

Puzzlement replaced her initial annoyance at the intrusion. "Yes, I am."

The man flipped open a leather case to show a police badge. "I'm Detective Connor McLean from the Port Dare PD."

The woman displayed identification. "Gail Cooper from Child Protective Services. May we speak with you and your husband? Is he home?"

Beginning to feel wary, Mariah said, "Yes, he's watching the Mariners."

Neither asked about the score, even though the game was critical to the Seattle Mariners making it to the World Series and most people were at least mildly interested.

"What is it?" Mariah asked. "Is something wrong?"

"It might be best if we spoke to you and your husband together," the woman said.

"Well, then…" Apprehension raised a lump in her throat as she backed up. "Come in."

They followed her into the living room. Simon, a man with dark hair and the broad cheekbones of his Slavic heritage, tore his gaze from the TV and stood politely. Three-year-old Zofie, in the midst of tumbled plastic blocks and miniature people spread over the carpet, paused with a red block in one hand and stared at the visitors.

Mariah swallowed but failed to dispel the lump. "Simon, this is Detective McLean from the Port Dare police and Ms., um…"

"Cooper," the woman said pleasantly. "Gail Cooper. I'm from Child Protective Services."

His expression didn't change, but Mariah felt her husband's immediate tension. She supposed she was feeling it herself. It was so strange, having a police officer and a social worker drop by without calling, and at this time of the day.

"What do you want with us?" he asked. "Is this about someone we know?"

"In a way." Ms. Cooper smiled at Zofie, who was alarmed enough to scramble to her feet and race to clutch her mother's leg. "It might be best if we could talk without your daughter hearing."

Real fear gripped Mariah now. Not questioning the suggestion, she boosted Zofie into her arms. "Honey, I need you to play in your room for a minute, while

Mommy and Daddy talk to these people." She started down the hall, as though her request was matter-of-fact, keeping her voice soft. "Okay?"

Zofie popped her thumb into her mouth and stared over Mariah's shoulder at the strangers until her mother turned into the toddler's bedroom.

Mariah set her on the floor beside her small table and chair. "I loved the drawing you made today. Can you draw me a new picture?"

Zofie hesitated, then sat down. Around her thumb, she mumbled, "Okay."

"I'll leave the door open so you can call if you need me."

Thumb out of her mouth, the three-year-old was already reaching into her crayon box. "Okay," she said again, obligingly. Thank heavens, she was almost always good-natured and compliant.

Simon and the two visitors stood exactly where they'd been when she'd left them, her husband stiff and still expressionless. He had turned off the baseball game.

"All right. What's this about?" he asked, voice harsh, the moment he saw her.

Mariah gave him a reproving look. "Please. Sit down. Can I get you a cup of coffee?"

The man looked at her, his light gray eyes somber. "No coffee. Thanks."

The two sat at either end of the sofa. Mariah chose the chair facing them. Simon planted himself behind her, his hands gripping the winged back of the chair.

The police officer spoke. "A child who plays with your daughter has been sexually molested."

Mariah pressed a hand to her mouth. "Who?" she asked faintly.

"Lily Thalberg."

Zofie's preschool classmate was an animated little girl with wild blond curls, bright blue eyes and enough energy and grace to make her "most likely to become a cheerleader," as her parents joked. She and Zofie weren't best friends, but these past few months they'd played at each other's homes a couple of times.

"Oh, no," Mariah breathed. "But...how? She wasn't kidnapped, was she?"

"No, her molester was apparently an acquaintance." Ms. Cooper looked straight at Simon. "I'm afraid she's named you, Mr. Stavig."

The chair jerked as Simon's grip tightened. Mariah couldn't breathe.

"This is insane! I hardly know who this kid is, and you're claiming she pointed her finger at me?"

"I'm afraid she did," the police officer said stolidly. "We're obligated to follow—"

"You dare to come here, into my home, and accuse me on the word of a three-year-old?"

"At this point, nobody is accusing you," the social worker soothed. "We simply need to ask you some questions, and inform you that we will be conducting an investigation."

"An investigation!" He shoved violently at the chair, moving it several inches despite the fact his wife sat in it. Pacing, he snapped, "How can you *investigate* something like that? It's ludicrous that you're here at all. The kid can't even talk! I can't understand a word she says." He stopped to glare at them with narrowed, glittering dark eyes. "Tell me— can you?"

The police officer's jaw muscles knotted. "Yes,"

he said, voice very level. "Even in a terrified whisper, 'Zofie's daddy,' was clear as a bell.''

Mariah's head swam. She felt distant, as if she looked down on a scene she didn't fully understand and had no part in.

Lily. Pretty, comical Lily, touched...sexually? The idea defied imagination. How could anybody do something so horrific to a child so young?

And...Simon. They were saying *he* had done it. Mariah's husband. The very idea was ridiculous! Mariah couldn't believe this was happening. Had Lily ever even met Simon, except at preschool events like the Halloween party, where too many people were around for something like this to happen?

She'd missed a couple of exchanges.

Simon was shouting, "Maybe you should be looking at *her* daddy. Did you ever think of that?"

Mariah stared at him in shock. He and Tom Thalberg had talked about the Mariners in front of the house just recently. Tom was a nice man.

Seemed to be a nice man. These people wouldn't be here if Lily hadn't been molested. *Somebody* had done this unspeakable thing.

She heard her own voice. "Was she raped?"

The police officer's cold stare for her husband turned to something gentler when he looked at her. She read sympathy in his eyes. For her, which scared her even more.

"No. We can be grateful, because she would have been injured badly if an adult male had actually penetrated her vaginally. From the standpoint of the investigation, however, the ability to gather DNA would have been helpful."

"Oh." Penetration... No. She would not imagine

Zofie, instead. No. "Then…then what?" she asked, just audibly.

He told her about oral sex and objects pushed into Lily, things Mariah wished she'd never heard. She glanced at Simon, expecting him to look as shocked, but all he did was stand across the living room from the tableau the rest of them made, his nostrils flared, fury written across his face.

"My husband would never do anything like that," Mariah said stoutly. "We have a daughter. You saw her. Zofie is fine. Surely a man who would molest another child would do the same thing to his own daughter."

"Yes." Detective McLean's voice was very soft, the gaze he kept on her husband very hard. "Unfortunately that's usually true."

They started talking about how she needed to take Zofie to the hospital to be checked, and that for her safety, Simon should move out of the house and not be alone with her while the investigation proceeded.

Simon exploded. "You want to take my wife and home and child from me? You have no evidence and no right!"

The police officer rose to his feet, his bulk suddenly menacing. "We have the word of the victim."

"Get out of my house now!"

"Daddy?" In her bright red overalls, her dark hair ponytailed, her small face pinched, Zofie stood in the hall. "Mommy? Why is Daddy yelling?"

Simon's head swung as if he were an angry bull. "Go back to your room! Now!"

Her breath hitched and tears filled her eyes. With a muffled sob, she ran.

Mariah sat rooted, unable to go after her.

Taking advantage of the interruption, Ms. Cooper said, "Mr. Stavig, if you'd just answer some questions…"

"I will answer no questions! Get out."

"Mr. Stavig, you might be able to clear this up in half an hour if you would cooperate," the social worker tried again.

"Simon," Mariah whispered. "Please."

He didn't even glance at her. "I've never been alone with this girl, I hardly know who she is. Look elsewhere for your monster."

"Monsters," Detective McLean said, "can take many forms, Mr. Stavig. Even that of a man like you."

Face contorted with anger and, Mariah thought, an effort to hide fear or even tears, Simon stalked to within a few inches of the police officer. "Out," he snarled.

The detective inclined his head. "Certainly. But we will be back, and you will answer questions." Those light, compelling eyes turned to Mariah. "Mrs. Stavig, please try to persuade your husband to help us instead of hindering. And consider taking your daughter and staying elsewhere if you can't persuade him to leave the house for the new few weeks."

They walked out. Neither Mariah nor Simon followed. She sat frozen, stunned, reluctant to look at her husband. She heard him breathing as hard as if he'd been running, or fighting.

The front door closed quietly. From down the hall came the sound of quiet sobs.

Mariah waited for Simon to say, *How can they think I would do such a thing?* Or, *Help me remember. I've never even been alone with this girl, have*

I? She waited for him, to come to her, perhaps kneel in front of her and take her hands and beg her to believe him incapable of being the monster Detective Connor McLean had named him.

Instead he turned that furious face on her and said, "You will take Zofie out of preschool so that no one else can accuse us." And then he picked up the remote control and turned on the television, as if nothing had happened.

Stiff and tired and feeling terribly afraid, Mariah stood and went down the hall to her daughter's room.

"Martinez is rounding third," the commentator crowed.

She wasn't sure Simon had even noticed she'd left the room.

If he had asked her, *Help me remember,* she would have had to say, *Last Saturday, my students did a Sunday matinee of* The Diary of Anne Frank. *You agreed to watch both Zofie and her friend Lily Thalberg. I know nothing happened, but you were alone with the girls.*

But he had not asked that or anything else. He had not been grieving for Lily, nor bewildered at such a terrible accusation. He had been in a rage that anyone would believe the word of a three-year-old child.

A child the age of his own Zofie, who was just as pretty as Lily Thalberg.

CHAPTER ONE

"Ms. Stavig? Can i talk to you?"

Mariah looked up with a smile. "Tracy! Of course you may. Come on in."

A seventh- and eighth-grade literature and drama teacher, she kept her classroom door open during her planning period specifically so that students would feel free to drop by. Most often it was the theater enthusiasts who hung around her classroom during breaks, but she wanted to be available to kids like Tracy Mitchell who were falling behind with their assignments, too.

Mariah had been grading papers in which her eighth-grade advanced lit students were supposed to be analyzing *To Kill A Mockingbird*. Josh Renfield's opening sentence was a tangle with no subject. He liked big words and multiple clauses, but basic grammatical structure apparently eluded him. Mariah laid down her red pencil with relief.

"Are you here to talk about your missing assignments?" she asked.

"No. Um…" Tracy fidgeted in front of the desk. "Can I tell you something? I mean, something…well, that I'm not supposed to?"

"Not supposed to?" Was Tracy mature enough to realize that a friend was in over her head with drugs or boys, that some secrets weren't meant to be kept?

"Mature" was not the word that leaped to mind with Tracy Mitchell, who tended to spend classes passing notes and giggling.

"Yeah." Her blond hair swung down, a curtain hiding her face. She spoke so softly, Mariah had to strain to hear. "This guy made me do things. He said no one would believe me if I was stupid enough to talk. I've been…I've been really scared."

"Scared," Mariah echoed, a chill hand closing on her heart. "Somebody threatened you?"

"I didn't think anybody *would* believe me." The girl looked up, her blue eyes full of hope. "But Lacy Carlson says you will. That you *listen* to kids."

No. Please not me, Mariah begged silently. *Choose someone else to tell.*

Even as she had the pitiful thoughts, Mariah knew she was being selfish. Tracy had come to her because she had developed a reputation among students as trustworthy. She should be glad that the teenager felt she *could* safely tell her story. She should even be flattered that the girl had chosen her. It meant she had done something right as a teacher.

But, oh, she didn't want to hear it. Not if the hearing meant she had to report the story to authorities and loose them on some man and his family.

Showing none of her inner turmoil on her face, she rose to her feet and closed the door to the hall. Coming back to the girl, Mariah placed a gentle hand on her arm.

"Why don't we sit down." She pulled a student desk to face the one Tracy chose. "Okay. Whoever 'he' is, it sounds like he doesn't want you to think anybody will believe you. Which doesn't mean they won't."

Tracy thought about that. "Maybe. Except—" she blushed "—I'm not a very good student. And I dress kind of…"

Like a slut, Mariah filled in. Aloud she said, "Provocatively?"

Tracy knew that word. She nodded.

"It's against the law for a man to rape a prostitute, you know."

"You mean, a whore?"

"That's right. In other words, your clothing or even, in the case of a prostitute, your profession do not constitute an invitation. No one can touch you without your permission." She paused a beat. "Is that what happened?"

Tracy's blue eyes filled with tears. After a moment, she gave a jerky nod.

"Will you tell me about it?" Mariah asked gently.

"The first time, he, um, just touched me."

"Where?" She kept her voice patient.

"My…well, my breasts. And, um, he kissed me."

"Did you mind? Or did you like it?"

"I guess I kind of… I mean, he's older and everything," the thirteen-year-old mumbled to the desk.

"You were flattered."

Tracy squirmed. "Kind of."

"Okay. Any of us might be."

"Only then, um, the next time he unzipped his pants and he made me touch his…you know." She was crying in earnest now, and her nose began to run.

Mariah stood long enough to grab a box of tissues and hand her several.

Tracy blew her nose.

"He made you fondle him."

"And…and put my mouth on him. He tasted…it was really gross. Especially when he…"

Mariah hid her shudder.

"Did anything more happen?" she asked quietly.

"Last time he…" She stole a look up. "He made me have sex. It hurt so bad! And I'm afraid I'll be pregnant!" With her face puffy and wet, she looked like a frightened eight-year-old, not the teen she was.

Mariah took her hands and squeezed them. "How long ago did you have sex?"

Tracy snuffled. "It was…it was the day before yesterday."

"There are morning-after drugs to keep you from being pregnant. That's the first thing we'll have to see to."

Her voice lightened. "You mean, I don't have to be pregnant?"

"No, you don't have to be pregnant." Mariah hesitated. "Tracy, is this man related to you?"

Her head ducked immediately, but she shook it no.

Actually, to the best of Mariah's knowledge, Tracy's biological father wasn't in the picture. On the two occasions when Mariah had called the mother in for a conference, she had left a different unsavory-looking boyfriend lurking in the hall. Mariah wasn't as surprised as she wished she could be that one of them, or another just like them, had molested the pretty young girl who dressed in tiny miniskirts and baby Ts that showed rapidly ripening breasts to superb advantage.

"Will you tell me who he is?"

"Will he have to know?" she whispered.

"If he's an adult, he should be punished. In the eyes of the law, you're a child. He cannot force you, or even persuade you, to have sexual relations. You did say he's older?"

Fresh tears flowed. "He's a teacher."

Mariah's heart sank even as her mouth made an *O* of surprise. Not one of the boyfriends.

A teacher. This was going to be ugly, and she wanted no part in it. Teachers were so vulnerable to these accusations. Look at her now: alone in the room with Tracy, the door closed. A student could say anything happened, and how would it be disproved?

"Oh dear," she said weakly.

"He…he told me he'd give me a good grade if I…you know. And if I didn't, he'd flunk me."

"I wish you'd reported him then and asked to be transferred from the class." She immediately regretted saying even that; she didn't want poor Tracy to feel as if what happened—assuming it had happened—was her fault in any way.

Tracy's head went down again. In a choked mumble, she said, "I thought it was kind of cool that he liked me. Even though he's *old*."

Mariah squeezed her hands again. "Who is it, Tracy?"

The seventh-grader murmured something.

"I'm sorry. I couldn't hear you."

"Mr. Tanner."

Mariah couldn't suppress an, "Oh, no."

Tracy's chin shot up. "Do you think I'm lying?"

"Did I say that?"

She yanked her hands away. "You sound like it!"

"No. I'm only…sorry. I thought he was a well-liked teacher."

"You mean, well-liked by *you*," the girl said spitefully.

"Tracy, I know him only as a colleague. We aren't personal friends. I'm on your side. I won't abuse your trust, I promise."

The flash of fear and anger faded. "Oh."

"Can you repeat your story for Mrs. Patterson?"

"The *principal?*" she said in dismay.

"She'll have to hear it, you know. And then I'm afraid you'll have to tell the police or a social worker. You may even have to testify in court."

"In court?" Tracy shrank back. "They can't just fire him?"

"It's not that simple. How can he be fired on the basis of one student saying he did something? He'll likely be suspended while an investigation goes on, but unless he admits to having relations with you, he may have to be convicted of a crime before he can be fired."

The teenager looked genuinely frightened now. "But…what if I won't talk in court?"

Mariah hated having to tell the poor girl what she'd set in motion by choosing to come to a teacher.

"Now that you've told me," she said sympathetically, "I *have* to report your story. That's the law for teachers. It would certainly be hard to convict Mr. Tanner if you won't testify. That would leave him free to molest other girls. Do you want that?" She gave Tracy a moment to reflect, then levered herself out of the student desk. "I'm going to call Mrs. Patterson to come here right now. Please stay and tell her, just like you did me. The worst is over, Tracy. It'll be easier this time, I promise."

Tracy sat hunched and small while they waited. Feeling out of her depth, Mariah talked gently about boys and how nice kisses were when both parties wanted them and how inexcusable it was for an adult to compel a child to have intercourse.

Noreen Patterson was a plump woman of perhaps forty filled with good cheer that didn't disguise her willingness to command.

The good humor faded the moment Mariah said gravely, "Tracy has something to tell you."

Tracy did haltingly tell her story for the principal. Afterward Noreen hugged her and said, "I'll call your mother. We need to talk to her."

"Will you fire him?"

The principal explained again about the necessity for an investigation, which Tracy took as an insult.

"You don't believe me!"

As Mariah had a class, Mrs. Patterson took Tracy away. She paused to murmur, "Will you come to my office at the end of the day?"

"Yes, of course."

Her seventh-graders were reading *As You Like It* aloud, stumbling over unfamiliar words and requiring constant explanations of Shakespearean language. Perhaps Shakespeare was too difficult for them, she thought, but then a student would read a passage with sudden understanding and relish for the rich language, and she would decide she'd been right to challenge them.

Today it was very difficult to keep her mind on the reading. Several times she was recalled by a loud, "Ms. Stavig? Ms. Stavig? I don't get it."

She avoided the faculty room during her break to be sure she didn't run into Gerald Tanner, the computer teacher. He was likely to seek her out, as they'd talked about doing a joint project that involved Internet research in his class and a paper in hers.

She liked Gerald, who was new at the middle school this year. A tall bony man who made her think of Ichabod Crane, he was in his late thirties and had been teaching at a community college before he'd decided to "get 'em young," as he'd put it.

Sexually? she wondered now in distaste.

But what if Tracy was lying for some reason? She might be afraid of her mother's current boyfriend who had raped her, or mad at Gerald because he was flunking her, or... The possibilities were endless. She had seemed genuinely distraught, but Mariah had thought before that Tracy, who was in her beginning drama class, had real talent on the stage.

The accusation alone could be enough to ruin Gerald's career as a teacher; such stories tended to follow a man.

She had reason to know.

Simon had lost his job after rumors got around, even though the accusation was never substantiated and he was never taken to trial. The excuse for firing him was trumped up, and he had known the real reason, but he couldn't do anything about it. Now, three years later, he lived in Bremerton, where nobody whispered, but he'd had to take a job working at the Navy shipyard that wasn't as good as the one he'd lost.

He'd lost his wife, too, but she didn't want to think about that. Not today.

This was different, Mariah told herself; the victim was old enough to speak for herself, and it might not be too late for doctors to recover sperm and therefore DNA. This wasn't anything like a child's perhaps wild—or perhaps not—accusation.

Zofie's daddy.

She would hear the quiet accusation until the day she died. Not in the little girl's voice, because she'd never seen Lily Thalberg again. After the notoriety, after the investigation had stalled, the Thalbergs had moved away, wanting a fresh start, a friend of a friend had told Mariah. No, Mariah heard her husband named as a molester in the deep, certain voice of that police officer. Detective Connor McLean. He'd believed Lily Thalberg, she could tell. It was partly his certainty that had eaten at Mariah in the days and weeks following his initial visit, when Simon became furious at her smallest, meekest question and when she began to look at Zofie and worry.

She hated remembering. Second-guessing herself, feeling guilt again because she hadn't stood behind her husband.

Why did Tracy have to come to her? she wondered wretchedly.

Her last student was barely out of the classroom when Mariah followed, locking the door behind her. In the office, the secretary said, ''Mrs. Patterson is expecting you,'' and waved her down the hall where the counselors and the principal and vice principal had their offices.

Both Mrs. Patterson and Mr. Lamarr, the vice principal, were in the office, she saw as she opened the door. But they weren't alone. A second man who had been standing by the window turned as Mariah entered.

Her breath escaped in a gasp and she stopped halfway inside, clutching the doorknob.

As the big man with short, reddish-brown hair faced her, his light gray eyes widened briefly just before his expression became utterly impassive.

Anyone but him, she thought wildly. His voice would live forever in her nightmares and as the kernel of her guilt. If it had occurred to her he might be sent... But it hadn't.

She heard herself say hoarsely, "I'm sorry, I can't..." as she began to back up.

Noreen Patterson half rose from her chair behind the desk. "Mariah, what is it?"

Her wild gaze touched on *him.* She was breathing like an untamed creature caught in a trap. "I...I just can't..." she said again, her voice high and panicky.

He said nothing, only waited at the far end of the office. A nerve spasmed under one eye, the only visible sign he understood her distress or felt it.

The vice principal had reached her. Gripping her arm, he said, "What is it? Are you sick, Mariah?"

Sick. She seized on an excuse no one would dispute.

"Yes." She swallowed. "I'm sorry. I'm not feeling very well."

Detective Connor McLean abruptly turned his back so that he looked out the window rather than at her.

"The flu is going around," Ed Lamarr said. "Here. Why don't you come in and sit down."

In? She couldn't.

But it seemed she could, because she allowed herself to be led to the chairs facing Noreen's desk. Sinking into one, she tried not to look at the broad, powerful back of the man gazing out the window.

The principal sank back into her seat. "Do you feel well enough to talk about Tracy for a minute?"

Mariah breathed in through her nose, out through her mouth. Slowly, carefully. She could be strong. He had never threatened her, never raised his voice.

He had only destroyed her marriage and her belief in both her husband and herself.

No. Her fingernails bit into her thighs. Be fair. It was childish to hold him responsible. He was not the accuser. If he had not come, it would have been someone else. He was only the messenger. The arm of the law.

Lily Thalberg's voice.

As now he would be Tracy Mitchell's.

"Yes." Miraculously Mariah heard herself sound calm, if far away to her own ears. "I'm fine."

"Ah. Well, let us know if it gets the best of you."

Mariah sat with her knees and ankles together, her spine regally straight. Poised. A lady, who would never let anything get the best of her. "Of course," she agreed.

"Then I want you to meet Detective Connor McLean of the Port Dare Police Department."

Had he recognized her, or only seen that the sight of him upset her?

He turned.

She said stiffly, "How do you do."

He nodded. "Ms. Stavig."

Noreen smiled at Mariah. "Tracy Mitchell chose to come to Mariah. She tells me 'everyone' says you can be trusted."

Mariah focused fiercely on the principal, blocking out her awareness of the police officer.

"In this case, of course, I couldn't keep what she told me confidential. In the future, students may not think I can be trusted."

"She understands that you did what you have to do."

"Did she ask you to keep what she told you confidential, Ms. Stavig?" asked Detective McLean.

Mariah stared fixedly at the pencil cup on the principal's desk. It was a crudely made and glazed coil pot, a child's effort. "No," she said. "What Tracy wanted, I think, was for Mr. Tanner to be fired. She must have realized I didn't have the power to accomplish that. She did get somewhat upset at the idea of the police becoming involved, and particularly that she might have to testify in court."

From her peripheral vision, she saw him pull a notebook from an inside pocket of his well-cut gray suit coat. "Will you repeat what she told you to the best of your memory, Ms. Stavig? I believe she may have been more expansive with you than she was with Mrs. Patterson."

"Yes. Okay." Mariah took a deep breath and began, at first disjointedly, feeling herself blush at the recitation of physical details, before pulling herself together to conclude like the articulate teacher she was.

"What was your first reaction?" the detective asked.

"That one of her mother's boyfriends…" Mariah stopped herself and felt heat in her cheeks.

The principal smiled ruefully. "The same thought occurred to me."

"Is it possible she's accusing Mr. Tanner as a smokescreen?"

When no one else responded, Mariah did. "Anything is possible."

He continued gently, relentlessly. "Tell me what you know of her home life."

Mariah did, watching from the corner of her eyes as he took detailed notes.

"Do you know Gerald Tanner well?"

Surprised and made uneasy by the question, Mariah was unwary enough to look at him. Their eyes met briefly, and she turned her head quickly.

"Well, um, no," she fumbled. "He's new this year…"

"Aren't you planning a project together?" Ed Lamarr asked.

"Yes." Mariah explained. "We've never had any discussions I'd consider personal, however. I don't even know if he's married or has children."

"Actually he's single," Noreen contributed. "No children."

Mariah didn't want to know that or anything else about her colleague. She wanted this never to have happened.

"What will you do?" she asked the principal.

"I've asked him to come to my office. I'll have to tell him about the accusation, of course. Tracy has gone to the hospital for an exam, and, um…"

Mariah nodded.

"Unless DNA is recovered, however, the exam won't be conclusive. Well," she corrected herself, "unless she's never had sexual intercourse at all and the entire story is fabricated.

"Detective McLean will be conducting an investigation. I fear parents will demand that Mr. Tanner be suspended during the course of it. I'm undecided about that yet. Students have been known to make frivolous accusations. I don't want to overreact."

"Tracy's grades are suffering in my class," Mariah said. "She may be flunking his."

"And yet, the fact that she is a poor student can have no bearing on our response to her allegation," Noreen Patterson pointed out. "In fact, I suspect her failing grade explains why she responded to his…um, blackmail. He wouldn't have had the same leverage with a better student."

Mariah nodded. "Yes. I understand. It's just that…"

"That?" the principal prompted.

"It occurred to me today while we were talking that she and I were alone in a classroom with the door shut. She could have claimed I'd said or done anything. How will you ever know the truth?"

The police officer stirred. "I doubt a thirteen-year-old girl who is a poor student has the sophistication to have built an airtight case. She'll have talked to friends, for example, possibly bragging about how she was going to get rid of her computer teacher and make everybody feel sorry for her. Clearly she didn't understand that her accusation would go outside the school. In the stress of having to repeat her story to me, other officers, somebody from Child Protective Services, even a D.A., she'll likely slip up."

"If she's not telling the truth," Mariah felt compelled to say, surprised at her sharpness.

He lifted a brow. "Exactly."

She started at a rap on the glass inset in the door. Galvanized, Mariah leaped to her feet. She said hastily, "I know you'll want to talk to Gerald without me here. Unless you need anything else, I'll be going home now."

Detective McLean's light eyes flicked from her face to the man who stood behind her.

"Actually, Mariah, I was hoping you could stay." Noreen cleared her throat. "I'd like your thoughts."

Thoughts?

She was backpedaling, careful to avoid looking at the police officer who remained by the window, as though he imagined he could ever be unobtrusive.

"I don't know what else I can add." *Please don't make me do this,* she begged the principal with her eyes. *You don't know what you're asking.*

But *he* did. And, damn him, remained silent.

Noreen Patterson said firmly, "I'd appreciate it if you would stay."

Mariah stood for a moment, so near rebellion that she trembled. Nostrils flaring, she stared at Detective McLean, knowing what was coming, hating it and him. He could have rescued her, could have said in that quiet voice, "I don't think we need Ms. Stavig to be here."

But he said nothing of the kind, and after an intense inner battle Mariah went back to her seat and waited, head bowed.

Noreen Patterson raised her voice. "Come in."

"You wanted to see me?" Gerald Tanner looked wary.

The principal asked him to take a seat. The remaining one was right beside Mariah. She stared down at her hands.

"Mr. Tanner, one of your students has accused you of trading a passing grade for sex."

His body jerked, as though he'd been struck by a bullet. *"What?"*

Sounding calm, nonjudgmental, Noreen Patterson summarized Tracy's story.

"Who is the student?" he asked, strain making his voice shake.

"Tracy Mitchell."

"God." He bowed his head and squeezed his eyes shut. "I've had conferences with her—I know she can do the work if only she'd try—but I've never..." He drew a breath that was painful to hear.

Unable to prevent herself, Mariah turned her head to see the bewilderment and shock on his face.

"You don't seriously think I..." He looked from face to face and saw that they did. "Oh my God. This can't be happening!"

"I'm afraid it is, Mr. Tanner." Detective McLean spoke quietly. "Any accusation of this magnitude has to be taken seriously."

"But she's thirteen years old! A...a child!" His Adam's apple bobbed. "I have never been interested, would never be interested..."

They began to ask questions, and Mariah watched his horrified disintegration.

"You're going to take her word over mine?" He shoved his chair back. His frenzied gaze encountered Mariah. "Why is she here?"

Mariah opened her mouth, but nothing came out.

"The student chose to confide in Ms. Stavig," the principal said coolly. "Since she's involved this deeply, I asked her to stay."

He looked at her with deep hurt. "You couldn't have come to me?"

"I..." Her voice stuck, unstuck. "You know I have to..."

"Set up an ambush?" He shot out of the chair as if he couldn't bear to be so close to her.

"Ms. Stavig did nothing but what she is required

by law to do, and you know it," Mrs. Patterson said sharply.

"This is unbelievable!" He paced, his agitation making his gait jerky and his bony limbs look like sticks strung together. "Do I even get a chance to answer these charges? Does anybody care if I'm innocent?"

"Of course we care..."

He swung to face Detective McLean. "Are you going to arrest me?" he shouted. He stuck out his arms. "Here! Handcuff me now. Let's get it over with. Apparently we can skip the trial, too. The judge and jury are right here!"

He had passed the point of listening to reason, and Mariah couldn't blame him. They *had* ambushed him, and she understood his terror as the snares whipped shut on his ankles.

No matter the outcome, his life would never be the same again. Rumors would start, whispers would follow him. Even his best friends would feel doubt. Everyone would wonder: Did he do it? Even if Tracy Mitchell eventually recanted her story the doubts wouldn't be completely erased. Maybe she was afraid of him; maybe that's why she says it never happened. Maybe...

"I'm sorry," Mariah whispered.

The only one who seemed to hear her was Detective McLean, whose mask slipped briefly to reveal a flash of—what? Compassion? Some inner anguish?

Or was it pity, because twice she had been fooled by monsters who walked as men?

The next moment he looked back at Gerald Tanner and said in that quiet, steadying voice, "Mr. Tanner, I have every intention of hearing your side. Teenagers do make up stories like this. You will not be rail-roaded, I promise.''

Mariah stood up and left, not caring whether the principal would be annoyed.

God help her, she would never look at Gerald Tanner again without hearing the whisper of doubt.

Already those doubts murmured in her ear as she made her way blindly through the office and out the double doors to the parking lot.

But the ones that were not content to murmur, that clawed deep, had nothing to do with a high school computer teacher. Always, always, they had to do with Simon, the man she had loved.

If he had done what they said—of course he hadn't, but if he had—would he one day touch Zofie in a way no father should?

She got into her car, locked the door and rested her forehead on the steering wheel. She tasted the salt of her own tears.

''What else could I do?'' she asked aloud, and didn't even know if she was talking about Simon or Gerald Tanner.

CHAPTER TWO

CONNOR TOOK A LONG SWALLOW of beer and announced, "I'm starting to hate my job."

He and his brothers, policemen all, had gathered for their traditional weekly dinner and couple of beers at John's. John was the only one of them with children and a wife, which meant the sofa coordinated with the leather chair and the Persian rug, the kitchen table wasn't covered with old pizza boxes and takeout Chinese cartons, and instead of an overflowing hamper, the bathroom had clean, matching towels and, tonight, even flowers in a stoneware vase.

Connor was beginning to think a life of domestic happiness didn't look so bad. Not that he had any prospects for marriage, but...hell, he could buy a house. A man didn't need a wife for that.

Right now, the three were slouched in the living room. Natalie, John's wife, had shooed them out of the kitchen and insisted that she and their mother would clean up. The kids were doing homework upstairs. Whether Mom was here or not, somehow Natalie always managed to give the brothers time to talk. After finishing in the kitchen, Mom usually left, while Natalie was likely to pop in long enough to kiss their cheeks and wish them good-night, exchange a slow, deep look with her new husband, and disappear upstairs to read in bed. And wait for John, who would start getting antsy in an hour or so. Who could blame him, with a luscious woman like Natalie waiting?

Even the idea of a wife wasn't sounding so bad to Connor. Must be a symptom of age, he figured; his thirtieth birthday had come and gone.

His comment about his job still hung in the air when his mother appeared in the doorway. Voice sharp, she said, "Don't say things you don't mean. You sound like a teenager, making too much of some little complaint."

Surprised by her agitation, Connor raised his brow. "How do you know it's a little complaint?"

In the act of snatching up a coffee mug left on the end table, she demanded, "Well, isn't it?"

He shrugged. "Just a case I was going to tell Hugh and John about."

"Hardly your 'job,' then," she chided him. A regal, fine-boned woman, Ivy McLean departed for the kitchen.

After a moment of silence during which none of the brothers moved, Connor cleared his throat.

"What's with Mom?"

John gave him a look. "You know how important she thinks our work is. You aren't supposed to bitch. You don't have a job," he said dryly. "You have a calling."

"We're making the streets safe, et cetera, et cetera," Hugh added.

Connor grunted. As a kid, he hadn't been conscious of pressure from Mom to become a cop, the way John claimed to. He'd become one because his big brother had. There was no question, however, that Mom was proud of the fact all three sons were in law enforcement. And maybe she had no understanding of the need to grumble. A stoic herself, she had raised her three sons alone with grit and without whining.

John gave himself a shake. "Back to your job. Why are you starting to hate it?"

Hugh, the youngest and best-looking of the three McLean brothers, slumped lower in his chair. "It's that fuzzy, did-he-or-didn't-he crap," he announced. "Here's free advice—go back on patrol. Do some *real* police work."

John grabbed an empty and tossed it, connecting with Hugh's chest. "You don't think raping a thirteen-year-old is a crime? Arresting a rapist isn't real police work?"

Unoffended, Hugh crumpled the can in one hand. "I listen to Connor. These cases aren't clear-cut. This one with the schoolkid isn't a rape, it's a…jeez, I don't know." He gestured vaguely.

"A knife at the throat isn't the only kind of force," Connor said. "The power an adult—and at that a teacher, a figure of authority—wields over a kid is considerable."

"I know that. I'm not excusing it. I'm just saying, you may never know who's lying. Don't you ever hunger for a good, old-fashioned shooting at a convenience store?"

Connor grunted. "Maybe."

"Maybe" wasn't the real answer; "no" was. Sometimes he wasn't sure he was cut out to be a cop at all. Going back into uniform didn't appeal, and he wasn't sure investigating murders or arson or bank robberies as a Major Crimes Unit detective like John would make his view of the world any sunnier.

He was a cop, he was good at his job, and what else would he do? Until recently he'd never questioned any of the above, but lately he had felt restless. No, worse than that: he saw himself for the home wrecker he was.

Today, he'd seen it in Mariah Stavig's eyes. She hated him for what he had done to her family. And the little girl Simon Stavig had supposedly molested? She was probably still in counseling. She'd probably have hang-ups her entire life, and he, Detective Connor McLean, had done jack for her.

John got the conversation back on the track. "Something getting to you about this case?"

Connor rolled his beer can between his palms. "Just a weird coincidence."

They waited.

He told them about Mariah Stavig, the teacher the girl had chosen to confide in, and how he had investigated her husband three years before.

"Her face was familiar so I looked up the file." He continued his story. "The case was ugly. A three-year-old girl who said Simon Stavig molested her, but without corroborating evidence we were never able to arrest him."

John studied him thoughtfully. "But you think he did it."

"Oh, yeah." Connor shook his head in disgust. "He was one of those guys who got seriously pissed because we'd come knocking on his door. He wasn't shocked, the way you'd expect. I mean, wouldn't you be stunned if you were accused by some friend of Maddie's? Nah, this guy wasn't surprised. He was angry that we'd take the word of a kid that age."

John grunted. "This Mariah Stavig is still married to him?"

"I don't know. Now, *she* was shocked. I can still

see her standing there waiting for her husband to say, 'I didn't do it.' Getting more anxious by the minute when he didn't. Big eyes, you know.'' They were a mixture of green and brown that might make a poetic man think of the mossy floor of the rain forest. Not that he was poetic. "She was scared and puzzled. Even she recognized that his reaction wasn't right.''

"And now she had to call you to investigate some other guy.''

"Yup.'' Another swallow of beer seemed appropriate. Tonight he almost regretted that he wasn't really a drinking man; the two or three beers that were his limit didn't do much to drown the mocking voice that had lately been asking what good he was to the world. Irritably muting it, Connor said, "And she was damned upset when she saw that the luck of the draw had brought me.''

"She blames you.''

Connor shrugged. "Probably.''

They all sat in silence for a moment. The syndrome was familiar to them all. The battered wife called the cops, then was angry at the one who responded for making her husband madder, for jailing him, for letting the neighbors see the trouble behind the facade of her happy home. The storekeeper didn't blame the punks who robbed him, he blamed the cops who offered inadequate protection, who couldn't make an arrest. People called the police reluctantly, then saw the officers who responded not as saviors but as symbols of whatever bad thing had happened.

"You going to beg off the case?'' Hugh asked.

Connor frowned. He'd considered it. He couldn't exactly be said to have a conflict of interest, but certainly this investigation would be hindered by Mariah

Stavig's hostility. On the other hand, Port Dare was small enough that he often encountered people he knew. The sexual crimes unit was all of two officers strong. Penny Kincaid had plenty to do without taking on a call that had been his by rotation.

Besides, he was already hooked. He wanted to find out whether Tracy Mitchell was lying and why. And he wondered what had happened to Mariah Stavig in the three years since the case against her husband had been dropped. Despite her bewilderment at Stavig's strange reaction to the investigation, had she maintained faith in her husband? Did she trust him with their pretty little girl? Or had she left the son of a bitch, and now had her struggles as a single mom to blame as well on the cop and social worker who'd come a'knocking with an unprovable accusation?

"Nah," he said, with another shrug that expressed more indifference than he felt. "She called us. She'll cooperate."

Hugh was apparently satisfied. He laid his head back and gazed dreamily at a wall of books.

Big brother John, however, studied Connor with slightly narrowed eyes. "Reluctant cooperation from her is going to eat at you, isn't it?"

Connor pretended surprise and ignorance. "Why would it bother me?"

"Could be I'm wrong." John's gaze stayed unnervingly steady. "But I don't think so."

Connor swore. "I don't know what you're talking about." He, too, crushed his beer can in his hand, getting more profane when a jagged edge bit into his palm.

"Sorry." John didn't sound repentant. He did,

however, switch his gaze to his youngest brother. "So, what's with this blonde you're seeing?"

Nothing was with her, Connor could have told him. She'd go the way of all the other petite blondes their baby brother dated. Hearth and home did not yet interest him.

Truthfully Connor had a hard time imagining Hugh ever letting himself be vulnerable enough to experience anything approaching true love. Even with his brothers, he backed off from expressing emotion or admitting weakness. John thought Hugh had been hit hardest by their father's murder; Connor privately thought the opposite, that Hugh had been young enough to be oblivious to much of their mother's agony and to what he himself had lost.

Either way, Hugh did more than avoid commitment; he made sure the issue never had a chance to arise. He'd been damn near raised by his big brothers. Hell, maybe he wasn't capable of softer emotions. A man was what he'd learned to be. Honor mattered to Hugh. Duty. Family. Probably friendship. But tenderness and romantic love? Nah.

Right now, Connor was just grateful for the change of subject. John was too perceptive.

Yeah, Mariah Stavig's shock and hatred *had* gotten to Connor today. Probably she and her reaction to him were symbolic; he'd walked into too many living rooms to spread distrust, bewilderment, even fear, then walked away without a backward glance, much less resolution.

Mariah Stavig was the face that represented all the others who had been left to pick up the pieces after he shrugged and said, "I don't have enough evidence to take to the prosecutor."

Connor wanted to know what he had done to her life, and he wanted her forgiveness. It was ridiculously important to Connor that he somehow make her understand that he'd only been doing his job.

Suddenly the face his memory flashed like a slide in a projector wasn't Mariah Stavig's. The hatred and terror that blazed at him weren't hers, but rather a teenage girl's.

How could you do this to me? I trusted *you,* the girl in his memory had cried.

He could still hear his own stumbling response. *I thought it was the right thing to do.*

There it was in a nutshell, his credo: Do the right thing. Black and white. Right in this column, wrong in that. He understood the agonized choices and tragedy that lay between, but had never let those deter him from pursuing justice.

Trouble was, what did a man do when he began to wonder whether the credo he lived by was a simplistic piece of crap?

Making a sound, Connor got to his feet. "I'll see you, okay?"

John stood, too, a frown gathering on his brow. "Are you all right?"

"I'm fine." To convince his brothers, Connor set up for a shot, released the empty beer can and crowed when it dropped with a clank into the brown paper bag by John's chair. With their good-nights following him, he paused only long enough to stick his head in the kitchen, thank Natalie for dinner and say good-night to her and his mother before heading out to his car.

He was thirty years old. Almost thirty-one. Hell of a time to discover he had spent most of his adult life trying to vindicate a decision he'd made when he was seventeen.

I trusted you.

Connor revved the engine as he started his car. Swearing under his breath, he backed out of the driveway, then drove away just under the speed limit. He knew better than to think he could outrun a ghost.

MARIAH WAS UNSURPRISED to find a pink message slip in her mail cubby in the school office.

Please call Detective McLean.

Did he remember her? She'd bet on it. Did he feel any guilt about making accusations he could never prove, about leaving her family to live with doubt and whispers and questions? Or did he believe complacently that he held no blame for the disruption left in his wake?

She stared with burning eyes for another moment at his name, then crumpled the slip in her fist. It would be a cold day in hell before she would ever call him.

On a shuddering breath, she turned blindly and left the office, hoping nobody had noticed her distress. She was glad she'd come early, so she had half an hour to compose herself before her first class poured into her room.

The pink slip still crumpled in her fist, Mariah exchanged greetings with other teachers and aides as she made her way through the halls. Port Dare Middle School was badly in need of being bulldozed and replaced. Timber played a big role in the local economy, however, which meant luxuries like new schools were no more than dreams these days. This building was the original high school, now housed in an equally inadequate campus built in the fifties. Until a new industry could be coaxed to this isolated small city to replace the dying business of logging the Olympic rain forest, Port Dare School District would have a tough time passing bond issues. In the meantime, middle-schoolers—and their teachers—coped with a four-story Depression-era building with wonderful murals painted by WPA workers, decrepit bathrooms and insufficient classroom and locker space.

Mariah's room was on the fourth floor, which kept her in shape. The English teachers didn't complain, because they stayed the warmest in winter when the inadequate heat the ancient furnace pumped out all rose to their floor, making it comfortable while the math classrooms in the basement were icy.

A student, then a senior at the high school, had come back several years before to paint a minimural of Shakespeare surrounded by actors costuming themselves on the wall outside her classroom. Today she paused, her key in the classroom door, and stared at the lovingly created mural.

Her students liked her. Remembered her. Trusted her.

Tracy Mitchell had trusted her. Had come to her for help.

How could she let one of her students down because her own scars weren't fully healed?

She turned the key and went into the classroom, for once locking the door behind her. Empty or full, this room was a refuge. Bright posters and glorious words decorated the walls. Old-fashioned desks formed ragged rows. Mariah absently traced with her fingers one of the long-ago carved notes that scarred them: JB+RS. Morning sunlight streamed in the wall of windows. She even loved the old blackboard and the smell of chalk and the uneasy squeak of it writing on the dusty surface.

Her meandering course between desks brought her to the one where Tracy Mitchell sat from 10:10 a.m. until 11:00 a.m. every day. Sometimes she whispered with friends or used her superdeluxe calculator to write notes for them to read. But once in a while, she actually heard the magic in words, saw the wonderful, subtle hues they conjured, and she would sit up straight and listen with her head cocked to one side, or she would read her part in a play with vivacity and passion if not great skill.

Mariah stood, head bent, looking at the desk. Tracy had a spark. She had promise she would likely never fulfill, given her family background and her tight skirts and her sidelong glances at boys. But it was there, and teachers were sometimes wrong about who would succeed or fail. She did not deserve to be blackmailed, to have her budding sexuality exploited, to have to feel that this, of all things, was her fault.

With another sigh, Mariah went to her desk and dug in her tote for her cell phone. Apparently, despite the sunlight, warm for October, it was really a cold day. A very, very cold day.

Somewhere.

She picked the wadded-up message from the otherwise empty waste can, smoothed it out on the desk and dialed the number.

"Detective McLean."

"This is Mariah Stavig. You asked me to call."

His voice was calm, easy, deep, and agonizingly familiar. "I wondered when you have a break today so that we could talk."

"I take lunch just after eleven. Or I have a planning period toward the end of the school day."

"Eleven?"

"School starts at 7:20." Why did he *think* she was returning his call so early?

He made a heartfelt comment on the hour, with which she privately agreed; students would learn better with another hour of sleep. But Mariah said nothing except, "You must start work early, too."

"Actually I just got up." He yawned as if to punctuate his admission. "This is my cell phone number."

"Oh." Oh, dear, was more like it. Obviously he wasn't at the moment wearing one of those well-cut suits he favored. More likely, pajama bottoms sagged low on his hips, if he slept in anything at all. An image of Connor McLean bare-chested tried to form in her mind, but she refused to let it.

"Eleven, then," he said. "Where do I find you?"

She hesitated for the first time, hating the idea of him in here. But the teacher's lounge was obviously out, late October days, however sunny, were too chilly to sit outside, and short of borrowing another teacher's classroom—and how would she explain that?—Mariah couldn't think of another place as private as this.

"I'm on the top floor of the A building. Room 411."

"Can I bring you a take-out lunch?"

Annoyed at his thoughtfulness, she was glad to be able to say, "Thank you, but I packed one this morning."

"See you then."

She pressed End on her phone and stashed it again in her tote. Her heart was drumming. Ridiculous.

The door to the classroom rattled, and she glanced up to see a couple of blurred faces in the mottled glass. Startled, she saw that the clock had reached seven-fifteen without her noticing.

She let in the eager beavers. Probably eager not for her brilliant instruction, but for the chance to slump into their seats and achieve a near-doze for a precious few minutes before she demanded their attention. Most did, however, drop last night's assignment into her in-box as they passed her desk.

This ninth-grade crowd was reading *Romeo and Juliet.* She was big on Shakespeare. She'd let them watch the updated movie version last week, the one with Claire Danes and Leonardo DiCaprio and guns and swimming pools, which she personally detested as much for what it had left out as for the interpretation. But she'd found it effective with the kids, helping them to understand that the words were timeless. Now she was making them read the original, not cut to suit the constraints of moviemaking budgets and filmgoers' limited attention spans.

Tracy wasn't in her seat for Beginning Drama. Was she too scared or embarrassed to come to school now that the cat was out of the bag? Or had her mom made her stay home? The principal might even have suggested she take a day or two while the police investigated.

The class passed with Tracy's empty desk nagging at Mariah. The bell had rung and students were making their way into the hall traffic when Detective McLean's head appeared above theirs. Under other circumstances Mariah might have been amused as he tried to force his way upstream in a hall so packed, kids shuffled along in file with their backpacks protectively clutched tight. Stopping to visit with friends was impossible, the equivalent of an accident during rush hour on a Seattle freeway.

His progress would have been even slower on one of the lower floors. This was the bottom of the bottle, so to speak, tipped up to empty. Students were fleeing it for the commons or the covered outdoor areas where they could hang out for the lunch hour.

"God Almighty," the detective muttered when he finally stepped into her room. "What if there was a fire?"

"That," Mariah said, "is our worst fear. There is a fire escape on each end of the building, which would help, but since going down that would be single file, evacuating all four floors would still take way too long."

He looked back at the stragglers in the now-emptying hall and frowned. "The fire inspectors have been here between classes?"

"What are they going to do? Condemn the building? Where would we go?"

He growled something and closed the door on the hubbub. Mariah fought an instinctive desire to step back. Connor McLean was a very large man, easily six-two or six-three, with bulky shoulders to match. While she watched, he strolled around her classroom reading quotations, scrutinizing photos, smoothing a big hand over a desktop just as she'd done earlier.

"Place hasn't changed at all."

She raised her brows. "Since?"

"I went here. Smells the same, even."

"I like the smell." She was sorry immediately that she'd let herself get personal.

He inhaled. "Yeah. Creates instant memories, doesn't it?"

Yes. Yes, that was exactly it. Floor polish and books and chalk dust could release a kaleidoscope of memories of herself behind one of those student desks. The rustle of a note being passed, the wonder of the passage a teacher read with deep feeling, the stumbling recitation of a report before bored classmates, the glow of seeing a huge red *A*—good work!—on the top of her paper. Days and weeks and years spent in classrooms like this, the time happy enough that she had chosen teaching as a career. No wonder she loved the smell of school.

"Yes," she said stiffly. "I suppose it does."

He stood before the window for a moment, looking out. "This town doesn't change."

"The strip malls and Target and Home Depot weren't here when you went to Port Dare Middle School."

He gave himself a shake, as though ridding himself of memories she wasn't so sure were good. "No, or the developments in the outskirts. But the view from here hasn't changed an iota."

"Unless we tear down all the Victorian houses or allow new development on the waterfront, it never will."

Detective McLean turned abruptly, his gaze focusing intensely on her. "You didn't grow up in Port Dare, did you?"

She wasn't sure what business it was of his, or why he cared, but answering seemed harmless. "No. I'm actually from California. Sacramento. I came to college up here, met my husband and stayed."

"Where did you go?"

Was he going to check her college transcripts? "Gonzaga, in Spokane. Then Washington State University for a masters degree."

He made an interested sound as he strolled to the front of the room. "Why Port Dare?"

She looked at him steadily. "Simon found work here."

"You're still married?" He sounded casual, as if he didn't care. And why should he?

"No." Acid corroded her voice and her heart. "You did manage to destroy my marriage. Is that what you wanted to know?"

A muscle jumped in his cheek, but he didn't look away. "I hoped you were divorced. For your little girl's sake."

Mariah tasted bile. "Now Zofie gets to spend weekends with her daddy. Without Mommy around at all."

A frown gathered his brow. "He gets unsupervised visitation?"

"Of course he does!" She stared at him with dislike. "You never even arrested Simon. You never proved a thing."

"It's almost impossible when the victim is a child that young."

She clutched the edge of the desk for support, listened to her voice shake. "Then what's the good of making accusations you can never substantiate? If there is no sperm, no witnesses, why start something you can't finish?"

His mouth twisted. "How can we not? He might have given something away. You might have been able to prove your husband was never alone with the child and her identification of him was wrong. You and he had a right to know he had been named. Would you really have wanted to go on with your marriage in ignorance? Maybe have had more children with him?''

The sound that came from her was nearly a sob. ''I don't know! How can I even remember life before you came and spread doubts like…like salt in a field?'' Mariah drew a shuddering breath and fought for composure. ''I hate what you did to Simon and me and Zofie. I had to say that once. Now let's do what you came for and not talk about the past again.''

''It's my job.'' Did he sound hoarse?

''We all choose how we spend our lives.'' She, in turn, was cold, unforgiving.

''Someone has to stop child molesters and rapists.''

''Just know that you do bad along with the good.''

He gestured toward the rows of empty desks and said scathingly, ''Don't you ever let down a student? Maybe not connect, because you don't want to change how you present your material? Could it be you're so sure everyone should appreciate Shakespeare, you ignore those kids who can't read well enough. Or, hell, maybe you don't listen, because you're too busy or you don't like that student anyway?'' He stalked toward her, predator toward prey. ''Fail her on a test, when she needed you to understand that her mom walked out last week and she's cleaning house and doing the laundry and putting dinner on the table and taking care of her little brothers and crying when she should be sleeping? Maybe just failed to reach a kid, period, no matter how hard you tried? You've never done any of that?''

She winced inside. What teacher didn't have regrets? Who was perfect? But she hadn't chosen a profession where she destroyed more often than she built.

Chin high, face frozen, she asked, "Are you admitting that you 'failed' my family?"

That betraying muscle beneath his eye jerked, but he said quietly, "If I failed anyone, it was Lily Thalberg."

Now Mariah did flinch. Sometimes she almost forgot Zofie's small playmate, the child who had started so much when she whispered, "Zofie's daddy."

"You believed her."

"Yes."

"Did you ever question her identification of my husband? I mean, seriously question it?"

"Did I consider that she might be transferring the terror from her own daddy to someone else's? Is that what you're asking?"

"I..." She swallowed. "Yes. Or from her granddaddy, or..."

"Or someone. Anyone but your husband."

Her mouth worked. Put that way, she sounded childish. Blame anyone but Simon. "He didn't...he couldn't..."

Harshly, Detective McLean said, "And yet, you left him."

"Yes." Now she froze inside as well as out. "To my eternal shame."

He let out a ragged breath. "Ms. Stavig..."

"No." She straightened behind the desk. "It is far, far too late for recriminations." Not for guilt. Never for guilt. "I shouldn't have started this. I'm going to ask you to leave if this is what you came to talk about."

He moved his shoulders as though to ease tension. "You know it isn't."

"Then tell me what you need to know."

"So you *can* ask me to leave?"

"So that my students don't still find you here when they arrive for class in—" she glanced at the clock "—twenty-five minutes."

His gaze followed hers to the clock and he muttered an incredulous oath. "That's not long enough."

Although he would loom over her, Mariah pulled out her chair behind the large teacher's desk and sat. "I suggest you take advantage of that time," she said crisply.

Frustration and something else showed in his gray eyes. "All right," he said abruptly. His tone took on an edge, a sneer. "Here's a question, Ms. Stavig. Why do you think, when Tracy Mitchell decided to tell her story, she chose *you* of all teachers to hear it?"

CHAPTER THREE

MARIAH STAVIG'S FACE was gently rounded, far from classically beautiful. She lacked the dramatic cheekbones or lush mouth that were currently in vogue. Her extraordinary eyes, gold and brown with flecks of green, framed by thick dark lashes, more than compensated, in Connor's opinion. She had delicate features, pale, creamy skin and thick, dark hair worn in a loose knot on her nape.

Her face of all others had haunted him for years.

Now she stared at him with the intense dislike he had seen in his dreams. "Precisely what does that mean?" she asked sharply.

Still dogged with frustration and the bone-deep knowledge of wrongdoing, because he *had* played a part in destroying her marriage, Connor said, "It was a question. Nothing more. Why you?"

"My students trust me," she said stiffly.

He half sat on a student desk in front of hers, letting one leg swing. "Tracy Mitchell is a seventh-grader. Right? You've had her now for...what?" He pretended to think. "Seven, eight weeks? I gather she's not a top-notch student. How many students come through here a day? Be honest. How well can you even know the girl in that length of time?"

"Not as well as I do some of my eighth- and ninth-graders, of course. But Tracy is...noticeable. She dresses and acts older than her age. She's smart but not a good student. She tends to talk back, speak out of turn, exchange loud comments with friends at inopportune moments. But sometimes there's also something a little...sad about her. Do I know her well?'' Ms. Stavig tilted her head. ''Not yet. Do I know why she's the way she is? No, but I can guess, having talked to her mother several times.''

''Already?'' He hoped he didn't sound as surprised as he was. ''She a real troublemaker?''

''No. Simply an underachiever. I find it best to ride herd on kids from the beginning.'' Her mouth firmed. ''Now tell me what you meant to imply. What possible bearing does Tracy's choice of me as the teacher to tell have on anything?''

''I thought maybe rumor told her you had escaped marriage to a sexual molester. That she assumed you would be sympathetic and not question her motivations or the...details of her story.''

Emotions flashed across Mariah Stavig's expressive face before she narrowed her eyes. ''But, you see, most people at school didn't know Simon. I have no reason whatsoever to think Tracy Mitchell was aware that my ex-husband was accused of sexual molestation. And if she did know, she would also know that I supported him when he said he was innocent.''

''Did you?''

She ignored the question, although anger flared in her eyes.

''In fact, she would know that I think this kind of accusation rather resembles a witch hunt. Too often, it's all emotion and little truth. If she were smart, she would have chosen another teacher. When I realized what she wanted to talk to me about, I almost asked her to do so."

"And yet," he mused, "you did listen and you went to your principal."

Her face became expressionless. "I am legally obligated to report Tracy's story."

"If you weren't?" He leaned forward. "Would you have told her to forget it? Maybe suggested she just ask to change classes? Chalk up the sex to experience? How *would* you have handled it, Ms. Stavig?"

She bent her head as if in rapt contemplation of her hands, flattened on her desk blotter. "Tracy's situation is...different." She spoke very quietly. "Of course I would have taken action."

He didn't say, *Just as I had to take action.* He didn't have to. She looked up, shame staining her cheeks.

"I do realize that you had to do your job." Now her hands knotted on the desk before she seemed to notice and moved them to her lap, out of sight. Her voice was low, halting. "I'm sorry for what I said earlier. It's not your fault Lily accused Simon or that you couldn't prove either his guilt or innocence. I do know that."

Now he felt like crud. This whole interview had been about him. He'd desperately wanted her to say just this, and manipulated her until she did. If he had never seen Mariah Stavig before, he would have approached her very differently.

"No," he said abruptly. "I'm sorry. You have every reason to harbor...bitterness toward me. Probably I should have bowed out of this investigation because I knew that. Instead I've been making little jabs, just to see a reaction.''

She stared, her lower lip caught between her teeth. ''Why?'' she whispered finally.

Connor closed his eyes for a moment. ''Because I couldn't take the way you looked at me yesterday. As if I were another kind of monster.''

''Why did you care?''

He could barely make himself meet her gaze. ''Because I do have a conscience, believe it or not. I knew what I'd done to you, the decisions I'd left you to make. Every day I leave people to make those decisions. You were…symbolic, I suppose.''

''You wanted me to say it wasn't your fault.''

His grunt was meant to be a laugh. ''Yes. How small we can be.''

''Yes,'' she said softly. ''We can be, can't we? My decision to leave Simon was mine alone. But I wanted to blame somebody so I didn't have to take responsibility. The funny part is, I can hardly remember the social worker from CPS.'' She made a ragged sound. ''Not even her name. That is funny. I chose *you* to hate.''

Brows together, Connor studied her in genuine perplexity. ''Why?''

Her gaze skittered from his. ''I don't know. I didn't even realize…'' Her breath escaped. ''No, I do know. You dominated. Compared to you, she was a shadow. And then there was the way you said it. 'Even in a whisper, Zofie's daddy, was clear as a bell.' You see, I remember that, word for word.''

He swore.

Mariah gave a crooked, sad smile. ''That's why I hated you. Because you were Lily's voice.''

"I'm sorry," he said again, inadequately.

"No. You did what you had to do." Visibly composing herself, she glanced at the clock. "My next period students will start arriving in just a few minutes. I'm afraid we've wasted our time."

He shook his head. "I don't think so. We had to get past this."

She gave him a brief, almost vague smile. *Class dismissed.* "I'm going to eat my lunch, very quickly, if you don't mind."

"No. Listen. Can I come back later? After your last class, maybe? Or do you have to pick up Zofie right away?"

Pulling a sandwich out of her brown paper bag, Mariah shook her head. "I do have that planning period, remember."

"Oh, right. One o'clock?"

She agreed.

He stood. "I'll get out of here, then, so I don't start whispers."

Mariah looked surprised and as innocent as he suspected at heart she was. "Nobody is talking about Tracy yet."

What he'd meant was that they might whisper about *her.* He didn't say so. "Good. I want to get to her friends before she can. Her mother promised she wouldn't let her call any of them until I say it's okay. I'll do some interviews here at school, others tonight in the kids' homes."

Her brow creased. "I'm not sure I know who her best friends *are.* Her crowd, sure, but if she had a really close friend…"

"I'm sticking around school today to talk to some of her other teachers, too."

"Oh. Of course." She tried to smile. "Poor Gerald."

"Maybe." Connor hadn't made up his mind yet.

He left, then, to hit up the next teacher on his list.

The consensus among the faculty, he found, was in agreement with Mariah's brief sketch of the girl. "A smart mouth," the math instructor said. All equivocated when asked about her academic potential. "She's got the ability," conceded the social studies teacher grudgingly. "If she'd ever pay attention."

Several had also had meetings with her mother. They were guarded in their assessment, but having met Sandy Mitchell, Connor could read between the lines. She was apparently still married to the long-missing husband, which didn't stop her from replacing him with a rotating succession of men. She claimed to want the best for her daughter, but she let Tracy baby-sit until the wee hours on school nights, wrote excuses for skipped classes and apparently paid more attention to her current boyfriend than she did to whether her daughter had missed assignments or flunked tests.

When asked how truthful they thought Tracy was, each and every teacher hesitated. But once again, there was general agreement. "Hard to say," the social studies instructor said at last. "She's darned good at making up excuses for late assignments. I bought a few of them before she tried one too many."

Her art teacher was a standout. This was the one class where Tracy excelled. Even Connor could see real talent in the sketches Jennifer Lawson showed off. "Look at her clay project compared to the other kids'," she said, leading him back to a worktable beside a kiln.

He studied the rows of squat pots, as yet unglazed, constructed with coils. Only one had character and unexpected grace; it was both taller and narrower than the others, the neck taking an intriguing curve. Connor indicated it, and Ms. Lawson nodded.

"She's very focused in here. I don't get the excuses from her I know the other teachers do." She added simply, "Tracy Mitchell really has artistic ability. I hope she chooses to use it."

Tracy's mother had given permission for him to read her daughter's school file, starting with a pre-kindergarten assessment—"bright and eager"—and ending with the sixth-grade report card, which consisted of *B*s and *C*s. There had been up years and down years, he discovered; teachers who had seen promise in the girl and worked hard to cultivate her enthusiasm and ability, and teachers who had disliked that "smart mouth" and early budding of sexuality.

Nobody particularly noted lying as a problem. Yeah, she probably made up excuses for undone homework, but what kid didn't? Connor knew he had.

His one interview with the girl had left him undecided. Usually he had a gut feeling. Strangely, this time he didn't. Sitting in the living room of the apartment where she lived with her mom, she had told her story in a disquietingly pat way. But then, Connor had reminded himself, this was the third time in one afternoon she'd been asked to tell it. Wouldn't be surprising if it didn't come out by rote after a while.

If she was lying, she was smart enough not to let any smugness or slyness seep through. He had detected some real anger at the teacher, but not the distress a girl raped at her age should feel. If she was already sexually active, the actual act might not have disturbed her as much as it would have your average thirteen-year-old. Even so, how much experience could she have? Shouldn't she be traumatized?

But he wasn't making assumptions too quickly. Sometimes the trauma was buried. It could take time to claw its way to the surface. Or, hell, maybe she'd seen her mother trading sex for favors over the years, so this swap, a grade for a quickie, had seemed normal to her, something a girl did.

Could she, at thirteen, *not* be traumatized by forced sex with a man three times her age?

Connor was more depressed by that possibility than by any of the others. Damn it, a thirteen-year-old was a kid. A little girl, who shouldn't be seeing R-rated movies, far less be numbingly sophisticated about sex.

Anyway, assuming she was that sophisticated, why had she decided, after the fact, to tell her drama teacher what had happened? Because she was upset? Or because Gerald Tanner hadn't kept his side of the deal? Say, he'd decided she should put out a few more times if she wanted that passing grade?

The bell rang. Knowing better this time than to try to force his way up three flights of stairs against the lemminglike plunge of the middle-schoolers toward their next classes, Connor waited outside in a covered area. Shoulder propped against a post, he watched thirteen- and fourteen-year-olds flirt, gossip with friends, struggle to open ancient metal lockers and act cool.

On the whole, they hadn't changed since his day. Haircuts and clothing styles were a little different, but not the basic insecurity that was the hallmark of these young teenagers.

He didn't see a girl hurrying by who would have been as calm as Tracy Mitchell, talking about the first time her computer teacher exposed himself to her.

The crowd was thinning out, the next bell about to ring. Connor shoved away from the post and through the double doors into the tall A building with its Carnegie-style granite foundation and broad front entrance steps. Stragglers on their way to class cast him startled looks. He was an alien in their midst, an adult who wasn't a teacher or a known parent. He smiled and nodded when they met his eyes.

Tracy could be lying, all right. She wouldn't be the first teenager who'd decided an allegation of sexual molestation was the way to bring down an adult she hated.

But Gerald Tanner was also the classic nerd who had probably been hunched over his computer when his contemporaries were developing social skills. Not to mention fashion sense. Even Connor, who didn't give a damn about clothes, had shuddered at his polyester slacks, belted a little too tight and a little too high on his waist, and the short-sleeved white dress shirt and tie. Okay, Tanner didn't have a plastic pocket protector, but the black-framed glasses made him slightly owl-eyed. Who wore a getup like that these days? Hadn't he ever heard of contact lenses?

The point was, Gerald Tanner fit the profile of a guy who felt inadequate with women his own age. Here were all these teenagers, as awkward as he was with the opposite sex, the girls developing breasts, experimenting with makeup, learning to flirt and to flaunt what they had. What could be more natural than the realization that *he* was more powerful than they were? That he could fulfill his fantasies without having to bare himself, literally or figuratively, with a real woman?

Connor reached the top floor and paused briefly outside a classroom with its door ajar. The teacher was talking, but damned if any of the kids seemed to be paying attention. Some of them were studying, one girl was French-braiding a friend's hair, a couple of guys were playing a handheld electronic game, while others drifted around the room. Connor shook his head in faint incredulity. In his day, you were in deep you-know-what if you were caught passing a note, never mind openly playing a hand of poker in the back.

The teacher raised her voice. "Everybody got that assignment on their calendar? Remember, the rough draft is due Tuesday."

One or two students appeared to make notations in open binders.

Still shaking his head, Connor moved on.

What kind of teacher was Gerald Tanner? Did he wear any mantle of authority? Or did the kids see him as a computer geek, too?

Connor's stride checked as it occurred to him that maybe times had changed. This was Microsoft country, after all, and Bill Gates was the Puget Sound area's biggest celebrity. Hell, maybe jocks weren't the only object of teenage girls' lust these days. Maybe visions of the next computer billionaire danced in the heads of thirteen-year-old girls.

He'd have to ask Mariah.

Her door stood ajar, too. She sat behind her desk, papers spread across the surface, a red pen in her hand. Her concentration seemed complete. Connor wondered if she'd forgotten he was coming back.

But, although he didn't make a sound, he was no sooner framed in the doorway than her head shot up. For a moment she stared at him with the wide-eyed look of a doe frozen in car headlights. Was she afraid of him?

But then she blinked, her face cleared, and he told himself he'd imagined the fear.

"Detective. I thought maybe you'd gotten lost."

"Just avoiding the rush."

"Smart." She started stacking the assignments, her movements precise, the corners all squared. "What can I do for you?"

"Tell me what you know about Tanner."

"Gerald?" Her hands stilled momentarily, then resumed their task. "Well…not very much, actually. As I said in Mrs. Patterson's office, I didn't even know whether he was married. We simply haven't become that personal."

Connor sat as he had that morning on a student desk in the first row. "Is he shy?"

"Um…" She considered. "No, not really. He's friendly in the teacher's lounge. He's surprisingly funny."

Okay, Connor thought, torpedo the stereotypes. Horn-rimmed glasses did not mean a man was humorless; skinny arms did not mean he was pathologically shy.

"We've sat together to eat lunch several times, especially since we've started a discussion on doing a joint project coupling writing skills with Internet research."

"Have you seen him teach?"

She pursed her lips as she thought. Connor was

annoyed to find himself fixated on the soft curve of her mouth. Scowling, he tore his gaze away.

"Only briefly. Generally, of course, he isn't lecturing like I might do. The students work on computers, beginning ones on keyboarding skills, more advanced on computer animation or simple programming. So he tends to be wandering, looking over their shoulders, responding when they ask for help." She shrugged. "That kind of thing."

"Do they pay any more attention to him than the students down the hall—" Connor nodded toward the next classroom "—are to that young blonde?"

Mariah started to rise to her feet. "Is she having trouble?"

He waved her back. "If you mean, are they rioting, no. Are they hanging on her every word? No." He told her about the activities he'd seen going on.

Sounding rueful, Mariah said, "Karen is a student teacher. She probably won't be alone with the class for more than a few minutes. When Rich Sadow pops back in, the cards will vanish."

"Ah. The substitute syndrome."

"Exactly."

"To get back to the point..." he prodded her.

"Gerald? He is new this year, remember. But I'd say the kids are pretty enthusiastic. He brought some very cool programs with him, I understand. Stuff that's way beyond the school budget."

Glancing around the classroom, Connor muttered, "Is there a budget?"

She wrinkled her nose. "No, now that you mention it. But, to get back to Gerald, he seems passionate about computers as tools, and that kind of enthusiasm almost always gets through to kids. Besides," she added, "they like computers these days. They're a lot cooler than books."

"Does he always dress so…" He hesitated.

"Yes." She frowned, as if annoyed at herself. Firming her mouth, Mariah said, "I don't see what his choice of clothing has to do with your investigation."

"Just trying to…create a picture. See the whole man, so to speak."

"I honestly don't know him very well." Ms. Stavig sounded very businesslike this afternoon. "You're going to have to look elsewhere for help with your portrait."

Was she unable? Or unwilling? Connor couldn't tell.

"All right," he said agreeably. "On to Tracy. I took a look through her school record."

Some of Mariah's visible tension dissipated as she sighed. "It's full of ten-inch-tall warnings, isn't it? Here's a girl who needs lots of attention, who is lacking positive reinforcement at home, who will get lost if you ignore her. And then what did half her teachers do but ignore her."

"I noticed that," he agreed. "She yo-yoed—is that a word?—from year to year. Her sixth-grade teacher downright disliked her, I'd say, reading between the lines."

Mariah nodded. "Roberta Madison has, um, a reputation for doing better with boy students. The good little girl who can sit quietly in class is okay with her, too. A Tracy Mitchell apparently offends her sense of what's right."

Connor shook his head. "Okay. Let's go back through your talk with Tracy."

He had Mariah repeat yet again every word as close to verbatim as she could recall. She had a good memory—perhaps photographic, as she would pause, gaze into space with those tiny puckers gathering her brow, and then give a line of dialogue or describe an expression with certainty.

As she thought, Mariah Stavig seemed unaware that he was watching her. He found his mind drifting more than it should from what she was saying.

Light didn't play off her hair the way it normally would. The texture wasn't sleek and smooth, but more…downy, he decided. Connor imagined her hair loose, a fluffy, soft cloud like cotton candy, but less sticky.

Or he'd contemplate her long, slender neck, bowed gracefully when she gazed thoughtfully at her desktop. He liked her carriage, too; her back was always elegantly straight, her shoulders squared, as though someone in her childhood had impressed on her the importance of posture.

Mariah Stavig was a fairly tall woman, five-seven or -eight, he guessed, but slender. She was small-breasted, but he wasn't a man who liked more than a handful, anyway. Her fingers were long, her wrists narrow, her legs… Well, with her sitting behind the desk, he couldn't see them, but once, three years ago, when he had come to her house she'd been wearing jeans and he'd seen despite himself how long her legs were. A man's fantasy, those legs.

Mariah would have been too tall to be a ballerina, but that's what she made him think of. Delicacy and strength mixed together, grace coupled with innocence and unconscious sexuality. That's what he saw when he looked at her.

Which he had no damn business doing, he thought in exasperation. Connor moved restlessly and the desk creaked beneath him. Mariah, pulled from a momentary reverie, cast him a surprised glance with those catlike eyes, as if she'd forgotten he was still there.

"So you mentioned the possibility of her having to testify in court," he said gruffly. "And Tracy didn't like the idea."

"No." Mariah's brow crinkled again. "It obviously had never occurred to her that her complaint might go that far. 'Can't he just be fired?' she asked."

Mariah went on to tell him what she'd explained to the girl. Connor tried hard to listen and get his mind above his belt.

What in hell was he thinking? Mariah Stavig hated him! He'd broken up her marriage. She despised what he did for a living and was cooperating now only reluctantly, because of a sense of duty and a knowledge of the law. He hated to imagine how she'd react if she knew how intensely he was aware of her.

"Okay," he said finally. "I'll be talking to her again this evening. We'll see whether she's forgotten any of her story, or decides to embellish it a little."

"Do you think she's lying?" Mariah asked.

"At the moment, I have no idea," Connor admitted.

"Has she, um, been examined by a doctor yet?" She sounded timid. "I know it's probably not any of my business, but…"

"No, it's okay," he said. "Yeah, she had the works. Looks like she did lose her virginity in the past few days. No bruising or obvious signs that force was used. It was probably too long ago to recover DNA, assuming a condom wasn't used."

"She was afraid of being pregnant."

"She's thirteen years old," he said bluntly. "When I asked whether he might not have put on a condom before they had intercourse, she stared at me with complete blankness. In theory she knows what one is. Unless it was neon-green, I'm not convinced she'd have noticed if he put one on quickly, with his back to her."

The distaste and even embarrassment on Mariah's face might have been comical, under other circumstances. "She was probably trying not to...look." She was being very careful to keep her gaze fixed on his face, too.

A fact that stirred him uncomfortably.

Frowning, he said, "Exactly." Looking at the bank of windows, he made himself think about Tracy Mitchell, not the prim teacher behind the desk. "I need to start talking to kids. Hard to do without lighting a bonfire of rumors."

"Impossible, I imagine." Mariah looked worried. "If word gets out to parents, they may want Gerald suspended."

"Unfair as that could be," Connor acknowledged, "I'm hoping to find answers soon. Dragging this out will only make it uglier."

"You're mostly counting on her making a mistake, aren't you?"

"Or confessing all to a friend who has more conscience than she has."

Mariah didn't like that. "What if it's the truth?"

"Then my guess is we find that Tracy Mitchell isn't his first victim." Connor's voice hardened. "I'll be talking to his former colleagues, students, neighbors... You name it. If he's a pedophile, he'll have offended before. *And* found he liked it, which would explain his taking a job where he'd be working with all these young girls.''

''Oh.'' Her eyes were huge and alarmed, making him wonder how feral his expression had become.

He rose to his feet. Time to get out of here and do his job, not hang around wishing for the impossible.

''If I have more questions, I'll be in touch, Ms. Stavig. Thank you for your help.''

''You're welcome.'' She almost sounded as if she meant it. He felt her gaze on his back as he left her classroom.

He headed for the office, where the principal would have students called to talk to him one at a time, starting with Lucy Carlson, the girl who had suggested Tracy tell all to Mariah in the first place. He wasn't halfway when it occurred to Connor that he'd committed more than foolishness in lusting after a woman who hated him.

He'd committed a sin. He had to have lusted after her three years ago, when she was married and he was investigating her husband. Why else would he have remembered her face so well? Noticed her gloriously long legs in snug jeans to the point where he could still close his eyes and picture her walking away from him?

He might not have acknowledged his attraction, but what if it had affected his judgment, his objectivity? Looking back, he knew it had increased his abhorrence and animosity for Simon Stavig. Question was, had his peripheral but powerful awareness of Stavig's beautiful, puzzled, hurt wife changed the way he'd conducted the investigation? Had he done something differently, because he'd disliked the son of a bitch for wounding his wife?

He growled in his throat.

Did it matter what he'd felt for Simon Stavig, when lately he'd begun to wonder whether his reasons for going into this line of work in the first place had prejudiced him beyond hope? Hell, wasn't he already afraid he'd become a sort of avenger rather than a dispassionate investigator?

What was one more small sin added to the weight on his conscience?

Shoving through the double doors to let himself outside, Connor told himself it was time he found another job.

One that let him sleep at night.

CHAPTER FOUR

ZIPPING THE SMALL pink-and-purple suitcase, Mariah called, "Zofie, Daddy will be here any minute. Are you ready?"

Her six-year-old daughter appeared in the bedroom doorway, her small face set in a pout. "Do I hafta go?"

Mariah felt a familiar mix of potent emotions. Petty exultation—*she loves me best*—swirled with fear—*is she afraid of him?*—and finally a parent's familiar impatience.

"You know you do." She hesitated and added carefully, "You can always talk to me about Daddy and anything he says or does when you're with him. Sometimes there are reasons kids *can't* visit their parents, but as long as you don't have a special reason besides missing Renee's birthday party, you do have to go. Your dad loves you and wants to spend time with you, too."

Her daughter hung her head. "It's not just Renee's party. It's...sometimes Daddy..."

Mariah's heart jerked as if she'd touched a live wire. She fought to keep her voice calm. "Sometimes what?"

"Sometimes he's *boring*." The first-grader sighed heavily. "He doesn't *do* stuff with me."

Mariah sagged. Of course Zofie would have told

her if Simon had touched her like that. She had to quit scaring herself by reading something into nothing!

"I can't always do stuff with you, either," she pointed out, her voice only slightly shaky.

"Yeah, but then I can go to a friend's house or something," Zofie argued. "Or I have my toys."

"I know perfectly well you have toys at his house, too." Mariah raised her eyebrows and nodded at the bag in the hall. "Not to mention everything you just packed."

Zofie squirmed. "Yeah, but…" She flung herself at her mother and hugged her hard. "I like being with you!"

Mariah dropped to her knees on the throw rug in front of her daughter's bed and hugged back. Tears stinging her eyes, she said, "Oh, sweetie, you know I like being with you, too."

Zofie sniffed and nodded hard. "But Dad loves me, too," she mumbled.

"That's right." Mariah hoped and prayed Simon did, that he would always put the child they shared first.

One more sniff, and her petite daughter straightened, lifted her chin and said with resolution, "I'm okay."

Mariah smiled, hoping her tears didn't show. "Good."

Zofie cocked her head. "Is that Daddy? Did you hear a knock?"

"No, but let's go see." Mariah grabbed the child's suitcase from the bed and hurried with Zofie to the front door.

Opening it, her daughter cried, "Daddy!" with

complete delight, as if she hadn't just been bemoaning the necessity of seeing him.

Mariah stood back watching as he bent and lifted Zofie into his arms, a grin warming his saturnine face. For a moment he was the handsome man she had married, his dark hair tousled, his thin nose and wonderful cheekbones making him movie-star handsome. She had the jarring sensation of a temporal shift, as if this was once-upon-a-time, and he was just coming home from work, and he'd be looking up and smiling at her any minute…

Instead, over Zofie's dark curls, his cold gaze met hers. "I take it she's ready?"

Mariah forced a smile. "Yup. Zofie's all packed."

"Wait!" She wriggled in his arms. "I've got stuff to play with. I left it in the hall."

"Run and get it." He let her down and bent to pick up her suitcase.

The silence felt uncomfortable. Trying to sound friendly, Mariah asked, "Do you have any plans this weekend?"

Simon straightened to stare at her with an emotion near hate. "Are you asking whether this is the weekend I'm going to molest my daughter?"

She closed her eyes for a moment. "You know that's not what I meant. I was just making conversation."

"Yeah." His mouth curled. "Sure you were."

"Really…"

From the rear of the apartment, Zofie called, "I'm going to get something else, Daddy! I'll hurry."

If he heard, he didn't show it. His glittering eyes never left Mariah's. "Let's not play games. I know what you think about me. I'm not going to let you steal my kid from me, too. She'll be spending every other weekend with me for the next thirteen years. So get over it.''

Mariah gritted her teeth, anger saving her from shame. "'Get over it?'" she echoed in a low, furious voice. "I'm to quit worrying about my child? Don't you *want* me to worry about our daughter?''

"When she's with me, she's mine. Not ours." His dark eyes now held satisfaction and, perhaps, pain.

Mariah's fingernails bit into her palms. "Simon, please," she begged. "This isn't a competition. Can't we do our best together to raise Zofie?''

"Together?" He took a step forward, familiar fury twisting his face. "If you wanted us to raise her together, why are we divorced? It's because you didn't want to raise her with me at all. Did you? So now I have to take what I can get—two days out of every fourteen." His voice was a whip. "And, no, we're not raising Zofie together." He looked past her. "Ready to go, kiddo?''

"Sure." Zofie paused to hug her mom briefly. "Bye.''

How badly Mariah wanted to hold on and not let go! Reluctantly she lifted her hand from her daughter's fragile shoulder, touched her soft hair and forced a smile and light tone. "See you Sunday, sweetie.''

They were gone with a slam of the door and the sound of Zofie's high chatter receding. Mariah stood just inside, her hands knotted at her side, trembling all over.

In the early years, she'd been afraid every minute when Zofie was with Simon. But she'd talked to Zofie often about inappropriate touching, emphasizing it could come from anyone, asking her to promise to tell no matter what if anything like that ever happened. And now three years had passed, and Zofie had never even hinted that her daddy was anything but a regular daddy.

As time passed, Mariah felt relief. Surely if Simon had abused three-year-old Lily, he wouldn't have been able to resist Zofie. So her safe passage into elementary school must mean he *hadn't* been the one to do those terrible things to Lily Thalberg. That meant Mariah didn't have to worry. He loved his daughter. He would take good care of her when she was with him.

But shame followed on the heels of relief, because that must mean Simon was innocent all along when she, Mariah, had doubted him, her own husband. She'd left him so that he couldn't hurt their daughter, a terrible insult to a man she had promised to cherish and obey for as long as they both shall live.

He was always angry now, and she didn't blame him. Wasn't the whole foundation of marriage trust? A husband saw his wife without makeup and in childbirth and complaining about her mother and her best friend, and she trusted him not to betray her and to respect and love her despite her petty weaknesses. Just as she knew that he had fears he would never confess to his friends, and that his hot, brief anger meant nothing, and that he was embarrassed by his father's crude manners, but she would never tell. A husband knew you, as no one else ever had or would, just as a wife knew him. She should know, on a deep, instinctive level, whether he would ever have committed such a crime.

Only Mariah hadn't known, not with the certainty she should have felt. At first, she'd told herself it was

Simon's fault; if only he had talked to her, she never would have wavered. But why had she needed the words, *I didn't do it?* Why hadn't she loved him enough to trust him?

Mariah still couldn't answer that and was ashamed every other weekend when she saw in Simon's eyes what her doubt had done to him.

Worse yet, she was still afraid every minute when Simon had Zofie. Not *as* afraid; she could shop, clean house, go out with friends, without fear tearing at her nonstop. But the worry was there, a nagging, quiet ache that never left her until Zofie came running in the front door, singing, ''I'm home!''

This weekend, the anxiety was more acute. Meeting that police detective again had brought it all back. She saw the way he frowned and said in consternation, ''He gets unsupervised visitation?'' And when she asked whether he had believed Simon to be guilty, he said, ''Yes,'' without even a heartbeat of hesitation.

Once again, his certainty worked at eroding her confidence in what she should believe unshakably to be true: that Simon would never molest his own child.

And so she stood and shook until she heard Simon's car drive away, and she faced the fact that she would be alone in this apartment for almost forty-eight hours. She couldn't race after him and demand Zofie back, or shadow them and lurk under the windows of his rented house peering in windows.

She could only endure the weekend, as she had endured so many others, and try to convince herself that Zofie was safe, her daddy loved her, that he was angry because he felt betrayed and not because he also felt guilty.

On a breath that hitched in her throat and might almost have been a sob, Mariah turned away from the door that had closed behind a cheerful Zofie going off with Daddy, and went to the kitchen to make a dinner she didn't want to eat.

THE GIRL CAST CONNOR a frightened glance before bowing her head again and mumbling to the floor, "Tracy said he gave her the creeps."

The girl's father was staying out of it, just listening from his seat on the piano bench behind his daughter.

Connor dutifully noted, *Gave her the creeps* in his notebook. "Did she say why?" he asked.

Her brow crinkled. "Whaddaya mean, why?"

"Did she say whether Mr. Tanner had said something? Touched her?" Connor spread his hands as if to suggest other possibilities.

She shook her head.

Stifling a sigh, he asked, "What were you talking about when Tracy said that about Mr. Tanner? Did it just pop up at lunch? 'He gives me the creeps'? Or did something lead up to it?"

She mumbled something else.

Most cops tried to wring the truth out of scumbags at a biker bar. Connor's fate was to politely coax it from shy or sly teenagers.

"I'm sorry, I couldn't hear you."

She stole another look up, making him realize momentarily that she might be a pretty girl if she'd brush her hair back from her face and smile.

"We were, um—" she rolled her eyes toward her father "—talking about whether any of the teachers who are guys—you know, the male teachers—are hot." She drew a deep breath and launched into a spate, her cheeks pink. "Just, you know, talking. Because lots of the girls think Mr. Garrow, who teaches choir, is really cute. I mean, he's old, but not *that* old. It's like his first year of teaching."

Translation: he was twenty-two. Connor made an encouraging sound.

"And we were trying to think of all the guy teachers, and somebody said Mr. Tanner, and Tracy said, '*Eeew,* he gives me the creeps.' Like that."

"And she didn't say anything more?"

She gazed anxiously at him. "I don't think so."

"She's never talked to you about Mr. Tanner otherwise."

She shook her head.

"Do you know whether Tracy has had a boyfriend recently?"

This provoked another burst of speech. Tracy didn't really have a *boyfriend,* not like they were actually *going* together, but Jesse Rodriguez liked her, and last week she said this junior at the high school was flirting with her and said he'd sneak into the next dance. So guys *liked* her, see?

Too well, apparently.

Feeling he'd learned all he could, Connor thanked the girl and her father and left.

In the car, he looked at his notebook. Amy Weinstein was next. She lived, by coincidence, in the same apartment complex as Mariah Stavig.

Which meant nothing. He wasn't going to casually drop in at her place and say, "Hi. Just happened to be in the neighborhood."

Connor did, however, note her apartment as he wended his way through the complex looking for Building D. Mariah was in B103: ground floor, with a small patio. The first two were bare concrete slabs; hers was a small, luxuriant garden. Big wooden half barrels held topiary trees or boxwoods or something, below which ivy tumbled out. Terra-cotta pots and urns crowded the edges of the patio, flowering plants cascading out and clambering upward on wire trellises. He thought there was a round table and chairs in the midst, but his slowly cruising car took him past the corner of the building, and he lost sight of her oasis.

Amy's parents were less enthusiastic about their daughter being interviewed by a police officer, although they conceded the necessity.

Sitting to each side of her on the couch, they started answering for her almost immediately.

"Amy doesn't really see Tracy that much," Mrs. Weinstein assured Connor. "I don't know why anyone suggested her at all."

He smiled vaguely at them, then carefully watched the pale, thin girl as he asked, "Has Tracy ever mentioned Mr. Tanner to you? Beyond complaining about homework or whatever?"

She gazed back at him with odd composure. "She hates him."

Her parents rushed into speech, the mother first. "I can't believe Tracy hates anyone!"

Mr. Weinstein said loudly, "Not liking a teacher is hardly 'hating' him."

"Why does she dislike him?" Connor asked.

The girl gave a cool shrug. "Most of the teachers take late assignments, and he won't. Plus he doesn't like what she wears. Once he made her change. She says he picks on her."

The parents tried to downplay her every word—of

course Mr. Tanner didn't pick on Tracy! Why would he? Just because he expected the best of his students was no reason for them to dislike him. Why, they should be grateful that he cared! They certainly hoped Amy was.

Amy didn't say a word. She sat between them, a shadow, yet they seemed not to exist for her. She waited politely for the next question, her hands folded on her lap.

"Are you in her computer class?"

Amy was.

"Does it seem to you that he treats her differently than the other students?"

She gave it serious thought. "Um, I don't know. I sit on the other side of the room."

"Has she stayed after class to talk to him?"

"A couple of times, I guess."

"Did she say what they talked about?"

"She doesn't turn stuff in. And we're doing keyboarding, and you take these tests, and you're supposed to take so many a week, but I know she doesn't."

"Have you seen her right after she's stayed to talk to him?"

"You mean, like, when she comes into lunch?"

He nodded.

Amy shrugged. "I guess."

"Did she seem upset? Excited? Anything different?"

Amy didn't even blink. "I don't know. I guess she was kind of quiet or something."

He had the feeling she was lying, but he couldn't tell whether she hadn't noticed anything different about Tracy or whether she'd seen more than she wanted to say to him. Or wanted to say to him in front of her parents.

On the subject of boyfriends, she was more relaxed. A couple of guys had asked Tracy "out," but she wasn't interested.

"I hope her parents wouldn't let her date any more than we would you!" Mrs. Weinstein said indignantly.

"I don't think they actually date when they go out," Connor said.

But Amy's mother sniffed. "They're twelve years old! They're barely getting interested in boys."

Amy said quietly, "Tracy is thirteen."

"Big difference," her father scoffed.

Connor's eyes met the girl's, and they shared a moment of silent astonishment at her parents' naivete.

"There was this older guy at the dance," Amy offered. "Tracy said before that she might make out with him."

Over her parents' cries, Connor probed. "Older?"

"I don't know. Like, a high school kid?" She sounded uncertain. "I didn't really see him."

Connor eventually thanked her, handed her a business card and said, "If you hear anything, think of anything, please call me."

Her mother snatched the card and said, "Of course we will, Detective, but I can't imagine what Amy would hear. As we've been trying to explain, she and Tracy aren't really friends."

And wouldn't be in the future, if she had anything to do with it.

He nodded and left them all gathered in the open doorway, young Amy still calm, watching him gravely as he thanked them and left.

If he was going to hear from any of Tracy Mitchell's friends, Connor thought, it would be Amy Weinstein. The kids he'd interviewed at the school that afternoon hadn't offered any useful clues. If they were to be believed, their friendship with Tracy was casual. Lucy Carlson had insisted she hardly knew Tracy.

"We were just in a group when she started asking if there were any teachers you could really trust, if you had to tell something big. I said Ms. Stavig."

Now dusk was settling as he backed his car out of the parking slot. Driving out of the complex, Connor slowed again as he passed Mariah Stavig's building. This time, lights were on inside the greenhouse kitchen window and the sliding glass door. He saw movement inside, and his foot touched the brake.

The next second, he gritted his teeth and deliberately speeded up. He couldn't knock on her door and ask her out to dinner. So he sure as hell wasn't going to peep in her windows.

Frowning, jaw still clenched, he turned onto the road without looking in the rearview mirror.

Time to grab another wholesome meal on the job, courtesy of Burger King, and go visit Tracy Mitchell herself one more time.

THE POLICEMAN TRIED TO ACT really nice, but Tracy knew better. He was hoping to trick her into saying she was lying, but she wouldn't. It wasn't fair! she thought resentfully. Teachers could do anything, and everybody believed them. Nobody believed a teenager.

Her mother the traitor let him in when he rang the doorbell, even though Tracy had cramps and was scared and sad and had been huddled in her bed most of the day.

"Tracy!" Mom called. "Put on your bathrobe and come talk to Detective McLean."

"I don't feel good!" Tracy yelled back.

There was a murmur of voices. Ten seconds later, the bedroom door shot open.

"Tracy Ann Mitchell," her mother hissed, "when a policeman comes to talk to you, you drag yourself out of bed even if you are sick." Her tone made plain that she knew perfectly well Tracy wasn't.

"I already told him everything," she mumbled.

"Then tell him again," Mom snapped, and went back into the living room.

Tracy said the F-word and got out of bed. Down the hall she heard her mother laughing as if he'd made some incredibly funny joke. She probably wanted him for her next boyfriend. After the big fight, Jason hadn't been back. Mom couldn't *live* without a boyfriend.

"Just because I like having a man around..." Mom always said when Tracy complained because some jerk was going to move in.

Tracy did put on her bathrobe and even brushed her hair. Eyeing herself in the bathroom mirror, she decided she looked sweet and pretty without makeup and with her hair all shiny and loose. Alice in Wonderland.

Clutching the robe around herself, she went barefoot to the living room and curled up on one end of the couch.

He started to rise from where he already sat in the recliner that matched Mom's and belonged to whichever boyfriend lived here. Both of them faced the TV.

Whenever Mom was home, the TV was on. Soaps or talk shows in the daytime, whatever stupid sitcom she could find in the evening. Even if she was cooking dinner or on the telephone with a friend, the TV would be on.

"I like the company," she'd say.

But she had turned it off for the cop.

Tracy looked at him and waited.

He smiled easily at her. "I talked to some of your friends today."

She hugged herself. "Yeah? So?"

"Tracy!" her mother said sharply. Her face looked pinched. Yesterday she'd been all maternal and worried and mad at that SOB who had touched her little girl. Today she just wanted it all to go away, so Tracy could go back to school and be out of her hair.

"One of them remembers you saying Mr. Tanner was a creep," the cop said.

She tucked her feet under her. "He is."

"She says you were discussing which male teachers were 'hot.' Do you remember that?"

"Kind of. I guess." She tossed her hair. "Does it matter?"

"Just curious what he'd done or said at that point to make you think that."

She gave a shudder. "He's always *helping* you at your computer. Which means he can hang over your shoulder and breathe on your neck and 'accidentally' bump his mouth against your cheek. Any of the girls can tell you."

It was true. She was grossed out when he came up behind her and practically hugged her so he could put his hands on the keyboard to each side of her hands. He smelled. And the other day, when he helped her,

she suddenly wanted to scream. It reminded her—
She gave another shudder. He was a creep. After the
way he had totally humiliated her in front of everyone, he *deserved* to lose his job!

"When did Mr. Tanner first—" Detective McLean
seemed to choose his words carefully "—become interested in you?"

"I don't know." Tracy looked down at her hands.
Her knuckles were white, and she realized her fingers
were clenched on the bathrobe. She couldn't seem to
relax; it was like her hands were frozen in a death
grip. "School only started September third."

"Uh-huh." He waited.

When? "Um...I don't know. Like, maybe after the
first week or two, he kept wanting to help me. And
talk to me after class."

"Did he have any legitimate reason to keep you
after class?"

"What do you mean, legitimate?" Weren't babies
legitimate if their parents were married and bastards
otherwise?

"Real. Something he could defend to the principal.
Say—" his gaze was sharp "—missing assignments,
or a bad attitude in class, or..."

"I'm really slow at keyboarding. Mr. Tanner
claims I'm not doing enough of his little tests, where
you type like DFG over and over. Or something. I
can't help it if I'm not very good at it. Who wants to
type anyway?"

In this honeyed voice, Mom said, "Now, Tracy,
you know how many jobs require typing and computer skills. What do you think you're going to do,
become a movie star?" The last had a little snap, like
the end of a whip uncurling.

Tracy stared at her sullenly. "I want to be an artist."

"We've talked about this. You have to be practical…"

The cop interrupted her. "Ms. Lawson showed me some of your work. You have talent."

She was angry at herself for feeling a flush of pleasure. All he was doing was buttering her up. *I'm your friend,* he was saying. *Trust me. I'll help you get out of this mess. Just admit that you're lying.*

He led her through her story again. Three weeks ago, Mr. Tanner had touched her breast when he kept her after class. He told her she was really pretty, so much more grown-up looking than the other girls. He was having trouble thinking of her as a student.

The next time, he took her hand and made her feel him and then unzip his pants and do other things. When she tried to make an excuse to leave, that's when he said she was flunking his class, but that could change.

She tasted blood and realized she was gnawing on her lip. "And I thought, it wasn't so bad. For a good grade."

Her mother said absolutely nothing.

Tracy swallowed. "Only then, the next time, he made me do it. And it hurt, and I hated it. And so I told."

He asked her why she'd chosen to talk to Ms. Stavig, and she said because she didn't know any of the teachers that well, but Ms. Stavig seemed nice and an eighth-grade friend told her Ms. Stavig was the best if you ever needed help.

Finally, after what seemed forever, the cop got up to leave. His eyes serious, he said, "I know this is hard for you. I'm sorry, Tracy. Please believe me. But sometimes people do lie, and Mr. Tanner is telling me one thing and you're telling me another. My job is to be absolutely certain who is telling the truth. So you'll have to be patient with me.''

She nodded numbly.

''Then we'll be talking again,'' the cop said, and left.

Tracy and her mother sat without talking or moving for a long time.

Tracy broke first. She jumped to her feet, screamed at Mom, ''There! Are you happy?'' and ran to her room.

CHAPTER FIVE

MONDAY MORNING, when Mariah walked into the teacher's lounge, a dozen low-voiced conversations stopped and then started again only after everyone checked out the new arrival. She'd never seen so many of the teachers and staff in here at once except for special luncheons.

Pouring a cup of coffee, pretending to a casualness she didn't feel, she asked Jennifer Risotti, the Family Life teacher, "Why the buzzing?"

The tall brunette sipped her coffee. "I hear you know more than the rest of us."

"Oh, dear," Mariah said involuntarily.

"Is Gerald really being investigated?"

"I'm afraid so. And, no," she said hastily, forestalling the next question, "I really can't say anything else."

"So you do know."

"I know Noreen hoped it could be resolved over the weekend."

Resolved, she thought with distaste, escaping the lounge and taking her coffee up four flights to her classroom. What an unemotional, euphemistic word for the completion of an ugly process that would leave everybody involved forever tainted. For Gerald Tanner, none of this would ever be resolved.

By lunchtime, she knew he wasn't teaching today.

A substitute had taken over his classes. Tracy, too, was still missing from her desk in Drama.

Mariah was just taking her brown-bag lunch from her tote bag and debating whether to go to the office and find out what was going on, when Noreen Patterson came in.

"Do you have a minute, Mariah?"

"Of course." She continued unwrapping her egg salad sandwich.

The principal shut the classroom door and came to her desk. "I wanted to keep you abreast of the investigation. Perhaps you've heard that Gerald isn't here today. I felt it best to suspend him with pay for the moment."

How quickly a man's life could be destroyed.

Hiding the flash of mingled anger and guilt, Mariah asked, "Do you know any more?"

"No, and I made plain to him that I was taking this action primarily to protect him from whispers."

"You heard from parents all weekend," Mariah said dryly.

Noreen Patterson grimaced. "Unfortunately." She chose the same desk as had Detective McLean and sat, her green-and-blue broomstick skirt pooling around her. "There's simply no way I can have him continue to teach with this kind of allegation outstanding. It's terribly unfair to him, I know. But what can I do?"

Mariah was silent for a moment. "There wasn't anything else you could do, I suppose."

"I don't know him well. I can't even say, 'Look at this man's record in his twenty years of teaching in the Port Dare district.'" She looked unhappily at

Mariah. "My instinct is always to back up my teachers, but this time…"

Mariah nodded. *This time, the allegation is too ugly. The students too vulnerable.* That was what the principal meant. And it was true.

"In this country, we're supposed to be innocent until proven guilty." She made a sound. "That's a naive thing to say, isn't it?"

"No." Noreen Patterson looked her age and more today. "No, it isn't. This is the only crime where the accusation alone has almost as much weight as a conviction."

Mariah made herself take a bite of her sandwich. When she'd swallowed, she asked, "Is he angry?"

"Oh, yes." The principal gave a heavy sigh. "How do you know if a man is capable of something like this?"

She tried to sound detached. "From the outside, I'm not sure you can ever tell. Even if you think you know him well."

She must have given herself away, because Noreen looked at her strangely. "You sound as if you've experienced something like this before."

Mariah bit her lip. "My ex-husband was accused. It was never proved. Simon said…" She tried to smile. "Well, you can guess. It was pretty much the same thing Gerald said. The word of a child against his. How can anyone ever know?"

Compassion in her eyes, Noreen said, "How painful for you."

"For all of us," she said quietly. "At least Gerald doesn't have a wife and child to lose."

"No." Expression troubled and soft, the principal

said, "I'm sorry you got involved in this. I didn't realize."

"I'm okay." She ate another bite, didn't taste it. "Has the police officer learned *anything*?"

"He says it can easily take weeks for this kind of investigation."

"Weeks." Mariah imagined Gerald Tanner's torment. What was he doing, sitting home in some bleak apartment staring at the wall, scared, envisioning the loss of his teaching certificate and his reputation? Seeing jail bars closing behind him?

Noreen sighed and struggled out of the student desk. "I'd better let you finish your lunch. I just wanted you to know what was happening."

Mariah nodded numbly. "Thank you."

"If you need...support, come and talk to me."

She tried another smile and nodded.

By the end of the day, she'd heard other rumors. Detective McLean was on campus talking to students and teachers again. Kids were getting called to the office so he could ask them questions about Mr. Tanner and Tracy and the dance last week.

Somehow, she wasn't surprised when he appeared shortly after her last student of the day gave up explaining why he'd been too busy that weekend to write his book report and left in a sulk.

She was turning off the overhead when he said from the doorway, "Ms. Stavig?"

"Detective McLean," she said resignedly, and released the screen to roll up.

In absentia, he was an imposing presence on the campus. People were scared, awed. He turned heads and provoked whispers wherever he went. Turning, she half expected him to be diminished in person: smaller than she remembered, less commanding.

But, no. He strolled into the room as though he intended to make himself unthreatening. Hands in the pockets of corduroy slacks, he held his shoulders slightly hunched and his expression was conciliatory. Somebody should tell him it didn't work, she thought unkindly. He was a big man, with the shoulders of a laborer. And yet he moved with the grace of an athlete and the wariness of the cop he was. His head was always turning, his eyes sharp. He'd scanned the room, missing nothing, before looking at her with that amiable, I'm-a-regular-Joe look.

"More questions?" she asked.

"Nah." He paused to read a quotation on the wall and gave a brief laugh. "Mark Twain is one of my favorite writers."

"Is he." She erased the page numbers of an assignment from the board.

"Not Tom Sawyer or Huckleberry Finn. *Roughing It,* and *Life on the Mississippi.* And his essays. There's nothing like laughing even as you're wondering if he didn't just insult you."

She was almost disarmed. "A literate cop?"

"You're surprised?"

"I would have said it was an oxymoron."

He winced. "Ouch."

Mariah sighed. "You want something."

"No." He picked up and set a student desk back into the row. "Just wondered how you are. Have you been fighting off the curious all day?"

"No, I've succeeded in hiding up here." She put her hands on her hips and nodded at the second desk he was pulling into place. "The janitor will do that."

He carefully aligned it with the others anyway. "Are you leaving?"

"As soon as I gather some papers to grade tonight."

"May I walk you to your car?"

So formal! Mariah eyed him with suspicion. "Think of my reputation," she said, only half kidding.

Did he actually look crestfallen? "Being seen with me would blacken it, huh?"

"No." She straightened a pile of papers unnecessarily, squaring the corners. "At least among the faculty, it seems to be common knowledge that I have inside knowledge. Maybe a secretary in the office talked. Or, heck, maybe people have noticed how much you've been hanging around up here."

He moved another desk. "Are you a pariah now, too?"

"I can't tell," she said frankly. "I fled into hiding before I could get a real sense."

He moved his shoulders restlessly and prowled the room. "What do the kids think?"

"That the idea of an old guy like Mr. Tanner making up to one of them is gross." She frowned, her hands going still in the act of gathering student papers. "You know, I couldn't really tell whose side they're coming down on. Gerald is generally known as funny and pretty nice…"

"And he has those cool programs."

She smiled ruefully. "Right. While Tracy is popular only with a certain segment of the kids. Some of the others think she's…"

"Slutty?"

Mariah made a face. "What an awful word."

"But one suggested to me by a girl I interviewed."

She sighed. "Tracy does come across that way, I'm afraid. Well, I suppose you noticed."

The detective crossed his arms. "Actually, no. Remember, both times I've talked to the girl, she was at home. The first time, she was wearing jeans and some little T-shirt—skimpy, but all the girls wear ones that look a size too small to me. Her hair was in a ponytail, she had on a little makeup..." He shrugged. "Just a regular teenage girl. The second time, her mom said she didn't feel very well, and Tracy came out in a bathrobe, face scrubbed clean. She could have been ten years old."

"Is she okay?"

"Tracy?" In his roving, he paused to glance out the window. "I don't know," he admitted. "Tension seems to be seething between her and her mother. Maybe it always is. She's thirteen, right? Isn't that the teenage version of the Terrible Twos?"

"So it's reputed to be," Mariah admitted. "I kind of like kids this age."

"Why?" he asked, studying her. Since he seemed genuinely to want to know, she answered.

"They're half child, half adult, gawky and graceful, naive and wise, foolish and sensible, all big feet and skinny legs and exaggerated posturing, but you can see in each of them the promise of who he or she will become."

"The English teacher speaks," he mocked, a smile in his eyes.

"The English teacher?"

"Who he or she will become."

"Oh." He made her sound so pedantic. Warmth

crept into her cheeks. "I particularly dislike mixed singular and plural."

"Just kidding." His smile was friendly. "I particularly admire the proper use of language."

Her heart did a funny hop and skip. She said the first thing that came to mind. "I'm, uh, ready to go."

"To go?" His brows rose. "Oh. Yeah. Sure. Can I walk you?" He lifted one hand. "No, wait. *May* I walk you?"

"Yes, you may," she said primly.

His smile teased her. "Kids are gone by this time, anyway. No one will see us."

She knew better but, feeling strangely light-headed, didn't care. What did she have to hide? She'd done no more than any teacher was required by law and conscience to do, however she might agonize over her decisions.

Mariah closed her desk drawer, swung her purse strap over her shoulder and lifted her tote bag full of papers.

"Let me carry that." His tone was polite but determined. "I'll look like a cad if I let you lug that down all those flights of stairs."

"I thought no one was going to notice us." Good heavens, was she teasing him? Detective Connor Mc-Lean, the man who had shattered her serene world?

He took the bag, his knuckles brushing her hand. "Hey, I'm a cop. 'Always be prepared,' is supposed to be our motto."

When the classroom door clicked shut behind them, Mariah realized how uncomfortably close Connor stood. Although he wasn't touching her, the hairs on her nape stirred when he let out the soft exclamation.

This was insane. She was painfully aware of him

as a man. Her hand where he'd inadvertently touched her felt hot and tingly, as if she'd burned herself. The smile glinting in his eyes had created a fizz of bubbles in her chest, anticipation and excitement for something that *could not be*. Even assuming he was…well, interested, she could never, ever forget how she'd met him, the way he'd unrelentingly driven doubts between her and Simon as if they were crude, pointed stakes in the ground.

She heard her own harsh whisper. *You believed her. Yes.*

He knew no more now than he had then, but he still wouldn't say, *Maybe I was wrong.*

Oh, how she wanted him to be wrong!

Except, if her doubts were erased, then all she would be left with was her own apparent inability to feel the kind of faith and love a man deserved from his wife.

Fear for Zofie, or despise herself. Two unhappy choices, brought to her in a surprise visit by Detective Connor McLean.

She could not be attracted to him. She wouldn't let herself be. Surely she possessed that much self-discipline.

Careful not to back into him, she stepped aside and turned. "Shall we?" she said briskly.

The hall was empty, the banks of lockers closed. The linoleum floor still gleamed from the weekend polish. Her heels clicked on it, but Detective McLean walked lightly.

A few doors down, light and a masculine laugh spilled from Rod Cabot's classroom. He and a new young Social Studies teacher were conducting a flirtation, Mariah knew. She had felt a few pangs of…not jealousy, exactly, but wistfulness. It would be nice to be in love again.

Maybe that's all that was wrong with her today. Three years without a date was a long time. She hadn't been interested when a few men had hinted that they might be. But if her body was reacting this way just because she was alone with a well-built man who had an oddly sweet smile, it was time she consider reentering the dating world.

Relieved, she said, "Back to Tracy. She does dress a little differently than most of the girls. Skirts shorter, shirts tighter, more makeup... She acts more sexually aware than her peers. I assumed she was imitating her mother, who also tends to wear miniskirts and three-inch heels even when the other mothers are in jeans." Tracy's mother also wore her bleached hair teased high and her skimpy tank tops cut low.

"She's a cocktail waitress down at the Customs House Inn," he said, as if in answer to a question.

"I know."

She felt his glance.

"I asked."

They reached the third-floor landing. A thunder of footsteps warned them to step aside. A kid tore past them going up, his face red and his breath coming in gasps.

McLean turned to watch. "A gunman in the basement?"

"I'd guess he forgot something in his locker. Seventh-graders are unlucky enough to be assigned lockers on the fourth floor."

"You work your way down with seniority?"

"Exactly."

They continued down the broad, polished linoleum

steps with a peeling abrasive strip on each meant to prevent slips.

"I heard you were asking about the dance last week," Mariah said. "Do you mind telling me why?"

Voices rose from the stairwell below.

"Let me wait until we get outside," he said.

They reached the heavy doors on the second floor that opened outside to a grand porch and wide steps that curved in two directions. The air was damp but cool, typical for a Pacific Northwest autumn day.

Students still loitered on the sidewalk and narrow stretch of lawn between the building and the street, some waiting for rides, others hanging out with friends, some skateboarders doing forbidden jumps off the curb. The two adults were alone on the porch.

"Rumor has it," Connor McLean said, "that a high schooler—maybe even a junior—sneaked into the last middle school dance to see Tracy. A four year age difference—that's a big gulf in sexual sophistication. I'm wondering whether he didn't come for more than a dance."

"You mean, she had sex, but not with Gerald," Mariah said slowly.

"Exactly." He shrugged. "Could be it was consensual, but then she panicked thinking she might be pregnant. Or it could be she thought if she sneaked away with him, they'd make out, only he pushed it further."

Mariah ran her hand along the rough stone cap on the railing. "But if he raped her, why lie?"

"I was hoping you could tell me." He grimaced. "You understand teenage culture better than I do. So here's my question—if this junior is popular, a guy all the other girls think is hot, and suddenly Tracy claims he raped her, what would the reaction be among students?''

''You mean, would 'snitching' be social suicide?''

''Exactly.''

She thought. ''I don't know. I wish I could honestly say every single kid would be repulsed by a boy who would rape a seventh-grade girl. The truth is, teenagers still have some pretty old-fashioned ideas about sex and sexuality and even gender roles. I can just hear some of them saying, 'She was asking for it,' because she dresses the way she does and because she agreed to go behind the gym with him, assuming that's your scenario.''

His gaze never left her. ''Would it make a difference whether he's popular or not?''

''I don't know that, either. But frankly, I doubt a really popular junior in high school would bother with a seventh-grader—*that* might be social suicide.''

''In my day—'' his tone was dry ''—a certain set of boys kept track of how many virgins they'd had. You might have to hunt young for that.''

She shuddered. ''What a thought! And, yes, of course it's possible. Have you asked Tracy about the dance?''

''I'm looking for ammunition first.''

Her mind jumped. ''And why Gerald?''

''Because she genuinely does hate him,'' the detective said reasonably. ''What a chance to kill two birds with one stone! Get rid of a teacher you detest, and have an excuse parents and authorities will accept for maybe being pregnant.''

Mariah gazed sightlessly at the few students still

hanging around the front of the building. "Does she hate him just because he's giving her a bad grade?"

He hesitated. "I'm getting the feeling there's a little more to it than that. At this point, I'm just guessing."

She hugged herself. The day *was* cold. She had no reason to feel as if a ghost had brushed by her. Sure, she was a teacher, too, but she'd never had a student actually hate her.

Had she?

"Kids aren't the only ones who make fun of someone to get a laugh. Teachers do it, too. Or they sit in judgment on the basis of a narrow ideological focus."

She turned her head. "You're saying…"

He held up both hands. "I'm not saying yet. It's too soon."

"You told the principal it could take weeks."

"That's right."

She was clutching her purse to her breast like a shield. "Do you know how agonizing those weeks will be for Gerald Tanner as well as Tracy?"

Emotions moved in his eyes, giving her a glimpse of a conscience she had wanted to believe he didn't possess.

"Yeah." In contrast, his voice was utterly without emotion. "I know."

Mariah took a breath. "Just…hurry. Okay?"

Gaze intense on her face, he reached out and briefly gripped her arm just above her elbow. "I'll do my best. That's all I can do."

Her head nodded, puppetlike. She didn't move.

"Mariah…" His voice lowered, roughened.

"Yes?" she whispered.

Behind them one of the doors opened. "Detective

McLean!'' Noreen Patterson said. ''You're still here.''

He blinked, and the next moment Mariah wondered if she had imagined that moment of shimmering intensity.

''Start early, work late,'' he said easily. ''I had some questions for Ms. Stavig.''

Ms. Stavig. Not Mariah.

And why would she want it to be Mariah?

''Did you have something you wanted to ask?'' he continued.

''Nope.'' Noreen scanned the cars at the curb. ''I was hoping to catch Justin's mother. And there she is.'' She lifted a hand to them, then hurried down the steps and across the lawn toward a red minivan with the doors open to what looked like half a dozen teenage boys in soccer shorts and shin guards.

''I've got to pick up Zofie,'' Mariah said quickly. ''Unless you had anything else?''

''No.'' His voice was very quiet, very controlled. ''I didn't want anything else.''

''Oh.'' Foolish to feel letdown. ''Then I'll take my bag…''

He looked back at her, expressionless. ''I said I'd walk you to your car, and I will.''

''You really don't have to…''

He merely raised his brows. ''Which way?''

''I'm parked on the side.'' Mariah was embarrassed by her sulky tone. She pivoted abruptly and started down the steps, aware of him following.

He was silent until she was fumbling to get the key in the lock of her small red car.

Then, rather oddly, he said, ''I take it I haven't improved on acquaintance for you.''

Startled, Mariah turned, the car door open. "What do you mean?"

"I'm just gathering that you despise me as much as you did last week when you walked into your principal's office and realized I'd been called."

He sounded as if he didn't care, but his very stillness told her otherwise.

"What difference does it make?" she asked. "You don't need me for this investigation."

"I told you..."

"That I'm symbolic." For some reason that made her angry. "Well, find another symbol." She snatched her tote bag from him and tossed it onto the passenger seat.

Creases formed on his brow. "Now I've annoyed you."

"I want this not to be happening," she told him, a snap in her voice. "I want not to be a part of it, but you keep involving me."

His eyes narrowed. "You didn't seem to mind talking about Tracy."

"No. I...I'm curious. How can I help it?" She got into the car, feeling safer. His hand on the open door kept her from slamming it. Childishly she said, "That doesn't mean I *like* my role in this!"

"You mean, giving the cop ideas? Letting him bounce his off you?" Now his voice was silky. "What is it, too much like consorting with the enemy?"

She gripped the wheel and stared straight ahead at the granite and stucco wall of the school. "Do you blame me if I have mixed feelings?"

There was a moment of silence. He sighed. "No. I don't blame you. I hoped... Oh, hell. Never mind.

I do appreciate your time and thoughts, Ms. Stavig. Drive safely.''

He closed her door and was already walking away by the time she turned, her mouth open as if she were going to say…what?

"Damn," she whispered.

What had gotten into her? One minute, they'd been talking like friends. No, more. She would have sworn he'd been…oh, flirting with her. That was one way to put it. And then when Noreen came out, he shuttered his every emotion, and hers had come irrationally screaming forth.

Maybe he was right, and she *had* felt like a collaborator, whispering under the portico with the man investigating the school's secrets. That's how the other teachers would view their low-voiced colloquy, she knew it was.

She heard that low, rough, "Mariah."

Not a question, but perhaps the beginning of one.

But what had he intended to ask?

Or was she, once again, imagining things?

And if he *had* asked, what would her answer have been? And why had she been so afraid of the question?

CHAPTER SIX

"I'M GOING OUT FOR A PASS!" Evan yelled, running a zigzagging path across the open grass. "Breaking right..."

Connor let loose the football, an easy toss, sending it spiraling gently into his nephew's outstretched hands. Evan clutched it to his chest and raced the last few yards to an imaginary goal line, where he spiked the ball and did a victory dance.

Lazing on his side in a sunny spot on the park grass, Hugh called, "Good one, kid!"

Connor reached the "goal line" himself and picked up the ball. "Okay, why don't you throw me a few."

"Yeah. Cool." The seven-year-old's thin shoulders slumped. "Except mine wobble."

Connor made his shrug careless. "Of course your passes wobble. You have to grow into throwing a football. At the moment, your hand is too small to put the right kind of rotation on it. Time will take care of it. For now, you can work on accuracy and developing your arm."

"Really?" Evan looked hopeful, then downcast. "My friend Ryan can throw really great passes."

"Is he bigger than you?"

He frowned. "Well, yeah."

"There you go." Connor grinned. "Evan, you're

seven years old. Trust me, by the time you hit high school, you'll be ready to star.''

A big smile lit the kid's freckled face. ''O-kay!''

''Now, throw the ball.'' Connor broke into an easy lope, turning so that his pattern brought him into the path of the short pass. ''Good one,'' he called, and tossed it back. ''Another.''

Connor reveled in the normalcy of the scene and of John's son and his daughter, Maddie. She was off watching the soccer games and kicking the soccer ball with friends but within eyesight of her uncles. Hugh, who'd had a late night with one of his blondes, pretended to watch both kids while really catching some shut-eye.

Evan and Connor played catch until the boy was panting and red-faced. To be tactful, Connor said, ''I need a break. Let's go see what your uncle Hugh has in that cooler.''

Maddie arrived about the same time, dribbling the ball between her feet. She was playing on a special team this year that traveled all over the state to compete. Evan, perhaps recognizing that he wouldn't equal his sister's ability as a killer forward, had dropped out of soccer and started youth touch football.

''I'm hungry!'' Maddie announced, easily lifting the ball into the air with one foot and bouncing it from her forehead.

Hugh jerked and opened his eyes. ''Jeez! You scared me!''

''I think he should play goalie for you,'' Connor suggested ruthlessly. ''He's getting lazy.''

''Yeah!'' she exclaimed gleefully. ''We could practice penalty kicks!''

Hugh laughed. "You don't think you could get a kick by me, do you?"

His pretty niece dropped cross-legged to the grass. "You never even played soccer, did you?"

"I'm a good athlete," he said carelessly.

She gave him a piranhalike smile. "You're on."

Connor rubbed his hands together. "Oh, this is going to be fun. Whaddaya say, Ev? Shall we watch the slaughter?"

"Yeah!" his nephew exclaimed.

Hugh gave a kind smile. "You should take pity on your sister. Let's not embarrass her too much."

Evan fell to the ground with a raucous laugh.

Hugh lifted his eyebrows.

"You haven't been to one of her games lately, have you?" Connor asked. "They don't play like girls anymore. You're in deep doodoo, bro."

Evan thought that was funny, too. Hugh was less amused.

"Bunch of girls," he muttered.

Maddie was moved to heave the ball at him. He caught it in midair and grinned rakishly. "See? Won't catch me snoozing."

"We already did," she said with a sniff.

However sunny, no late October day could offer picnic weather, especially not on the Olympic peninsula at the foothills of mountains already gaining the foundation for winter snowcaps. The McLeans had brought one to the park anyway. John and Natalie had taken a ferry to Victoria for a romantic weekend getaway. Privately Connor suspected they wouldn't leave their room at the Empress. Hugh and Connor had offered to stay with the kids. Last night, Uncle Connor had been enough entertainment. By today

Maddie and Evan had begun to get antsy and whine about going to friends' houses. The picnic had been an impulse, but the kids had both jumped at it.

Yesterday Connor had worked, interviewing Tanner again and half a dozen more students from Port Dare Middle School. Today, he had decided to let well enough alone.

Tracy Mitchell and Gerald Tanner both could stew a little. The girl had missed a week of school now, and must be getting restless. The computer instructor's mood was swinging between anger and depression. Somebody was due to crack, Connor figured.

"Can we go to a movie tonight?" Maddie asked, unwrapping a sandwich. She seemed impervious to the wintry chill in the air and the cold ground that had barely thawed by midmorning. Her sweatshirt was tied around her waist, and she wore only jeans, a T-shirt and athletic shoes. But this was a girl who played soccer games in pouring rain and snowstorms. Her sport wasn't like baseball, postponed at the first drizzle. Officials never seemed to call a soccer game.

"Yeah!" Evan chimed in. "Cool! A movie would be fun. Can we?"

They had a rousing discussion about what was worth seeing, with both men knowing perfectly well they would end up at a PG snoozer. The trick was finding one that both a ten-year-old girl and a seven-year-old boy would enjoy. Maddie's tastes were starting to lean toward the preteen, while Evan was bloodthirsty and repulsed by romance.

"Hey, that's my team," Evan said suddenly. On the hour, players from the games that had just finished were heading toward the parking lot, while the teams to play the next game were warming up. A group of boys, filthy and grass-stained, were whooping and dribbling balls while their parents trailed, chatting and carrying lawn chairs and coats.

"You should have kept playing," Maddie said.

Evan shrugged.

"You can go say hi," Hugh suggested.

He shrugged again. "Nah."

Connor watched him with the tangle of pity and compassion and anger on his behalf that a parent might feel. Evan, scrawny and with huge feet, wasn't very athletic right now. He would grow into those feet in a few years, but right now he was struggling with a sense of inferiority.

Connor shared John's belief that their mother had contributed to it. She had baby-sat the kids often after their own mother had been struck with multiple sclerosis and forced to move into an extended care facility. The kids' grandmother still stayed with them when a case had John working hours that Natalie couldn't be home. For reasons none of them understood, she had always been harder on Evan than on Maddie. John had told Connor privately that he'd confronted her after Maddie told him "Grandma is mean to Evan."

Mom was trying. Connor could tell. She'd smile softly at Maddie, start to say something tart to Evan and then bite it back. Sometimes she even managed a compliment. But he was sensitive enough to hear what she didn't say.

"Do you miss playing soccer?" Connor asked quietly.

Evan plucked a clump of grass and began shredding it. "Not really."

Maddie, gifted athlete and sometime-bratty older sister, had the tact not to say, *You sucked anyway.*

Connor glanced back toward the boys who had been Evan's teammates, and just by chance saw a clump of little girls, maybe five, six years old, leaving another, smaller field. The one in the lead, a cute kid with a bouncy dark ponytail and skinny legs enveloped in too-big shin guards, was walking backward and talking to friends. Something about her tugged at Connor's memory. Big eyes he guessed were dark, a small heart-shaped face and an air of gravity noticeable even from this distance.

He felt a peculiar thump in his chest, and he immediately scanned the crowd, looking for someone else. Zofie Stavig's mother.

He found her, walking with another mother, each carrying a lawn chair in one hand and a cooler slung between them. Even looking at the back of her head, he was sure it was her.

"Excuse me," he said abruptly, shot to his feet and was halfway down the terraced slope to the soccer fields before he could think about what he was doing.

He caught up with the women and said, "Here, let me carry that."

Their heads turned; Mariah's eyes widened. "Detective!" she exclaimed.

Now the other woman's gaze was surprised and curious.

"Connor McLean," he said. "I'm with the Port Dare PD. I can't get *Ms.* Stavig here to call me by my first name."

She blushed, looking both annoyed and relieved that he'd gotten her off the hook from having to explain why she knew a cop.

"Lynn Kowalsky."

He and the other mother shook hands.

"I can carry that," he said again, patiently. When neither woman moved, he grabbed the cooler from them. "Your day to provide snacks?" he asked.

"Mine," Lynn Kowalsky said. "Mariah was nice enough to help me struggle across the field. After all, I couldn't watch the game without my coat, mittens, scarf and chair, too."

He lifted the cooler to his shoulder. "At least it's sunny."

They walked slowly, a woman to each side of him. He kept stealing looks at Mariah. She looked... different. Younger, lighter-spirited, less weighted by the sadness he had sensed in her every time he saw her. She was even prettier this way, whether because of mood or because of her casual Sunday clothes: blue jeans, white athletic shoes and a crimson WSU sweatshirt. Her hair was caught in a ponytail that bobbed at her nape as jauntily as her cute daughter's did.

On the other hand, Mariah had yet to say a word past that first exclamation.

Her friend glanced at her, apparently decided she wasn't going to contribute and chose to play nice. "Do you have a child in soccer, too?"

"Believe it or not," he said with what he hoped was a charmingly rueful smile, given to both women in turn, "my niece and nephew and brother and I brought a picnic to the park today."

Mariah was startled into saying incredulously, "A picnic?"

"My brother and his wife—they've only been married a year—went to Victoria for the weekend. My younger brother and I inherited the kids. My niece plays select soccer, doesn't have a game today, but she likes to hang out here and watch anyway. My nephew and I have been throwing the football.''

"You don't, um, have kids of your own?" Mariah's cheeks were still pink, and she sounded shy.

"Nope." But lately he'd realized that he wanted them. He wouldn't go so far as to say he was cooing over babies, but once in a while he'd watch John with his kids, or see a father passing with a toddler on his shoulders, and feel a physical pang of...envy. "I'm not married," he added helpfully.

"Oh. I didn't know..." She stopped in apparent confusion.

"Is that Zofie up there?"

Her gaze followed his. "Yes. She's a first-grader now."

He didn't let her think about the last time he'd seen Zofie. "Did your girls win their game today?"

"Three to two," said the other mother with satisfaction. "Zofie is a dynamite goalie."

"And Susan kicked the winning goal."

"Your daughter, I take it," Connor said.

She nodded to a freckled, sturdy redhead trailing Zofie.

"Before you know it," Connor said in a portentous tone, "those girls will be playing select soccer, and every weekend you'll get to drive to Yakima or Bellingham or Vancouver and rent a hotel room and spend all day hanging out on the sidelines."

Mariah actually looked at him. "You're kidding."

"Nope. John has been heard to wish he'd yanked Maddie from soccer while he still could."

She laughed. "I'm not sure I believe that."

Connor grinned. "Actually, he's proud of her. But he's a cop, too, which means he can't take every weekend off to get her to all those tournaments. Fortunately some of the parents with kids on the team take turns chaperoning a whole gang."

"Good heavens," Lynn said. "I don't think my Susan will ever play at that level, but Zofie..."

"Don't even say it," Mariah warned.

"This is my van right here." The woman unlocked the rear door and he deposited the ice chest inside. "Many thanks," she said, then called, "Susan! Let's go. You'll be late to that birthday party!"

Retreating, Connor muttered, "Maybe I don't want to be a father."

"What?" Mariah was right behind him.

"Talking to myself." He grimaced. "Is that how you spend every waking minute? Chauffeuring Zofie?"

"Pretty much." The momentary silence was a little awkward. "Actually, yeah. Especially since I'm a single mother—" She broke off.

He felt his face go stiff.

"I'm sorry," Mariah said quickly. "I didn't mean that the way it sounded. I wasn't blaming..."

"I know you weren't." Sure.

"Really."

He forced a smile. "Don't worry. Is Zofie going to the same birthday party?"

"No, thank goodness." As if automatically, she looked around for her daughter, saw her and relaxed. "We have lunch plans. Which probably means whatever fast-food place has the coolest toy with their kids' meal. She pays attention to the commercials."

"Boy, do I know what you mean." He hesitated,

told himself he was crazy and asked anyway. "You two would be welcome to join us. For our picnic, I mean. Evan's only a year older than Zofie."

She backed up a step, bumped against a log that edged the parking lot and started to fall. Connor lunged forward and grabbed her by both arms, setting her on her feet right in front of him. She was so close now, he could see how thick her lashes were and how blue smudged the delicate skin beneath her eyes, as if she hadn't slept well last night. Her soft mouth was parted in surprise, her eyes wide as she stared at him. God, they were gorgeous, he thought, the gold speckles in a brown-green iris so fascinating he couldn't tear his gaze away.

Let her go, he told himself. His hands stayed locked on her arms.

She took a deep breath. "Thank you," she whispered.

"You're okay?" he asked hoarsely.

Mariah nodded. The ponytail flipped against her neck. He imagined touching his mouth to the silky, pale skin of her throat.

Reluctantly, one finger at a time, Connor loosened his grip and finally lifted his hands from her arms. For just an instant, neither moved nor looked away.

"I..." She swallowed, backed up and bumped against the log again. This time, even as his hand shot out, she righted herself and laughed nervously. "I seem to be a klutz today."

He rubbed his hands on his jean-clad thighs. It should be too cold to break out in a sweat from even a vicious attack of lust.

"You're just jealous because the kids had an excuse to throw themselves around in the mud."

This laugh was more natural. "Oh, yeah. Speaking of which…" She looked past him.

Connor turned to see her daughter approaching. Closer up, he saw that her face was mud-streaked, her shorts and shin-guards filthy. Her gaze shied between her mother and the strange man talking to her.

"Zofie, this is…um…"

He could see Mariah frantically considering and discarding ways of introducing him.

"…a friend of mine. He's a policeman. Detective McLean."

"Hi," the girl said shyly. Under the dirt, she was exceptionally pretty, with those huge dark eyes and cheekbones that would make her a beauty when she grew up. "A police lady came and talked to my class about safety."

"I'll bet that was Officer Leary. Was she blonde? And so tiny she looks like that big heavy belt and all the equipment hanging on it is going make her tip right over?"

A giggle escaped Mariah's daughter and she nodded vigorously.

He lowered his voice. "She's tougher than she looks, you know. She's a brown belt at karate and can take down a bad guy faster than I can."

"The *boys* in the class all said she couldn't be a *real* police officer, and that's why she's the one who goes to schools. *They* think only boys can shoot people and stuff."

His eyes met Mariah's over the girl's head. "Well, you know what?" he told her. "We hardly ever shoot people, anyway. Mostly, we write traffic tickets." He bent down and pretended to whisper. "Does your mom ever speed when she's driving?"

Another giggle was his reward. "Not Mommy!"

"Oh, good." He straightened and grinned at her mother. "I don't know if I want to be friends with someone who speeds."

"But *you* get to," the six-year-old reminded him.

"Yeah, that's the most fun part of being a cop."

Mariah cleared her throat. "I hate to interrupt, but you, kiddo, are filthy and I'm getting hungry. Say goodbye to Detective McLean."

"You're sure you don't want a sandwich and cold s'mores?" he said. "We have plenty."

She looked at him as if he was crazy. "*Cold* s'mores?"

"Crunchy."

Mariah shook her head, but she was laughing again. "I think we'd better stick to McDonald's."

Zofie, bless her heart, looked hopefully at her mother. "S'mores sound good."

"He's having a family picnic, though. With his nephew and niece."

"How old are they?" Zofie asked.

"Evan is seven and Maddie is ten. I'll bet she could show you some goalie tricks."

Mariah's eyes flashed and her voice cooled. "That's nice of you to offer, but we can't today. Thank you, anyway. Goodbye, Detective."

Crap. He'd pushed too hard.

He smiled lopsidedly. "Bye, Mariah. Nice to meet you, Zofie. Your mom's right. You do need a shower."

"*After* McDonald's."

"Before," her mother said firmly, as they walked away.

Connor watched them go, but turned before Mariah

could look back. She probably already thought he was—what? Hitting on her?

Was he?

Brooding, he walked back up the hill to his family, who had finished sandwiches and were squishing cold marshmallows and crunchy chocolate bars between graham crackers.

Hugh was making horrible faces as he chewed. "It's just not the same."

"I'll bet they'd be really good if we froze them," Evan said enthusiastically. "Uncle Connor! You're back. These are really good."

"I'd better eat my sandwich first."

"So," his brother said, "who was it you went charging after?"

"Yeah." Evan cackled. "Was she pretty? That's what Uncle Hugh wants to know!"

"Sure she's pretty." Connor made a production out of grabbing his sandwich and a can of pop. "But it was just somebody I wanted to have a word with."

"I know the girl you were talking to," Maddie said unexpectedly. "My class reads to little kids and helps them with their reading. She's in Mrs. Kinnard's class. Her name's funny." She frowned. "Like…like Sophie." Her face cleared and she said in triumph, "Zofie! Isn't that a weird name?"

"Well, her last name is Stavig, which I think is Slavic, so maybe Zofie is a common name where they came from. Like if your last name is Moreno, you might pick Elena instead of Hortense for a first name."

"Hortense!" Evan thought that was hilarious.

But Maddie nodded seriously.

Creases deepening on his forehead made Hugh

look older. His tone, too, was grave. "So that was Mariah Stavig."

Connor grunted his assent.

"Is she divorced?"

"Yeah."

Hugh still wasn't happy. "She's not holding a grudge?"

"I think maybe she's getting over it."

"Was she mad at you?" their niece asked. "How come?"

"Back when she was married, I investigated her husband for something." Both of the kids knew what their dad and uncles did, and how people were funny about police officers, liking them a lot when they needed help, but being afraid of them, or even resentful, the rest of the time.

"Oh," Maddie said.

Hugh waited until Connor reluctantly met his eyes. "Is this smart?" he asked.

Connor thought about lying: *I really did have a question for her. Lighten up.*

But the McLean brothers had never lied to each other.

"I don't know," he said finally. "But it seems to matter."

Hugh thought about it and nodded. "There's more than one way to get wounded in the line of duty."

"I know."

Hugh was right: mixing business and pleasure was rarely a good idea.

Oh, yeah. There were plenty of reasons why Connor should leave Mariah Stavig alone.

But he was already planning what to say the next time he saw her.

MARIAH STILL COULDN'T believe she'd practically landed on her butt right in front of him. He always made her self-conscious. Wouldn't you think being self-conscious would make you *more* careful where you placed your feet, how you moved? Not her. He'd had to perform heroics to save her from a humiliating if not painful splat on the wet, cold ground, *and* he'd had the grace not to laugh at her.

"Is something wrong, Mommy?"

Mariah turned her head to smile at a now clean Zofie buckling herself into the car. "Not a thing. Did you decide for sure where we're going for lunch?"

"I think I want pizza. Can we have pizza?"

"We can have whatever you want," she agreed recklessly.

"Then pizza." Her daughter gave a decisive nod. "Rizzotti's."

"My favorite." Mariah gave her a hug before backing out of the driveway.

"I know," Zofie said smugly. She gave a small bounce on the booster seat she still, reluctantly, used. "That was a nice man at the soccer field. The policeman."

"Detective McLean?" She congratulated herself on sounding vague and surprised, as if she had to dredge his identity from her memory, so little had it meant to her to run into him there.

"Yeah. Him."

"He does seem nice."

Her daughter turned a puzzled face on her. "You said he was a friend."

"Oh, he's just the kind of friend you chat to when you meet. Not the kind you do things with."

"He wanted to do something with us. Eat cold s'mores."

"So he did." She managed a credible laugh. "Imagine how hard the chocolate bars would be."

Zofie frowned ahead. "It might have been fun."

"Yeah. It might have been. I just didn't want to intrude."

Even at six, Zofie knew that being polite included not "intruding." "You mean, he might have asked and not really meant it?" she questioned seriously.

"Well…" Mariah temporized. "I think *he* meant it. But we don't know his brother or niece and nephew, who were also there. They might not have wanted strangers joining them for lunch."

"Oh." Zofie nodded. "Maybe he'll ask us to do something when they're not there."

Mariah hoped she had conveyed without words that she did *not* wish to be asked again. She just wished she didn't have this tangle of mixed feelings: wistfulness and distracting physical awareness and a sort of throat-stopping knowledge that under other circumstances…

But this wasn't other circumstances, she reminded herself harshly, swallowing the lump in her throat. Detective Connor McLean was the man who three years ago walked into her living room and said a few quiet words that tore her family to shreds.

Anyway, she knew perfectly well she had no business remarrying. She'd promised to love Simon. Perhaps he had a hotter temper than she'd realized when she married him. Perhaps he was sometimes impatient, sometimes dismissed her as if her wants were insignificant next to his, but he was also a kind father, faithful to his wife, a good breadearner, a steady family man. He hadn't deserved her lack of faith. She had let a stranger's accusations have more weight in her heart than did her years with Simon.

What did that say about her?

Marriage was for better or worse. She had always despised the celebrities with their magnificent, romantic fourth weddings. Love was true and patient and stubborn and quite different from the wild excitement of romance.

She had promised the stubborn kind of love, and not delivered. How could she ever, in good conscience, walk down the aisle again and make a promise she hadn't kept the first time?

Casual dates, maybe. The anguish of love, no.

And somehow, Connor McLean didn't strike her as a casual man.

"You know, I may not even see him for ages," she said out loud to Zofie. "Besides, it's not his company I want for lunch."

"Whose do you want?" Zofie asked, half knowing, half liking reassurance.

"Yours, silly!"

Zofie giggled happily, forgetting the policeman.

Mariah wished he'd let her do the same.

CHAPTER SEVEN

SUNDAY AFTERNOON CONNOR took Maddie and Evan home and found John and Natalie already there.

"We missed the kids," big brother John said sheepishly, letting his wife take his place hugging them. "We caught an earlier ferry."

"You should have grabbed every minute," Connor said, as they all walked into the house. "When's the next time you'll have that kind of privacy?"

John gave an evil grin. "The kids know better than to surprise us in our bedroom."

"Ah. They've already had the visual aid part of Sex Ed 101, family style?"

"Nah. Just seen a few rustling sheets and heard Daddy snap, 'Whaddaya want?'"

"Good thing," Connor said, meaning it.

One of his most vivid memories, probably because the sight had been so disturbing, was walking in on his parents making love. He still had a snapshot tucked in his memory. He'd retreated silently, terrified by the seeming violence of the act and his mother's cries. It was years before he could put what he'd seen in context.

His cell phone rang.

"Damn," he muttered.

The caller's number didn't look familiar. "McLean," he said.

A short silence was followed by a girl's hesitant voice. "Is this, um, the police officer?"

His hunter's instincts sharpened. "Yes, this is Detective McLean. Who is this?"

"Amy Weinstein. You came and talked to me about Tracy."

"Right." He waved John on, staying outside on the arbor-covered brick patio by himself. "Did you think of something you forgot to tell me?"

"Well… It's something I didn't want to say in front of my parents," she said earnestly.

"Got you."

"The thing is, that high school guy we were talking about? He did come to the dance. I saw him."

Feeling an intense burst of satisfaction, Connor said, "Ah. I thought you might know who he is."

"Will he get in trouble?"

"Not if he didn't do anything that earns it."

"Oh." She was silent for a moment. "'Cause he's kind of nice. Funny and everything. You know? He doesn't look right through us just because we're middle-schoolers."

"I guess not, if he's interested in Tracy."

"She actually ignored him at the dance. I even heard her say, 'Why did *you* come?'—like it was really stupid of him or something."

Thus ticking the kid off, thought Connor. What she was telling him fit his imagined scenario as if he'd scripted it himself.

"So I don't see how he could have anything to do with…um, what you were asking about, but I thought I should tell you."

"Calling me was a responsible, smart decision, Amy. My job would be easier if people didn't keep secrets that often have nothing to do with the crime I'm investigating, not realizing how much time I waste trying to find out something that was irrelevant all along.'' He paused a beat before saying gently, ''I will need his name.''

''I know,'' she said in a small voice.

He waited.

''Chad. Chad Glazer.''

''Do you know where I could find this Chad?''

''Tracy says his parents have a really cool house in Old Town. That's all I know.''

''Amy, thank you.''

''Do you have to tell anybody I'm the one who told you?'' she asked in a rush.

''Nope,'' he assured her. ''My lips are sealed.''

She gave a gusty sigh. ''Okay. Goodbye.''

''Goodbye, Amy,'' but she was already gone.

Chad Glazer. Sunday evening would be a perfect time to catch even a teenage boy at home.

A quick look at John's phone book located Connor's target. Only three Glazers lived in Port Dare. A Robert A. had an address not ten blocks from John's place.

Connor stayed for dinner, a delivered pizza, with his brother's family, mainly out of reluctance to go to his empty apartment or grab a fast-food meal on his own. Afterward, he drove the ten blocks.

Tracy was right: the turn-of-the-century Queen Anne style house on a corner lot with a terraced yard and glassed-in conservatory was a beauty. On the way up the front walk, a distant bell rang in his memory. Didn't a Dr. Glazer sit on the hospital board and head Internal Medicine? Or was it Cardiac Care?

With night having settled, Connor was unseen on

the dark porch looking in a leaded-glass window at a dining room, where a slight man of perhaps forty was seated at the long mahogany table, pencil in hand and a newspaper spread in front of him. A crossword puzzle addict? He said something; somewhere, a woman laughed.

Irritated at himself, Connor still hesitated. How many contented domestic scenes had he walked into? How often had he left behind people whose lives would never be the same? Here he was, a man who lived in a bare apartment, who was unmarried, had no children, and his specialty was smashing families.

That was unjust, of course; he knew that. If sixteen-year-old Chad Glazer had raped a seventh-grader, he had to be called to account. Now. Not ten years from now when he'd raped a dozen women or more.

If this Norman Rockwell family behind the leaded glass was damaged, it wouldn't be Connor's doing. It would be the son's.

The woman who answered the door was pretty, with smile lines that made her likable from the get-go. She called for her husband right away. Despite his slight stature, he carried himself with an unmistakable air of authority.

"I'm Dr. Glazer. May I ask what you want with my son?" he asked, once Connor had repeated his request.

"Just to talk to him." Connor pocketed his badge. "I'm investigating an allegation of sexual harassment against a teacher. I'm talking to a number of kids who know the girl who made the allegation."

"I see." He didn't look altogether satisfied, but turned and called upstairs, "Chad! Please come down here."

"Sure, Dad!" Seconds later, a boy came bopping down, taking two steps at a time, one hand skimming the banister and his sneakered feet thudding on the stairs.

Heart sinking, Connor thought, damn it, he looked like a good kid. Cargo pants bagged, but his plain T-shirt more or less fit, no visible body parts were tattooed or pierced, his brown hair was short and a little spiky and his expression was pleasant.

He leaped down the last three steps. "Hey, what's up?"

"Chad, this is Detective..." The father hesitated and looked inquiring.

"McLean." Connor held out a hand. "Chad, I need to talk to you about a girl named Tracy Mitchell."

"Tracy?" he repeated, mouth hanging open. "She hasn't been in an accident or something, has she?"

"Nothing like that."

The woman, who had waited quietly to one side, said, "Why don't we all sit down."

"Thank you," Connor said.

"You won't mind if we stay," the boy's father said in a steely voice.

"Of course not."

The living room—or maybe parlor was the right word—was furnished with antiques, from leaded, glass-fronted bookcases to a cherry secretary that had to be nine, ten feet tall. Plushly upholstered settees clustered around a river-rock fireplace. Even the rug underfoot was valuable, if Connor was any judge; once vivid blues and golds were faded to umber and navy and cream, but it had a silky luster and a delicacy of pattern that you didn't see in the rug department of the local department store.

"I'm Mrs. Glazer," the woman said. "May I get you a cup of coffee?"

"Thank you, but no." As standard practice, Connor avoided accepting refreshments. It seemed wrong, somehow, to "break bread" with folks you might arrest.

The parents flanked the boy when sitting down, a form of protection he accepted without typical teenage resentment. Even now, while his expression was anxious it was also open and basically unafraid.

He wasn't a big kid. He was probably going to be built like his father and maybe not reach more than five-eight. He had the wiry strength of a wrestler or runner.

Connor asked, and the boy said, "Yeah, I run track and cross country both. Man, I wish I could be a hurdler, but I'm just not tall enough."

His dad smiled at him with pride. "Chad finished a half marathon this past summer."

"Good for you." Connor took his notebook from an inner pocket as much to signal that he was ready to get down to business as because he really needed notes. "Chad, how did you meet Tracy?"

"I don't know." Now *that* was standard teenage response. But he corrected himself immediately. "I guess she was hanging out with some people I know. I thought she was pretty, and we got to talking. I really don't know her that well."

"And how did you see her after that?"

The kid flushed. "Well, the first time I didn't know she was in middle school. She looks older. When I didn't see her at the high school, I asked."

"And then?"

"She's a walker," he said simply. "Like I am. I just run into her crowd downtown. You know. At Tastebuds, or places like that."

"Did you ask her out?"

The flush in his cheeks deepened. "She's only an eighth-grader."

"Actually," Connor said, "Tracy Mitchell is in seventh grade."

He jerked. "*Seventh?* You mean, she lied?"

"It would seem so."

Dr. Glazer said, "Is this going somewhere, Detective?"

"Yes." Connor looked straight at the boy. "I want to hear about the middle school dance you sneaked into."

The mother let out a small gasp; Dad only raised his eyebrows. "Is that a crime?"

"Not one that would interest me if it is," Connor said easily.

The boy kept his chin high. "A couple of the guys and I did. Just, you know, to see if we could."

"Tell me about it."

"We just, like, took turns hiding in the middle of a crowd all holding up their ASB cards. It was easy."

The principal would be thrilled to hear that, Connor was sure.

"How long did you stay?"

"I don't know." He shrugged. "Maybe an hour? It was boring."

"I understand that you told Tracy you were coming so you could dance with her."

The kid twitched a little. "Um, I might have said

something like that. Just…you know…to, um, flirt or something.''

''And did you dance with her?''

He didn't disguise the flash of hurt quickly enough; Connor's sharp eyes noted the look the parents exchanged.

This shrug was too elaborate. ''She kind of blew me off. It was okay.''

''In what way did she 'blow you off'? She didn't want to dance?''

''She said no, she was hanging with some friends.'' He shrugged again. ''Like I said, that was okay.''

''Did you dance?''

''Nah. Just…you know. Talked to some guys I knew. And then I left.''

''Did you leave the gym at any time?''

Chad looked puzzled. ''Well, when I left I did. You mean, before that? They don't let you out. Once you go out, you can't come back in.''

''Unless you sneak in,'' Connor said dryly.

He grinned. ''Well, yeah. But I didn't. 'Cause I didn't really want to get caught, you know? Anyway, why would I want to go out and back in?''

''To have a cigarette?''

''I don't smoke. Smoking's dumb.''

''To make out with a girl. Or talk to one.''

He was smart enough to catch on. ''Like Tracy. That's what you're asking, isn't it?''

''Yeah. Like Tracy.''

His eyes fired up. ''Did she say I did something? I never even talked to her again after she blew me off! Why would I?''

Connor leaned a little harder. ''Did you see her? Maybe watch her?''

The father stirred but said nothing.

Chad Glazer stiffened. "I don't like her that much. I saw her a couple of times, just dancing and hanging out. She didn't even look at me. And that's it."

"Did you leave with the friends you came with?"

"Yeah, we all decided we were bored. Nobody paid any attention to kids going out, just ones coming in."

"So you walked home together."

"Yeah," he said combatively, his chin thrust out. "We did. If you don't believe me, you can ask them."

"I might need to do that. If you could write down their names and phone numbers, I'd appreciate it." Connor kept his tone scrupulously polite.

Dr. Glazer asked, "Are you done with my son?"

"Yes. Thank you for your patience."

"Will you do us the courtesy of explaining why you're asking these questions?"

Connor hesitated, considered and decided that at this point there was probably no reason not to answer. Hell, he might learn something. "Tracy Mitchell has accused a teacher at the middle school of sexual harassment. And more. He denies it. We're just checking out the possibility that in fact she's covering up a different type of incident."

The boy's stare was incredulous. "Like I...raped her?"

The kid was sharp.

"Something like that," Connor said apologetically. He would have to check out Chad's story, but this time his gut told him he'd heard the truth. Chad Glazer didn't have the temper or ego problems to force a girl because she'd rejected him.

Mrs. Glazer's back had gone stiff and her voice icy. "It's ridiculous that you'd think for a minute my son would do something like that! He's a good student, a successful athlete and a nice boy! Any teacher would tell you so."

"Unfortunately even nice boys have raped, Mrs. Glazer." Connor put away his notebook. "Our culture still encourages boys to think that if a girl leads them on, they're entitled to take what they think they've been promised."

"I didn't think…" Chad stuttered. "I wouldn't…"

Connor stood. "I may confirm your story, but don't worry. This was…just a theory I was following up."

The boy's forehead furrowed. "This teacher… *raped* her?"

"That remains to be seen."

"Wow."

"I've told you more than is general knowledge. I'd appreciate it if you would keep what I've said to yourself for now."

Chad nodded. "Yeah. I mean, sure. Oh. I can write down those numbers for you."

Connor withdrew his notebook again and gave it and a pen to the boy, who scribbled quickly and handed it back.

"Thank you for your time."

Dr. Glazer saw him out, only saying quietly at the door, "His mother's right. He is a good kid."

Connor nodded. "Yeah. I got that impression. I'm sorry to have bothered your family."

A hell of a lot sorrier than his polite but professional tone suggested.

In the car, he used his cell phone to call the first of the boys, who confirmed that he and Chad Glazer had stayed together at the dance. "Yeah, we walked home afterward. I stopped at his place for a while to hear this new CD he has." His voice changed, became anxious. "Are we, like, in trouble for sneaking in?"

"No. I'd suggest you not try it again, but...no. This was about something else."

So much for that theory, Connor thought, putting away his cell phone, more relieved than he liked to acknowledge. Time to do some more serious investigation into Gerald Tanner's background.

TRACY DIDN'T WANT TO GO back to school, but her mom made her.

"Your grades..." Mom said, but Tracy knew Mom didn't really care. She got mad when teachers called her in to talk, but she had dropped out of school at sixteen herself, so it wasn't like *she* could talk. She just wanted Tracy to learn to type so she could be a secretary or something else respectable instead of a barmaid.

What Mom wanted was Tracy out of the apartment. She probably already had some guy waiting to "visit" when Tracy wasn't around.

Mom usually got what she wanted.

Resentful, Tracy dressed in her favorite tight boot-cut jeans, a hot pink T that said Meow on the front, and clunky sandals. People would notice her anyway.

"You'll be late," her mother called.

She shoved her binder and books into her pack. "I'm going!"

"Tracy! Wear a coat, for heaven's sake!" Mom said, when she saw Tracy heading for the door.

"I'm not cold." Tracy took satisfaction in slamming the door behind her.

She walked the ten blocks to the middle school really fast, goose bumps on her arms. Coats were a hassle; there wasn't really room in the locker, and she always ended up losing them.

"Tracy!" Jen waved, her expression awed. Clumps of kids turned to stare.

She sauntered. "Hey."

"Are you all right?" Her supposed friends clustered. "We've been so worried! Everybody said…"

"Why haven't you called?" Summer asked. Like *she'd* bothered to call.

"Did you know that Mr. Tanner has been fired?" somebody else asked. "Or suspended, or something."

"I knew you'd be so glad," Jen finished.

"I heard," Tracy said with a shrug. "Listen, I've got to go to my locker."

She escaped, but not for long.

"Tracy!" Rachel hugged her, and everybody else on the staircase closed in on her, just the same as outside. "You're back. Everybody has missed you *so* much."

Tracy felt weird, like she was having an out-of-body experience. She answered, sounding cool, like nothing had happened, but it was as if the real her was floating above looking down.

None of her friends really cared, she thought. She saw the avid curiosity in their eyes, felt the whispers that started behind her when she moved on.

Her first period teacher acted all concerned, but her eyes had that same look. It was creepy.

Ms. Stavig was different. She smiled when she saw Tracy, strolled down the aisle between desks and briefly laid a hand on Tracy's shoulder before circling the room again, still talking about the scene they were going to read today. She gave Tracy a good part, one where she was mad, which helped. She had a reason to yell. Afterward, she felt drained and a little more peaceful.

But the weirdness rejoined her outside the door of Ms. Stavig's classroom. She had Computers next, and it was all she could do to go in the room. A stranger, a woman, looked puzzled at the sight of her.

"I've been absent," Tracy said.

"Oh. Of course." She started explaining what they were doing, and Tracy was able to sink behind a computer monitor and pretend she was practicing her keyboarding.

Had Mr. Tanner really been fired because of her? Would they do that without any, well, proof? Tracy tapped at the keyboard, thinking furiously. That policeman hadn't been back to talk to her for days. He had sounded as if he wasn't happy with her story.

Her stomach knotted and she felt sick. Panic prickled on her skin immediately. Maybe she was pregnant, even if they had given her something they said would keep it from happening. Did it always work? What if she was the one person it didn't work for?

She stared blindly at the computer monitor. If Mr. Tanner was only suspended, he would be back. She couldn't come to class if he was here! They wouldn't try to make her, would they? She absolutely could not face him.

Tracy heard herself gasping for air and wondered distantly why nobody had noticed.

What if they really had fired him, and he didn't come back? Would he be able to get a job somewhere else, like Mom did when she was fired? Or was it different for a teacher? What if he could never get a job again, and it was all because of what she'd told them?

Her shaking hands dropped from the keyboard and she balled them in her lap.

"Tracy?" the substitute said kindly, stopping beside her. "Are you having problems? I know you must be rusty..."

"I feel sick. I have to go to the bathroom." Tracy leaped to her feet and bolted.

In the bathroom she tried to throw up, but couldn't. It was quiet in here. She crouched in front of the toilet and rested her forehead on her crossed arms.

She should never have told Ms. Stavig. She shouldn't have told anybody anything. She should have waited until the end of the month to find out if she was pregnant, and then if she wasn't she could have pretended it had never happened. She should never, never, never have started this.

Dropping to her knees, her tears wetting her arms, Tracy felt ten years older than she had a week ago.

How could she ever take back what she'd said, when she couldn't tell the truth?

Eventually, feeling gray and weak and almost numb, Tracy washed her face without looking in the mirror at the person she hated, and went back to class.

CHAPTER EIGHT

WHEN MARIAH LAID THE gentle hand on Tracy's shoulder, she'd seen the tears spring into the seventh-grader's eyes. The sight unsettled Mariah for the rest of the day. Tracy hadn't cried when she told the story in the first place. Was the investigation itself increasing her trauma? Or was something else going on? Were kids being mean? Surely not the teachers! Or was poor Tracy simply feeling…fragile?

After her last class, Mariah gathered the papers her eighth-graders had written about *Farewell to Manzanar* and stowed them in her tote. She should be planning for tomorrow, when she would be starting new units in two of her classes. Instead she glanced over her nearly bare desk, even though she wasn't really looking for anything.

Lockers were still clanging in the hall, voices calling to friends, feet thudding on the ancient floor. She wouldn't have noticed a footfall, but out of the corner of her eye she saw someone fill the doorway. With a sense of inevitability, Mariah looked up to see Detective Connor McLean walk in and close the door behind him.

Her eyebrows rose at his assumption that she wanted, or at least was willing, to be closeted with him.

"Yes?" she said, with a hint of tartness.

''I need help,'' he said bluntly, standing just inside the door.

Her heart skittered, a peculiar sensation that left her breathless. *Why him?* she begged, but got no answer.

''In what way?''

He sighed and walked toward her, not a handsome man, but one possessing a quality of powerful masculinity expressed without swaggers. She couldn't imagine him picking a fight, even shouting. He didn't have to. His control was so complete, it alone was intimidating. Banked fires, she thought, burned hotter than those that leaped for the sky.

He said, ''I'm hoping you'll talk to Tracy again.''

''You mean, encourage her to talk to me,'' Mariah said slowly. ''And then tell you what she says.''

''She's not going to open up to me.''

Mariah clasped her hands on her desk. ''Did it ever occur to you that she's telling the truth?''

''Yeah, it occurred to me. Maybe she is.'' Those brawny shoulders moved. ''I just think there's something she *isn't* telling.''

''Don't you have a female officer on your force who could talk to her?''

He stopped in front of her desk, four square and unavoidable. ''She knows you. Trusts you.''

Emotions tangled, Mariah said, ''I don't want to betray her.''

''How can settling this be a betrayal?''

''I don't know!'' She shot to her feet and walked to the windows, partly to escape him. A packed yellow bus lumbered onto the street, cars crowded the curb as parents picked up kids, walkers dawdled on the lawn to flirt while others dodged traffic to hurry away from the hated school.

She felt him behind her, so close she was afraid to take a deep breath.

"'The truth will set you free,'" he murmured.

What if she knew the truth about Simon and Lily Thalberg? Would she be free of this burden of guilt whatever the answer? Or would the knowledge of Simon's innocence increase the load a hundred-fold?

"All right," she said abruptly. "But I'll tell her that it's not confidential, that you've asked me to talk to her."

To his credit, he didn't hesitate. "Thank you."

"I take it you're getting nowhere."

"The high school kid who came to the dance didn't rape her."

Mariah swung around, stepping back at the same time so that she bumped the windowsill. He hadn't been as close as she'd imagined, but still she felt…crowded.

"What about the mother's boyfriends?"

He appeared relaxed but watchful. "There isn't one right now."

"But there was a couple of weeks ago."

"If he raped Tracy, why didn't she accuse him?" he asked patiently.

Mariah hugged herself. "I don't know."

He must be wondering why she was so perturbed. Lines furrowed his brow. "Do you still think I'm out to railroad Tanner?"

Mariah heaved a sigh. "No. I think…you're fair."

He didn't move. "Was I fair to your husband?"

The tangle of emotions seemed to be tightening into a solid knot. "I don't know. Maybe."

"Think," he said quietly, "about why you left him."

"Because I couldn't be sure..." Her voice shook. "For Zofie's sake..."

"I've investigated a lot of complaints like the one against your husband." He sounded thoughtful, a man musing aloud about a subject that had perplexed him. "Almost always, the wives back their husbands one hundred percent. Did you know that? Even when the son of a bitch has had every one of their daughters, night in and night out, the mothers deny that their husbands are guilty."

Her fingers bit into her upper arms. "Why are you telling me this?" Mariah whispered. "Don't you know how I already despise myself for not supporting Simon?"

"Yeah," he said. "I've gathered that."

"'The truth will set you free,'" she quoted bitterly. "But what if I never know the truth?"

"I think you already do." His voice was soft, lethal. "Or at least, the truth that counts to you. Here's my question, Mariah Stavig. Why *didn't* you trust your husband?"

She stared. Her mouth opened, but nothing came out.

Because you scared me. Because I always want everything in words, everything laid out, nothing unspoken. Because I'm not a loyal wife.

How many times had she asked herself the same question? How many times had she answered it, always in terms of herself, her own doubts and inadequacies.

She had always begun with the immutable fact that Simon was her husband. He deserved her support and faith. She had never turned the question on its side and asked, *Did I not trust him, not love him, even before I heard Detective McLean say those terrible words?*

Of course their marriage hadn't been perfect. Was any? But to believe something so dreadful...

"You're saying...that I *knew...?*" She trembled between shock and anger.

Connor shook his head. "I'm not saying anything. Only you know why you had reason to doubt him."

Mariah glared at him. "Why did you really come up here today?"

"To ask you..." He stopped. Swallowed. Rubbed the back of his neck. "To see you."

The confirmation of what she had guessed rocked her. "To see me?" Did she have to sound as if that was such an unlikely possibility?

He gave a painful smile. "I didn't make a big enough fool of myself the other day?"

"Fool?" She was beginning to feel stupid.

His gray eyes searched her face. "I wish we were meeting for the first time."

Her breathing was shallow, ragged. "I don't understand."

"I think you do." He rubbed his neck again, seeming to hesitate. Then he took a swift step forward, gripped her chin and lifted her face.

She had one fleeting glimpse of his eyes darkening, the twist of his mouth, the taut line of his jaw, before his mouth touched hers with startling gentleness. He brushed her lips, came back and did it again. Heat rushed to her belly and her knees almost buckled. She made a peculiar little sound, perhaps a whimper, and parted her lips so that he was able to kiss her properly. No, not *properly* at all, but slowly, deeply, his tongue sliding along hers, and oh, she was kissing him back, she knew she was, but couldn't seem to do anything to stop herself.

She clutched his powerful shoulders and felt the muscles harden beneath her hands. His cheek rasped hers, and the groan that tore from his chest as he lifted his head weakened her further.

"That," he said in a raw voice, "is why I came up here."

"Are you...are you supposed to kiss someone involved in..."

"I'm not investigating you," he interrupted. His fingers flexed on her jaw, and he abruptly kissed her again, hard, before he released her and stepped back.

Mariah sagged against the windowsill. The contact brought her to a panicked awareness of where they were. "What if one of the kids outside saw?"

"I'm not a student. I'm not another teacher or an administrator. Don't teachers kiss their husbands or boyfriends?"

"You're not..."

A muscle jumped beneath his eye. "But I want to be."

She stared helplessly at him. "This is crazy! I *hated* you! Did you know that?"

"Yeah." His voice became soft, almost blurred, as he wiped it of all expression. "People often do."

She bit her lip. It felt swollen, tender. She wanted to touch it, to marvel at long-forgotten sensations. "You're serious, aren't you?"

"Very." He looked much as usual, a big man with a stern face, but she had the sense that he was holding himself rigidly, braced for rejection.

"What..." Mariah had to clear her throat. "What is it you want?"

Of course she'd set herself up for the obvious. Humor came into his eyes, then as quickly left, leaving an expression of vulnerability. "For now, let's just say...the pleasure of your company. Would you go out to dinner with me, Mariah?"

A date.

"Zofie..."

"Would she mind a baby-sitter? Or is this Simon's weekend with Zofie?"

"We had to switch weekends. She's home." Mariah swallowed, then blurted, "I haven't dated since—" She clamped her mouth shut.

He looked startled. "In three years?"

"It just hasn't felt right."

He said nothing for a moment, only stood there with his hands at his sides. At last he asked quietly, "Does it feel right now?"

Mariah took a breath. "I don't know. But I will have dinner with you."

It was a second before he reacted, first blinking, then with a subtle relaxation of the muscles of his face. He looked less hard, less remote. "Thank you."

"When do you...?"

"What about Friday?"

That gave her four days to become terrified. She gave a jerky nod. "Okay."

"I'll pick you up at six?"

"Okay," she said again. She restrained herself from asking what she should wear. Half the girls in this school would have handled this with more social deftness! *They* knew how dressy any particular occasion would be. She must have known, once upon a time.

"You'll talk to Tracy, too?"

"Tomorrow," Mariah promised.

Connor nodded. He'd jammed his hands into the pockets of his corduroy slacks. His shoulders were slightly hunched. Was he again trying to be physically unobtrusive?

"You think I'm scared of you," she guessed aloud.

His brows rose. "What?"

"You look like one of my students when he's trying to be invisible."

His shoulders squared, and he smiled sheepishly. "Sorry. I've learned to make myself as unimposing as possible when I want someone's cooperation."

"You've never frightened me."

Furrows deepened on his forehead. "You sure as hell looked scared to death that day you saw me in Ms. Patterson's office."

"Shocked," she corrected him. "You brought it all back."

He watched her. "Is that so bad?"

"No," Mariah surprised herself by saying. "I'm starting to think maybe it's been a good thing. I had let it all turn into...oh, the monster hiding in the closet."

"What's in there instead?" he asked quietly.

She tried to laugh. "A mess! What else?"

There was the kindness in his eyes that she thought she was falling in love with. "It's all spilling out, huh?"

"Yup." She laughed again, more successfully this time. "Like I say, a cleanup is probably overdue."

"Good for you."

Mariah tilted her head. "You never talk like a cop. Do you know that?"

She'd jolted him. "What do you mean?"

"Have you ever in your life shouted, 'Freeze! Drop that gun'?"

His very sexy mouth twitched. "Uh, no. Now that you mention it, I don't think the occasion has arisen."

"I know hardly anything about you," she realized. "You poke and prod at me, but you don't give much away about yourself."

"Maybe I'm not very interesting."

"You're trying to hide your boring personality?" She amazed herself by teasing.

"Something like that." He sounded rueful. "Okay. Fair's fair. I know more about you than you do about me. We'll remedy that Friday. I promise."

"Good." The windowsill was beginning to feel awfully sharp-edged digging into her behind, but she felt safest glued to it. Not that she was scared of him; she'd told the truth about that. It was more what he made her feel that unnerved her.

Why him? she wondered again.

"I'll call you tomorrow?" Connor said. Asked. As if he needed her permission.

"Okay."

He seemed to hesitate for a moment, then dipped his head in a brief nod and left. Mariah had a moment of crushing disappointment that he hadn't kissed her again, even if she was framed in the classroom windows, in plain sight of the entire student body.

He'd kissed her the first time to make a point, perhaps to make her face her own feelings. Their relationship really hadn't progressed to the kissing hello and goodbye stage.

Their relationship.

A shivery, exhilarating kind of terror swelled in her chest, and Mariah heard herself breathing fast, in small gasps, as if she had just raced up all four flights of stairs. She was going on a date, with the man who had caused her more emotional turmoil than anyone in her life ever had.

Except perhaps Simon.

The very thought of her ex-husband chilled her, turning the butterflies in her stomach into nausea.

She wasn't the only one who had hated Detective Connor McLean. Simon would be enraged if he found out she was dating the police officer who had accused him. He already harbored so much anger and bitterness. Was it fair to do something that would upset him so terribly?

Here's my question, Mariah Stavig. Why didn't *you trust your husband?*

How Simon reacted to her decisions about her own life wasn't her problem, she told herself defiantly. She wasn't married to him anymore.

And this wasn't the time to confront the queasy, uneasy realization that, for the first time in the three years since she had asked him to leave, Mariah didn't know for sure why she *wasn't* still married to Simon.

But learning the answer could be all-important, not just for herself but for Zofie's sake.

Zofie. Mariah glanced at the clock. Heavens! She was late already.

She hurried to check that she had grabbed everything she needed to grade papers tonight and prepare for tomorrow's classes, then left the room. As she pulled the door closed, Mariah paused over her own reflection in the glass inset. Were her lips softer, fuller, because she had been kissed? For a moment she indulged herself by pressing her fingertips to her mouth, remembering. Then, shaking her head at her own foolishness, she walked quickly down the hall, her heels clicking on the scuffed floor, trying very hard to ignore a renewed swelling of exhilaration and almost-fear.

"I'M GOING TO BE HONEST with you," Ms. Stavig said quietly. "I won't—I *can't*— keep anything you tell me confidential. But I hope you'll talk to me anyway."

Tracy fingered the zipper pull on her backpack. "What do you want to know?" she asked warily.

"Just...how you're doing." The teacher's face was kind. "I know rumors have gotten around. They always do. How are the other kids treating you?"

Tracy shrugged. "Like always. Mostly."

"Mostly?"

"Some guys have said things. You know." They'd leave her alone if she cried, but she wouldn't. If they wanted to think she was a slut, let them. Maybe she *would* be one. Didn't most kids take after their mothers? Maybe she wouldn't be able to help it.

Ms. Stavig looked mad. "Have you reported them?"

Tracy rolled her eyes. "Oh, yeah, like that'd make me popular."

"It might be good for them to hear a few home truths."

Tracy shrugged and kept playing with the zipper pull.

"Your friends?"

"They're cool."

There was a small silence. Tracy didn't look up.

"What about your mother, Tracy? Is she being supportive?"

A hand clamped around her chest. "I guess," she mumbled.

"Has she considered getting you into counseling?"

Tracy shook her head. Tears burned at the back of her eyes.

"I know your mother works nights. I worry about you home alone. Are you scared? Or sad?"

She was glad her mother wasn't home. But scared, too, in case he came back. Mom kept saying she guessed she should change the locks, but Tracy could tell it was one of those things Mom would never do. Tracy always put the chain on the door, but she knew from TV shows that any guy could snap one of those in a second if he really wanted in.

"Scared. Sometimes," she said, her head down.

Ms. Stavig's hand came out to cover hers. "Does your mom have a boyfriend right now?"

Tracy's eyes widened and her head snapped up. "What do you mean?" she almost yelled.

The teacher looked startled. "Why…nothing. Only that it might especially bother you now if a strange man moved into your apartment."

Another guy who would check her out when she went down the hall in her nightgown or who would just *happen* to glance in when her bedroom door was open. Who would press too close when he passed her in the kitchen, or make a big deal out of hugging her or pulling her down to sit on his lap and her mom would smile because they were being *fatherly,* only Tracy could feel the woody pushing up against her butt.

Staring fiercely down at her pack, Tracy said, "Mom hasn't found anybody yet."

"Do the boyfriends ever…bother you?" Ms. Stavig said it delicately, as though it weren't really a subject fit for Tracy's ears, but as if she felt she had to ask.

Bother her.

She tried to look blank. "What do you mean?"

Surprising Tracy with her bluntness, Ms. Stavig said, "Make sexual advances."

"Like…like Mr. Tanner did, you mean?" His name stuck in her throat, but she forced it out.

The teacher pushed her soft brown hair back from her face. "More or less. Have any of them…oh, looked at you the way Mr. Tanner did, before he made advances?"

Tracy shook her head even as she stared down at the pack again. Nausea was rising the way it did every time she thought about what had happened.

Every time she lied about it.

She took a deep breath, fighting the upset stomach, telling herself she didn't have to throw up. But she knew she did.

Ms. Stavig was talking, but Tracy didn't know what she was saying.

"I've got to go," she said, jumping to her feet and backing toward the classroom door. "I just remembered I promised my mom I'd…do something."

Ms. Stavig rose, too, and watched her with eyes that were so…so *nice,* it made Tracy want to cry.

"Just remember," she said. "If you want to talk, you know where to find me."

Tracy nodded, backed out the door and ran for the bathroom at the end of the hall, making it just in time. Afterward, she was grateful that nobody was around to hear her puking her guts out.

Kneeling in front of the toilet, her face buried in

her arms, crossed atop the seat, Tracy cried. How could she tell?

She couldn't. She just couldn't! But she would hate herself for the rest of her life.

"SURE." CHUCK BERG STEPPED back. "Come on in. Have a seat. What do you want to know? I taught here with Gerald for…oh, six, seven years. I've given him a hard time about dummying down to the kiddie level."

A community college instructor who also taught computers, Berg obviously hadn't heard about his former colleague's troubles. Sitting down behind his cluttered desk, he raised his eyebrows. "What's this about?"

"I'm investigating allegations made by a student concerning Mr. Tanner," Connor said carefully. "I'd rather not be specific until I've heard your impressions about him."

Berg ran a hand over his sandy, thinning hair while he thought. "All right," he said at last. "Depending on what you ask."

"Have you seen him teach? Tell me what you think of his competency."

Connor heard about Gerald Tanner's creativity, thoroughness, enthusiasm.

"He actually enjoyed teaching the 100 level classes," Berg marveled. "We miss him."

When questioned, he said that he and Tanner had been casual friends, occasionally playing a round of golf together, having a drink, that sort of thing. "We didn't usually socialize in the evening just because he wasn't married. You know how it is." He looked uncomfortable. "Couples tend to get together with couples."

Connor nodded his understanding. "To your knowledge, did he date?"

Relieved to be off the hook, the instructor sat back in his chair. "Yeah, sure. I mean, he wasn't exactly Don Juan, but... Sure. I remember he was seeing a part-timer from the English Department for a while."

"Was he ever interested in students?"

That straightened Berg right up. "Good God, no! Strictly verboten."

Connor spread his hands. "That doesn't mean it doesn't happen."

"Guy was straitlaced. No. If you heard something..." He shook his head, appearing sincere in his disbelief. "No. I just can't imagine. Not Gerald Tanner."

Connor probed some more. No, they'd never discussed pornography, except maybe on a political level. He did recall them talking about an attempt by the city council in Bremerton to use zoning to outlaw topless joints. "We were both doubtful it would stand up in the courts," he said. "No, I didn't get the feeling Gerry felt strongly about the issue." He rested his forearms on the desk. "Now I think it's time you tell me what this is really about."

Connor told him.

Berg's shock showed. "You're taking this *seriously?*" He shook his head sharply. "Of course you are. You have to, don't you? And you wouldn't be here if you weren't investigating. But Gerald? No. He's a nice guy. I don't believe for a minute that he'd even look at a thirteen-year-old girl that way, much less rape her!" His thin, intelligent face set in older, harder lines, he looked squarely at Connor. "You wanted to know what I think. That's it."

Connor pushed himself to his feet. "I appreciate your candor."

"You've got the wrong guy." Berg said the same thing Connor had been hearing all day here on the campus of the community college where Tanner had taught for some years before quitting to take the job in Port Dare.

Having friends stunned at the very idea didn't, in Connor's experience, rule out the possibility that Gerald Tanner had been disguising a sexual interest in young teenage girls all along, but did make it less likely. Many of these people had known Tanner for years. The man they knew was maybe a little inept socially, but he did have friends, date, get along with his colleagues and have an outlet in the online world where geeks were gods. Connor's first impression of the guy as a classic failure who needed the feeling of superiority he got from being the older and stronger in a sexual relationship was shifting into something more textured and...hell, *likable*.

Damn it, he was getting a gut feeling at last, and it told him Tracy Mitchell was lying.

CHAPTER NINE

CONNOR RANG MARIAH'S doorbell, feeling nervous as a teenager picking a girl up for a first date. He'd wanted this more badly than he had realized. Damn it, he should have thought of something special for the evening, something to make *him* stand out from the crowd of other men who would be asking her on dates if she had decided she was now ready.

He'd considered a dozen possibilities from the Crescent Lake Lodge, tucked at the west end of the glorious deep-water lake in the Olympic National Forest, to any of several restaurants in Port Townsend, the nineteenth century port of call for the Puget Sound.

The trouble was Zofie. Mariah would be paying a baby-sitter, and might balk at a destination a distance away that would have her out into the wee hours of the night. He pretty much figured they'd better stay in Port Dare. Which meant taking her to a restaurant where she might have eaten a hundred times.

It was the company who counted, he reminded himself. A thought that didn't help. He could have used some teenage cockiness.

The door opened without any warning footfalls. Framed in the opening, Mariah was ravishing in a snug teal sweater above a wrap skirt that looked

South Seas to him with simple block-printed teal fish swimming around the hem of lustrous blue fabric.

"Hi," she said, sounding shy.

Maybe he wasn't the only one who was nervous. She'd admitted to not having dated since her divorce. She probably felt like a home-schooled kid being dropped into the unfamiliar public school system with no idea of the unwritten rules and mores.

"You look beautiful," Connor said.

"Oh." Her cheeks pinkened. "Thank you. Um, come in. I need to say goodbye to Zofie."

The baby-sitter appeared slightly older than Mariah's students, but too juvenile to cope with a crisis. On the other hand, Zofie smiled at him with complete poise.

"Hi, Decktiv McLean." She only stumbled slightly over the "detective."

"Hi, Zofie." He nodded at the baby-sitter, too.

She gave him a quick, scared smile.

Mariah hugged her daughter and kissed the top of her head. "I won't be too late."

He'd figured her right and was glad not to have to be coming up with a last-minute change of plans.

"Do you have a number where we'll be?" she asked him.

"I'll have to use your phone book." He wrote down the restaurant number on a pad by the phone.

"Call if you need me," Mariah told the baby-sitter. To her daughter, she added, "Be good for Christy."

Zofie rolled her eyes. "I'm always good."

Her mother laughed. "Uh-huh."

Finally she and Connor were out the door. "I hope The Lighthouse sounds okay," he said.

"I love it!" she assured him.

Yup. She'd eaten there hundreds of times. "I've only been twice," she added. "Ages ago. It's not exactly the place to take a preschooler."

He was pretty sure the host didn't hand out crayons and cartoon-printed place mats. "Probably not," he agreed.

They chatted about nothing during the short drive, adults practiced at making conversation with strangers. That's what they were, on one level: complete strangers. And yet they kept stumbling over their history.

The restaurant was a sprawling, shingled building that had grown from the original working lighthouse whose beacon had been turned off in 1922, when new technology made it redundant. You could still tour the building, climbing the circular wrought-iron staircase to see the huge lamp, tended by a keeper who lived in the dank, stone-walled apartment at ground level. It was now a museum, furnished as the keeper had left it, the walls hung with glass-framed newspaper clippings, brochures and tidbits of maritime history.

The restaurant was decorated in keeping with the history, the windows looking out at the rocky shoreline small-paned, the walls hung with ship's antiques. Brass navigational instruments, spyglasses, wheels and anchors all had the unmistakable patina of a century or more.

Seafood was the specialty, but they made some damn good pasta here, too. Mariah ordered a sea bass dinner, and he went for a pesto shrimp pasta he'd had before. The wine arrived, and they were left with candlelight and each other's company.

The moment of truth.

They both spoke at the same time, then laughed awkwardly when their words tangled.

"You first," she said.

"I just wondered if Zofie was okay with this."

"Sure. She remembered meeting you at the soccer field. It was the cold s'mores that stuck in her mind. Why wouldn't I want to go out with someone willing to take a niece and nephew for a picnic on a cold October Sunday?"

"I'm glad I met her approval." Connor hesitated. "You haven't told her..."

"Are you kidding?" Mariah looked shocked at the idea. "For one thing, kids her age have big mouths. She'd probably tell Daddy all about the man Mommy had dinner with." She couldn't hide a small shudder.

Connor frowned. "Does it matter if he finds out?"

"I'd rather he didn't," she said frankly.

His frown deepened. "Are you afraid of him?"

Her pause bothered him.

"No, of course not," she said, a beat too late. "I think it would hurt him to find out that, of all the men in the world, I chose to go out with you. You humiliated and threatened him. My being with you—" She gestured helplessly. "He'd see it as a slap in the face."

"Is it?" Connor couldn't stop himself from asking.

Her entire spine stiffened. "What do you mean?"

"You did say you haven't dated since the divorce. Did you choose, maybe subconsciously, to go out with me as a way of showing him?"

Her nostrils flared. "Showing him what?"

He shrugged. "I don't know. That he doesn't have any say over what you do? That you think he was guilty?"

Her narrowed eyes told him he was blowing it big time. "Do you realize how nasty and petty you're making me sound? Do you really believe I'm incapable of telling my ex-husband what I think? That I'd resort to 'showing him' in such a hurtful way?"

He felt like scum. "No," he said. "I guess it's my own inadequacies speaking. I've been wondering ever since you agreed to have dinner with me *why* you did. Why me?"

She stared at him for an unnervingly long time, seeing more, he suspected, than he was ready to bare.

"Maybe you're the handsomest man who has asked."

He made an impatient gesture.

"*And* the most persistent."

"I can be pushy," he admitted.

"And you kissed me. That helped."

"It did?"

She gazed seriously at him. "The truth?"

Connor reached out and gripped her hand. She turned it to meet him palm to palm.

"You've opened my eyes. Made me take another look at my choices and my life. Freed me, a little, from the guilt I've been carrying."

"So you're grateful," he said grimly.

She shook her head, then nodded, then shook it again. "Yes. No. It's…" Her mobile face showed her struggle for words. "You've stirred me. And, um, I'm attracted to you. Because of Simon, you're the last man I should be dating. But here I am anyway."

Gaze lingering on the color flaring in her cheeks, on the rich depths of her eyes and the delicate curve of her jaw, he said softly, "Thank you."

She wrinkled her nose at him and removed her

hand from his. "Tonight was supposed to be about *you,* not me. How did you manage to dissect *my* motivations again?"

Reassured for the first time that she shared the uncomfortable, maybe inconvenient, attraction he felt, Connor was able to grin. "You're so easy to rile."

She tried to glower. "Oh, thanks."

Their salads arrived, and conversation lightened as they ate. Connor told Mariah about his family as they appeared on the surface: three brothers, all cops, only the older one married and with children, their mother a lifelong presence in their lives.

"Is your father dead?" Mariah asked.

"Since I was a kid. Nine. He was murdered."

"Murdered?" she echoed in horror. "How? Why?"

"Dad was a loan officer at a bank. Some nut walked in, sprayed the place with bullets and walked out. Dad and two others were killed, a twenty-one-year-old teller was paralyzed for life and a couple of customers were injured." He was silent for a moment, remembering his mother's profound grief and his own childish bewilderment. "They never caught him."

"So you don't even know if your father was a target, or if it was random."

"You got it. That was tough on my mother." Understatement. "She couldn't understand, mourn, move on. She kept waiting for the who and why, only nobody could tell her. Dad died because..." He grimaced and held out his hands, palms up.

Tiny crinkles formed on her brow. "Is that why you all became police officers? To exact the justice and closure your family never had?"

He moved his shoulders uneasily. "That's the tidy answer. Probably even true."

She cocked her head to one side. "But you don't like it?"

On a spurt of frustration, he said sharply, "It's a ridiculous goddamn reason to choose a career."

Mariah looked thoughtful. "It beats chance, which is how most people wander into a career. At least motivation that personal implies a purpose. Even a passion."

"I used to think I had both. I'm not so sure anymore." Connor was shocked to hear himself admit as much. His brothers were his best friends, and he hadn't done more than hint to them at his increasing dissatisfaction. When he said, "I'm starting to hate my job," they took it as hyperbole, and he hadn't corrected them.

"What's changed?" she asked simply, pushing away her salad plate.

He leaned forward. "Some of your accusations pretty much nailed my problems with what I do. I'm a destroyer. It has to be done—nobody should get away with abusing a child or raping a woman. But the fact is, I often can't prove my case. Whether I do or not, I leave chaos in my wake. Doubts, fear, recriminations, guilt, marriages irretrievably shattered, kids taken from their parents..." He rotated his head to ease the tension in his neck. "I break. I don't pick up the pieces."

She'd have been within her rights to say, *I told you so.* Instead she said with quiet sympathy, "But how could you? That's not your job."

"No," he said. "It's not. And, as you pointed out, that was my choice."

Their dinners arrived, and as they ate he talked more about growing up, raised as much by John as by his mother, who'd worked two jobs to pay the bills and put food on the table.

"Sometimes I rebelled at having a brother only a few years older giving me orders, but I idolized him, too. He claims Mom influenced him to become a cop, but I can't say the same. She was hardly ever home. No, me, I followed in John's footsteps—four years at the University of Washington, then I applied for a badge. By that time, I'd been hearing big brother's stories. Hell, it was inevitable."

"And Hugh?"

"Oh, he was gung ho from the time he was a little kid. Like John, he got from Mom the idea that if cops had really done their jobs, Dad's murderer would have paid. Or maybe the shoot-up wouldn't even have happened, because the wacko would have been in jail for something else. There had to be warning signs. Hugh is on a mission to ensure the bad guys don't walk, so they can't commit evil another day."

"You make him sound like John Wayne."

Connor gave a grunt of laughter. "Actually he's sinfully good-looking and likes to play on his days off. Usually with a pretty blonde, although a redhead or two have slipped in there."

"What about you?" Mariah asked quietly. "You've never been married?"

He shook his head. "Just never came up."

"You haven't become…soured on marriage, after what you see in your job?"

"Maybe more cautious," he conceded. "Mom never remarried. I guess I'd like to be sure I've found my once-in-a-lifetime partner before I take the plunge.''

She nodded and bowed her head, pushing food around with her fork.

"Do you still love him?" Connor asked abruptly.

She looked up, eyes widening. "No! We've been divorced for three years."

"You might have left him only for Zofie's sake."

"How could I love a man I thought might have…" She stopped.

"But do you think he did it?"

"I don't know!" she cried. "I've said that a thousand times. I just don't know!"

Connor set down his fork. "I'm sorry. I shouldn't have asked."

"It's all right." Suddenly she sounded weary. "Of course you wonder. I don't even understand myself what I thought or guessed or knew. All I'm sure of is that if I had loved Simon the way I should have, I would never have doubted him and I certainly wouldn't have feared for Zofie. So…do I love him? No.''

The last word was clipped, tight. *Don't ask me any more.* But he heard grief in her conclusion, too, and some self-doubt he couldn't clearly make out. She'd already suggested that she judged herself because she hadn't stood by her husband.

Connor regretted fiercely that he hadn't been able to answer her questions for her. Like his mother, Mariah Stavig found it hard to live without that closure she'd talked about.

"Do you miss him?" he asked.

"Simon?" Emotions passed like ghosts across her face. "At first I did. It was hard to become a single parent overnight. When you're used to being married, suddenly being on your own is scary. There's nobody to talk to in the same way, nobody to count on if your car breaks down or you get sick or..." She made a face. "But I was the one who did the talking. Simon was the strong, silent type. I realized somewhere along the way how little he ever actually communicated to me. He didn't feel as if he needed to explain himself. Not ever. So, after you came that first time, it was like him just to turn the TV back on and pretend nothing had happened."

"But you must have asked him."

"He got angry," she said simply. "That's when I realized he always had, whenever I questioned him." Hair a dark halo, her face pretty and earnest, she looked at Connor as if she really wanted him to understand her SOB of an ex. "You know, Simon was actually born in Yugoslavia—well, Serbia, now. He has some old-world notions. His grandmother stayed with us once, and she wouldn't sit down to dinner while he was eating. She hovered, hurrying to refill his glass, asking if he wanted more of anything, waiting on him. Simon's mother isn't quite that bad, but she's deferential to his father. Maybe, in his view, a woman should never question a man."

And they had a daughter. Hadn't that ever worried Mariah? "Zofie seems pretty outspoken," Connor commented.

"Simon always talked about how she could be anything. A doctor, a lawyer, the president of the United States. I really think he expected his children to be American in a way he isn't quite, even though he doesn't even have an accent. Zofie has never hinted that he's squelched her. But apparently I was another story.''

''You were his wife.''

''Exactly.'' She smiled sadly. ''We'd been married five years, and I hadn't noticed that he didn't confide in me. Pretty dense, huh?''

Damn the bastard for making her sad.

''I wouldn't say that. The problem is, we look to be swept away by love. Analyzing someone's character, habits and values flies against the romanticized notion of love overcoming all. Maybe when you're older and considering a second marriage, you tick off the good versus the bad. I suspect very few people do the first time around. He must have had appealing qualities. Would you have listened if a friend had said, 'Hey, he's kind of old-fashioned about women. He isn't going to like being challenged by you'?''

''I didn't listen,'' Mariah said ruefully. ''My parents didn't like him at all. They're old-fashioned in a different way—Mom was forty when she had me, but I probably wouldn't have listened if they were young and hip. Or if my best friends had said the same things. I have to say, though, that Simon did talk to me more in the early days, about his family and growing up and what he hoped for in life. It was once we were married that he became more serious, more reserved, more impatient when I asked him for something he didn't think he should give. Men did *not*, in his view, wash dishes.'' She gave a wry smile. ''And why are we talking about my ex-husband? Do all trails lead to Rome?''

Connor lifted his wineglass to her. ''Ex-girlfriends, boyfriends, husbands and wives are one of those subjects couples have to get out of the way right up-front. Didn't you know that?''

''I'm not very experienced at this,'' she reminded him.

''Oh, yeah.'' He let a smile play around his mouth. ''Well, them's the rules.''

''Oh, are they?'' She tilted her head coquettishly. ''I haven't heard about *your* girlfriends yet.''

He sipped wine, shrugged. ''Nobody serious to tell about.''

''Never?'' Mariah looked incredulous. ''In your whole life, you've never fallen in love? What about…oh, sixth grade?''

He laughed. ''Yeah, I had a big crush on a girl in my class. Can't even remember her name. I do remember that she sat in front of me for a whole month, and her hair smelled like lilacs. I wanted to touch it so bad. When she wore it in a ponytail, I yanked it until she hit me.''

Mariah laughed, a merry sound. ''Weren't you a jock in high school? You must have had girlfriends.''

''I played football and basketball. Yeah, I had girlfriends.'' More like, a girlfriend.

He'd given something away. Mariah's eyes were dark and knowing. ''But not somebody you want to talk about.''

Why was he reluctant? Did too many years of silence on a subject rust your ability to talk about it? He tried not even to think about Becky, although he couldn't help doing so at odd moments. Hell, how could he *not,* given that his job was more a crusade in her name than in his mother's.

''I went with a girl named Becky for a couple of years.'' Even his voice sounded rusty. ''Her dad didn't like her dating, so we hung out at school, I'd drive her home, she'd sneak out sometimes at night.'' He shrugged. ''She was scared of him. I knew that. I thought he was just an SOB who'd ground her, maybe give her a hard time if he ever caught us. Talk about old-fashioned, not letting a sixteen-year-old date. Then she turned seventeen, and she still couldn't.''

Mariah watched him across the table, her expression compassionate. ''What happened?''

''I wanted her to go to the prom. She freaked. She couldn't possibly ask her father. I said I would.'' How clearly he remembered his teenage arrogance and blindness. ''That's when Becky finally told me she had been having sex with her father for years. Since she was about twelve. He was jealous. That's why she couldn't date.''

Mariah let out a small, anguished sound echoing the pain he had felt. ''What did you do?'' she whispered.

''Tried to talk her into going to the school counselor. Didn't she know how sick that was? I said.'' He shook his head, hearing the incredible insensitivity. Yeah, it was her father who was sick, but she must have known she could stop him, and she hadn't. At that age, she wouldn't have understood the difference in responsibility between the adult and the child, the power he had over her. Connor continued, ''Of course, she wouldn't go. Her mom was dead, her dad was all she had. No little sisters to worry about. She'd be out of high school in just another year, and then she'd move out of the house. She begged me to be patient.''

''But you weren't.'' Mariah said it as if she knew the rest of the pathetic story.

"In my defense, I don't think it was my own impatience driving me. I thought I was in love. I was the knight on the white charger. I was determined to save her. Hell, I knew what was right and wrong. The real trouble was my inflated belief that I could fix anything."

"You confronted him?"

"I was smart enough not to do that." He gave a harsh, humorless laugh. "I called Child Protective Services. Becky denied the whole thing, he beat the crap out of her and she ran away after telling me she hated my guts." Until his dying day, he would remember her swollen, battered face and the terrible sense of betrayal in her eyes. "I heard later she was pregnant, living with some sailor in Bremerton. The baby couldn't have been mine. I don't want to think about whose it was."

"Oh, Connor." Her hand crept across the table and shyly covered his. "I'm sorry. I could tell you didn't want to talk about her. I guess I'm pushy, too."

He gripped her hand, too hard, feeling the fragile bones under his fingers. "No. It's okay," he said gruffly. "It happened a long time ago."

She nodded, her face grave. "You couldn't have done anything differently, you know."

"I should have talked to her." A rough sound came from his throat. "I never imagined she'd lie to the CPS worker. Somehow, even though she wouldn't make the call herself, I was sure she'd be grateful to be rescued." He gave another harsh laugh. "Rescued. More like sending a lifeboat that drove right over the top of her."

"You had to tell," Mariah repeated.

"Yeah. I did." He tried to smile, felt how bleak

his effort was. "Right and wrong have never looked as clear-cut since."

Her forehead crinkled as her eyes searched his. "You face these dilemmas every day, don't you?"

"No, what I do is deal with other people facing them. It's never easy."

She bit her lip. "And they all look at you later the way I did."

"Most of them."

She squeezed his hand back, hard. "I think, Connor McLean, that you're a good, kind man. I'm sorry it took me so long to notice."

He hoped she found him a little more exciting than that implied, but he appreciated the thought.

"If we were anywhere else, I'd kiss you," he said roughly.

"Oh." Her cheeks flushed and her gaze wavered from his.

"Or do good, kind men not do that?"

Mariah firmly reclaimed her hand. "I don't know all that many." She sounded prim. "But since you already *have* kissed me..."

Too long ago. At odd moments the entire week he'd remembered her taste, the faint flowery scent of her hair, the quiver of her lips and her tiny gasp. He hadn't kissed a woman in months. The dating game had palled for him years ago. Every so often he met someone he liked enough to make the effort for. That seemed to be happening less and less often, which made him wonder if there was a reason he was thirty years old and hadn't fallen in love since high school.

Tonight, he was thinking he just hadn't met the right woman yet. Or, more accurately, he had met her and just hadn't broken up her marriage yet, he thought dourly.

Forget Simon, Connor told himself. She was single now. She wouldn't be getting back together with her ex. Why *shouldn't* he kiss her?

"And I'm looking forward to doing it again," he said, letting his gaze drift for a brief moment to her mouth.

Her blush was gratifying.

They sipped coffee and talked about politics at work and the school board and the city council, avoiding any more land mines. After he paid, they strolled out into a misty night, smelling the salt air and hearing the roar of the surf.

Mariah had already fastened her seat belt by the time he got behind the wheel.

"I was thinking," she said.

He glanced at her, keys in his hand.

"I promised myself I wouldn't talk about Tracy tonight at all."

"I don't mind if you have something to say."

"Well." Mariah pushed her hair back from her face. "It was what you said about your girlfriend. How determined she was not to rock the boat. To...protect her father, I suppose."

"Tracy doesn't have contact with her father."

"So she says." Her face was indistinct in the dark parking lot. "I was just wondering whether there was some chance she does, and her mother doesn't know."

Connor considered. "I asked about him. I didn't get any sense she was hiding anything, but what the hell. I'll locate him."

"You can do that?"

"It's harder than you'd think to disappear. And this guy doesn't have any reason to be hiding, unless he's skipped on child support. I had the impression from Tracy's mother that she's happier he's out of the picture."

Mariah sounded worried. "If it's not her father she's protecting…"

"She might be telling the truth," Connor reminded her.

"What do you think?"

He shoved the key into the ignition. "I think she's lying," he said baldly.

"Then…"

"Then if it's not her father she's protecting, I have to look at her mother."

Distress made her voice husky. "You think she *collaborated* with someone, or…"

"Or just turned her eyes the other way. Do you know how often that happens?" He sounded savage; couldn't help it.

"No. I've read…" Mariah drew an audible breath. "I'm sorry. I shouldn't have brought this up at all."

"No." He deliberately relaxed. "You're right. I'll find Tracy's father first. Then I'll have a talk with the last boyfriend."

"Thank you," Mariah said softly.

"Just doing my job."

As he hoped he'd done it when her husband was accused.

As was habit for a cop, he had stayed aware of their surroundings. He knew the parking lot was quiet, no one getting out of a car or exiting the restaurant. So he didn't hesitate when impulse had him reaching for her.

He wrapped his hand around the back of her head and covered her mouth with his, sharp-edged need making this kiss hungrier than it should have been. But instead of stiffening, she sighed and parted her lips. His other hand found her shoulder, traced the fragile line of her collarbone, stroked her throat, flattened on her chest just above the swell of cleavage. Damn, he wanted the plump weight of her breast in his hand, but he had enough restraint to know it was too soon, would scare her off.

He stroked her tongue with his, explored the soft contours of her mouth, nipped at her full lower lip. She kissed him back with a passion that seemed somehow innocent, unpracticed. It made him wonder what kind of lover her husband had been.

None of his business.

Yes, it was, damn it! The way Simon Stavig had treated Mariah was a part of the experiences that made up who she was, how she would react to another man's touch and promises and excuses.

Right now, Connor thought, nuzzling the hollow at the base of her throat, he couldn't complain. The quick rise and fall of her breasts, the ragged vibration of her pulse beneath his mouth, gave him intense satisfaction.

Whatever had come between them before, Mariah wanted him. She'd forgiven if not forgotten.

He was a lucky man.

With a deep-throated groan, he lifted his head, kissed her one more time and then reluctantly let her go.

"Time to get you home," he said.

"I..." Her voice was high, breathless. Attuned to

her, he felt her draw in a sustaining breath that allowed her to steady her voice. "Thank you."

The drive was too short. He asked her about her drama program, and she talked almost at random about auditions for the play to be performed in early December, *A Christmas Carol*.

In front of her house, before releasing his seat belt, he kissed her again, but didn't let it get serious. This was a first date. He had a chance, if he didn't blow it.

When he opened her door, she seemed to fit so naturally against him that he found himself sliding his hands down her back, gripping the soft curve of her buttocks, nipping at her mouth, finally losing himself in a long, drugged kiss.

She sounded dazed when they surfaced. "I should go in."

"Yeah." Her hair was fluffy beneath his cheek. "I didn't intend…"

Surprisingly she laughed, a delicious gurgle. "If you're claiming it wasn't premeditated, I don't think you'll get off. You did warn me, you know."

"I did, didn't I?" He found himself smiling, which made it easier to let her go. They walked to the front door hand in hand. "Can I take the baby-sitter home?"

"She lives in the complex."

"Then this is good night." One last slow kiss during which he savored her soft mouth, her slender neck under his hand and the pillow of her breasts against his chest. Then he let her go and backed away. "I'll call."

"Thank you for a nice evening, Connor." He was

pleased to see her fumble the key before she got it in the door. "Good night." She disappeared inside.

Walking back to the car, he wondered how soon before he could decently call. Was tomorrow morning pushing it?

CHAPTER TEN

IT TOOK CONNOR LESS THAN two hours in front of a computer to discover that Randy Mitchell had been dead for half of Tracy's life. When her mother and she said no contact, they meant it.

Although Saturday wasn't a schoolday, Tracy's mother did work, Connor knew, leaving at around four-thirty in the afternoon. He rang their doorbell at three-fifteen.

An eye peered at him through the peephole. A moment later, he heard the rattle of a chain being unfastened and a dead bolt being unlocked. Ms. Mitchell, dressed for work in a tiny miniskirt, fishnet stockings and three-inch heels, opened the door.

"I'm sorry it took ten minutes to let you in. That kid!" she said irritably. Over her shoulder, she yelled, "Tracy! Why did you fasten all the locks?" She shook her head and made an apologetic moue at Connor. "She's gotten so timid! Honest to God, I swear she'd put bars on the windows if the landlord and I would go for it."

"She was raped." He had to remind her?

"At school!" She shrugged. "If you can call it rape, when she went along with it."

Connor immediately developed a deep distaste for Tracy's mother.

As if reading his expression, she said hastily, "Not

that a teacher should have been seducing a little girl like my Tracy! I hope he's fired at the very least! Still, it's not as if a lock would have kept him out.''

He kept his tone stolid. ''Ms. Mitchell, I hope you'll consider counseling for Tracy. She's very young to have had this kind of experience. Her fear—'' he nodded at the door ''—suggests she feels very vulnerable. I know you work evenings, which leaves her here alone. Talking out what she really fears might help.''

She pressed a hand to her generous bosom, three-quarters bared by a plunging neckline. ''Do you know how much those robbers charge? I can't...'' She stopped and aimed a patently false smile past his shoulder. ''Tracy. See who's here to talk to you again.''

He'd missed her first reaction to his presence. Connor turned and nodded. ''Tracy. How are you?''

Dressed in jeans and a T-shirt that said, Surfer Girl, she gazed at him expressionlessly. ''I'm okay.''

''I'd like to talk to you again, if that's all right.''

Momentarily hopeful, she asked, ''Does that mean I can say no?''

''I know it's hard.'' He imbued his voice with sympathy. ''Unfortunately, going over and over your story is an unavoidable part of the investigation. I can't make an arrest until I have my ducks lined up, and you can help me do that.''

''Of course she wants to help!'' Steel in her voice, her mother wrapped an arm around Tracy and urged her toward a chair.

Her daughter dug in her heels, eyes widening with panic. ''I've said everything! I've said it and I've said it and I've said it!''

He made his expression grave. "We won't go over the whole thing again. In fact, I'm hoping you'll be more truthful with me today, Tracy." Let her stew for a few minutes, he thought.

Her mouth opened as if she wanted to flare defiantly back, but the fear in her eyes gave her away. She closed her mouth with a snap and sat down, hugging herself.

"Ms. Mitchell," Connor said to the mother, "I'd like to speak with you privately for a moment."

She nodded. "Sure. Come on into the kitchen."

From there he could see the top of Tracy's head in the recliner. In a low voice, he said, "Are you aware that your husband is dead?"

"Dead?" She gaped.

"You didn't know."

"I haven't heard from the bastard in years," she said bitterly. "He never paid a cent of child support, you know. He didn't want to be a father. Like I wanted to be a mother then! But I was raised Catholic, even if I don't go to Mass now, and I wasn't about to get an abortion. He hung around for a while, but he yelled when Tracy cried and got mad when I had to take care of her instead of him. One day, I got home from work and picking Tracy up at day care, and he was gone. Just cleaned his stuff out. The only decent thing he did was, he didn't take all my money. I guess he saw I'd need it. I never tried to find him."

Connor nodded. "I wanted to be sure he hadn't been in touch with Tracy. Maybe gotten curious about her. He died in the King County jail six years ago. He was in for thirty days after being picked up on a warrant—unpaid tickets. He was knifed by another inmate." Feeling it was called for, he said more gently, "I'm sorry to have sprung it on you this way."

"No." She took a breath and squared her shoulders. "I'm glad to know. I always thought he might show up again some day. I never actually got a divorce. I swore I wouldn't remarry." She gave a twisted smile. "Now I guess I might someday. I like having a man around. It bugs Tracy. I can tell she wishes I was some kind of Susie Homemaker, always making cookies and being Room Mother and that kind of stuff, but it's just not me. I am who I am."

"Tracy's at the age when being dissatisfied with your parent is normal."

"You mean, the one whose mother is the PTA president wishes she looked like me?" She cocked her hip and splayed one hand on it.

"Could be."

Her laugh was raucous and somehow sad, as if she knew he was lying. "I don't suppose Randy had any life insurance?"

"That, I don't know. You might contact the jail, see if you can't find out whether he was employed. He might have had insurance through a job. If you were still legally married…"

"Unless he got a divorce without me knowing, and I don't think you can do that, can you? Besides, he knew where to find me."

"Check it out," he advised her.

"Yeah. I'll do that." She stole a glance at the clock, her body language suddenly restive. "You probably want to talk to Tracy without me here, don't you? I gotta do things on the way to work. You being here gives me a chance to leave without having to tell Tracy every step I'm making."

What kind of mother, he thought again, would leave her daughter, obviously upset, to be interviewed alone by a cop? He contrasted her casual attitude with Mariah's willingness to sacrifice everything for Zofie's sake. But Ms. Mitchell's suggestion suited his agenda, so he nodded.

"Yeah, I would just as soon speak to her alone. She's more likely to open up." Translation: she was more likely to break when she felt more vulnerable, without her mom to back her.

"Hey, honey," the mother said blithely, bustling into the living room with her hips swinging. "The officer wants to talk to you alone, so I'm heading off for work now."

Following close behind her, Connor got a bird's-eye view of the way Tracy flinched from her kiss.

"Well." Her mother retreated, forced an artificial smile and went to the door. A huge handbag that looked like it could hold two outfits as microscopic as the one she wore hung over the top of the TV. She grabbed it, said, "Be good," and was gone.

Tracy sat stone-faced.

Connor chose the end of the couch closest to her chair. He picked his words carefully. "I shouldn't have implied that you're lying. I don't know that you are. I just want to make sure you understand what's going to happen to Mr. Tanner if we prosecute."

She didn't move, but she was listening.

"He will, of course, be fired. Losing his job for a reason like child sexual molestation will mean he can never teach again. It will certainly get in the way of him finding any work at all. He will have to pay a lawyer to defend himself. I have the impression that will take every bit of savings he has. Without a salary, he'll probably have to go stay with a friend, give up his apartment. Say the jury believes you and he's convicted. He'll go to prison. Probably not a real long term. Rapists never get the sentences we cops think they deserve. But he'll spend time behind bars.''

She shivered.

"If I were a woman, I wouldn't marry—heck, I wouldn't date!—a man who had been convicted of a crime like this.''

Tracy's mouth worked.

"His life won't be over, but it won't be the same.'' Connor leaned forward, elbows on his knees, and said gently, "Is that what Mr. Tanner deserves, Tracy? Because if it is, I'll get on with it. If he did this to you, that *is* what he deserves.''

A whimper escaped her, then another one. She seemed to crumple, drawing up her legs at the same time so that she ended in a ball, rocking as she sobbed.

Connor dropped to his knees beside her chair and tried to hold her as she cried. At first she resisted him, shutting him and everything else out in her misery, but finally she relaxed enough to cry onto his shoulders.

And at last she mumbled something.

He patted her back. "What?''

The swollen, wet face that looked up at him bore little resemblance to the pretty, brittle teenager he knew.

"He didn't do it. Mr. Tanner didn't do anything.''

SUDDENLY THE POLICEMAN thrust a huge white handkerchief at her. Tracy snatched it, then mopped her face and blew her nose.

"I lied," she said, fresh tears filling her swollen eyes. Why hadn't they just fired Mr. Tanner? Why did they have to call the cops?

"Tracy." Connor waited until she looked at him. "I didn't tell you what I did to make you feel sorry for your teacher. If he pressured you into having sex, I meant it when I said he deserves everything coming. Don't take back what you said now because you feel sorry for him."

"It was never him," she admitted miserably.

He got up from being on his knees in front of her and sat back down on the couch. It was as if he couldn't get away from her fast enough. "Then why did you say he did?" he asked.

Tracy blew her nose again. Tears ran unchecked down her cheeks. "I was afraid I was pregnant!" she wailed. "I had to say it was somebody!"

"Tracy, do you have a boyfriend?"

She shook her head furiously.

"Did you voluntarily have sex?"

Her face crumpled again. She pictured the dark silhouette in the paler rectangle of her bedroom door, the weight tilting her mattress, the hand that covered her mouth. Somehow she was rocking and couldn't seem to stop herself. Eyes downcast, she shook her head again.

"Who raped you, Tracy?" His voice was hard. He was mad, probably at her. She didn't even blame him.

"I can't tell you." She gave him one wild look. "I won't! You can't make me!"

"Why won't you tell me? Why would you protect someone who did that to you?"

She shook her head. Kept shaking it, until her hair

lashed her cheeks. If she stopped, he might make her talk, and she wouldn't. She wouldn't!

But his voice was soothing, as if he could tell she was about to break. "All right. Then tell me why you chose Mr. Tanner to accuse."

"Because he's such a jerk!" Her eyes flooded with tears, her mouth trembled, but this time she kept her chin up. "I hate him! I…I did hate him. I don't know anymore."

"Why did you hate him?"

"He makes fun of students. It's like, he's teasing, and everybody laughs, but it's not funny if you're the one he's…he's being mean to."

"What kind of teasing?" he asked.

Tracy sniffed. "Like, there's this boy in my class who isn't very smart. I think he does special ed part of the day. Mr. Tanner is always saying stuff like, 'Does everybody get this? Does even *Kyle* get this?' And, like, everybody thinks that's funny, but I see Kyle kind of hunch. You know?"

The policeman surprised her. "I was my current height when I was in seventh grade," he told her. "Tripping over my own feet, they were so big. I got teased, sometimes by teachers, too. They never seemed to recognize that I was sensitive about being different."

"Well, I'm kind of, um, *mature* for my age, too," she went on, cheeks red. "I mean, not tall, but…you know." She stole a glance up to see if he got it.

His glance swept over her, but not offensively. She thought maybe he did think of her as a child. That made her feel safe.

"The other girls will catch up," he said, as if she didn't have anything to be ashamed of.

"I guess." Her eyes felt grainy and so puffy it was like she was peering through a tunnel. "Sometimes he'd say stuff." She mimicked his voice. "'Miss America has joined us. Tell me, Tracy, is the bathing suit competition today?' The week before I went to Ms. Stavig, I wore this shirt of my mom's one day. *I* thought I looked pretty. Only I didn't know you could see through it. And I went to his class, and this really hot guy I like stopped to talk to me. Only suddenly Mr. Tanner was like, 'Tracy, stand up.' Everybody stared." She burned with humiliation at the memory. "And he says, 'I see you took me seriously about the bathing suit competition. Or…no. Is that a bra I'm looking at? Should we be glad you're wearing one? Or disappointed?' Even the guy I like was laughing and…and *leering*." She had to take several deep breaths before she could finish. "Then Mr. Tanner tells me to go to the principal's office and not come back until I'm *decent*. I ran out." Tears clogged her sinuses and leaked out of her eyes despite her effort to maintain her dignity. "That's why I hate him," she said intensely.

The big cop had this look on his face she couldn't read. After a moment, he said quietly, "I don't blame you."

"Really?"

"You know, if you'd reported him, he would have been in trouble for this kind of behavior."

She curled her lip. "Like anybody would listen."

"Ms. Stavig listened, didn't she?"

Suddenly ashamed, Tracy ducked her head again. "Yes," she whispered.

"This is his first year teaching middle school. He's used to college students, who are less sensitive about their appearances and whether they fit in. He may genuinely not realize he's hurting feelings.''

"But he's kind of, like, *nerdy* looking. He's got these thick glasses, and... Don't you think somebody made fun of *him?*''

Ms. Stavig wasn't the only one who listened. Tracy was scared of Detective McLean in one way, but she also noticed that he paid attention to what she said, thought about it and gave her answers that felt honest. This was one of those times.

"Maybe he's teasing kids now because he was on the receiving end of it a lot when he was a kid. Maybe it feels good to be the powerful one now.''

"That...that's...*cruel,*'' she said in perplexity.

"I don't know. I'm just guessing. Probably he doesn't know, either. Most of our behavior isn't consciously motivated. Things that happened when we were little, things we don't even consciously remember, motivate the way we respond to people, explain why we're afraid of...heck, flying or dogs or teachers who are too tall. Mr. Tanner might be able to change. He might even be sorry to know how much he hurt your feelings.''

Tracy pressed her lips together and thought. *Might.* That meant he might *not* be sorry, too.

"But after I lied about...him doing those things to me, nobody will listen.''

"I want you to tell Ms. Patterson and Ms. Stavig exactly what you've told me about why you chose Mr. Tanner.''

Terror made it hard to breathe. "Do I have to?''

He nodded, looking stern. "Lots of people are going to ask you, and you need to tell them the truth.''

"Like...like other kids?''

"There's been talk. You say, 'I got him in trouble because I thought he was mean to me, but I didn't realize how *much* trouble he would be in, and I'm sorry I caused it.'" He leveled his gaze on her. "Are you sorry?"

She couldn't see him through the tears, but she could nod.

"You could be in trouble with the law for making a false accusation, you know."

The fear was crushing her chest.

"What's important is that you tell me who did rape you."

Trembling, she shook her head.

"You know me, Tracy. I'll be back. I'll keep coming back until you tell me."

"I can't!" she whispered.

"Tell me why."

"I can't tell you that, either." If she did, he'd know everything.

"I'm thinking you're protecting someone." He sounded musing, as though instead of talking he really was thinking, but aloud. "You were strong, sticking to your story. Stronger than I thought you'd be. Some kid rapes you, I can't imagine why you'd care enough to protect him. Nah." He shook his head. "Seems to me it must be someone close to you. You haven't had contact with your father, you don't have other family you see much, do you, Tracy? No, it's mostly been you and your mom. There aren't that many people you care enough about to protect, are there, Tracy?"

She was breathing in huge gasps, just staring at him, waiting for him to pounce.

"What I'm thinking is that we need to talk about

your relationship with your mom," he continued, in
that same tone.

Her voice came out high and unnatural. "But my
mom...that's ridiculous. She's a woman. I thought I
could be *pregnant*."

"That's true." He nodded as though she'd said
something brilliant. "There's a man in this somewhere. I just don't think that's who you're protecting."

He knew. How could he know?

"Tracy, if your mom is somehow involved, you
will never feel safe here again. I know it's hard to get
her in trouble, but if she didn't take any better care
of you than to let you be raped, she needs help, too.
You cannot go on the way you are." His eyes were
serious, caring, seeming to see deep inside her. "The
locks don't keep her out, or anyone she chooses to
bring home."

She heard her own breath scraping in, whistling
out.

"I'm going to leave now, and I want you to lock
up tight behind me." He got to his feet, but his eyes
never left hers. "You do some thinking, Tracy. I can
help you, but not until you tell me what really happened."

She'd seen nature films. She was the mouse. Or the
rabbit, trapped away from the hole.

"I'll be back, Tracy."

He let himself out, quietly. She sat frozen. He'd
been gone for several minutes when she flung herself
at the door, her hands shaking as she pushed the button for the knob's crummy lock, then fastened the
dead bolt and finally the chain, even though that
would make Mom mad when she came home in the

middle of the night because she'd have to ring the doorbell and wait until Tracy got up to let her in. Finally Tracy checked all the windows to make sure they were latched, even though the apartment was on the second floor.

At last she went back to huddle in the chair, clutching the tear-soaked handkerchief he'd forgotten.

She wished he hadn't left. She wished she could trust him.

She wished she didn't know she could never, never tell anyone, even if he was right and she would have to be scared forever.

"ONE MORE STORY," ZOFIE begged.

"Nope." Mariah set the pile of library books on the coffee table. "*Cowardly Clyde* was supposed to be the last one. Come to think of it, so was *Rosamund.*"

Zofie scooted forward on the couch and grabbed for a book on the stack. "Yes, but we haven't read this one. See?"

"Tomorrow night," Mariah said firmly. "Time to brush your teeth. Come on."

"Oh, poop," her daughter muttered.

She widened her eyes. "Do you need to?"

"*Mo-om!*"

They shared a brief giggle.

While Zofie brushed her teeth, a task she had mostly taken over these past few months, Mariah put away the books and started cleaning up the kitchen.

Her gaze kept wandering to the telephone hanging on the wall, and once she thought she heard the beginning of a ring and lunged for it before she realized

Zofie had turned on a music tape down the hall in her bedroom.

She didn't know the etiquette for adults dating. But wouldn't it have been polite for Connor to call and say, "I had a good time"?

Maybe he didn't have a good time.

She'd sworn beforehand that she wouldn't talk about Simon or Tracy, either. Then what did they do but spend the entire evening talking about both! Not to mention his sexually abused girlfriend, a topic he'd tried to avoid.

Mariah moaned softly. She was a failure as a fun date.

"Live and learn," she said aloud, but she didn't want to learn a lesson she could only apply the next time a man asked her out. She wanted not to have blown it with Connor McLean.

Maybe it was meant to be, she thought miserably. She shouldn't have dated him. The very fact that they couldn't avoid painful topics should tell her something.

"Mo-om!" Zofie called. "I'm ready for you to tuck me in."

The phone rang at that precise moment.

"Just a minute," Mariah called back, and picked up the cordless. "Hello?"

"Mariah? This is Connor."

"Oh, hi." She tried to sound carefree, surprised that he had called so quickly. To her own ears, she failed wretchedly.

His voice became intimate, warm. "I'd like to have had dinner with you tonight, too, but I figured that was pushing you."

Pressing her hand to her warm cheek, she said, "I couldn't have left Zofie…"

"Yeah. I know you couldn't. But, if she were away for the weekend, would you have?"

Her mouth opened, closed. A sophisticated woman would undoubtedly tease, play hard to get. "Yes," she said finally, baldly. Truthfully.

"Good." His voice was rich with satisfaction.

"I shouldn't have said that, should I? I could have strung you along a little." She sounded breathless with relief, even if she was trying to flirt.

"I'm a straightforward guy. I'd rather you were honest."

From down the hall came Zofie's, "Mom! I'm still waiting!"

Guiltily realizing she'd forgotten her daughter, Mariah said, "Um, listen. I have to go tuck Zofie in."

His voice changed, became deadly serious. "I was hoping to talk to you about Tracy. I followed up today on your suggestion. Can I call you back in a few minutes? Or… No, I suppose it's too late to come over."

Her heart did a peculiar little flip. "Aren't you at home?"

"Actually I'm calling from the car. I just tried to track down Tracy's mother's last boyfriend. Turned out to be a flop."

"*Mo-om!*"

"Then come," Mariah said hastily.

"See you in a minute."

She hurried down the hall, resisting the impulse to dance. "Sorry," she said to Zofie, enveloping her in a big hug. "Did you do a good job brushing your teeth?"

By the time a knock sounded softly on the front door, she'd settled the six-year-old into bed, told her that Connor would be coming over and left her listening to a tape of gentle bedtime music sung by folk singers like Pete Seeger and Arlo Guthrie.

Connor stepped in, took a swift glance around, presumably to be sure Zofie wasn't in sight, and kissed her. When he lifted his head, he said huskily, "I've been thinking about doing that all day."

"Me, too," she admitted, her voice squeaking. "I mean, I've been thinking about you doing that."

"Good," he said for the second time tonight, with that same satisfaction.

Stepping back, she pulled herself together. "Can I get you something to drink? Did you have dinner? I could heat leftovers…"

"No, I'm fine." His mouth firmed, as if she'd recalled him to his reason for coming by. "Let's sit down."

She curled her bare feet under her on one end of the couch, while he sat beside her but not touching.

"Tracy admitted today that Tanner never touched her," he said without preamble.

"Oh!" Her first reaction was delight for Gerald's sake, her second dismay as she foresaw the fallout. And finally, she thought about Tracy, who had been afraid she was pregnant. "Oh," she said, more softly.

"She won't tell me who did rape her, but says it was rape."

"Poor Tracy!"

"I scared the crap out of her when I started dancing around the subject of her mother." The lines on his face deepened. "I'm not sure I want to know what we're going to find out."

"No." Mariah tried to imagine being so young and unable to trust her mother. "Did you find out anything about the father?"

"He's dead. Has been for years."

She gave an automatic nod. "Have you let Gerald Tanner know yet?"

"No, but I called Mrs. Patterson. She's arranging a meeting first with just you, Tracy and her on Monday morning. I want her to hear Tracy's story before she talks to Tanner." He told her, then, about the myriad cruelties dished out by the computer teacher. "I'd gotten hints from some of the other kids. I want to make sure Mrs. Patterson knows. How she handles it is her business."

"Tracy will have to be pulled from his class."

"Oh, yeah." He frowned in silence at the far wall for a minute. "He could insist that we file charges for making a false accusation, which she could hardly dispute."

"Will he?"

"I hope not. I doubt it, after the principal is done with him. At least, if I judge her right."

"He may have more compassion than you're crediting him with." She hoped.

"Could be." He sighed and took her hand, looking down at it as he traced the fine bones along the back.

She looked at his bent head and wondered why this man of all others made her feel so much. The merest touch, a clear, penetrating glance, the rumble of his voice, all were enough to make her feel light as air, as giddy as…as a woman in love for the first time.

No. She couldn't be in love with him. Not yet. And she'd loved Simon, or been in love with him, anyway. Somewhere along the way, what she felt died. Maybe she wasn't capable of permanency. Otherwise, why—?

Don't think about it, she told herself. Not right now. She didn't know what Connor felt or wanted yet. She was entitled to…to flirt and go dancing and maybe even have an affair, wasn't she?

The phone rang, a sudden, shocking sound, and she jerked.

"Excuse me." She took her hand back. On the way to pick up the telephone she'd left in the kitchen, Mariah felt Connor's gaze on her.

"Simon," she said, a moment later.

Connor half stood, then sat back down. His eyes were dark, steady.

As if he hadn't been so angry the last time, her ex-husband said, "I promised Zofie I'd come to her soccer game tomorrow. She wasn't sure of the time or where it is."

"Oh. Um…sure." Damn it, he'd wonder why she sounded so flustered, she thought. Turning her back on Connor, she went to the refrigerator where she'd posted the soccer schedule. She told Simon, "One o'clock at the far field at Meadow Park."

"Okay." He was silent for a moment. "I assume Zofie's in bed?"

"Yes, I'm sorry."

"No, just tell her I'll be there."

"No problem." Now she sounded so darn cheery and synthetic, she despised herself. "She'll be glad you're coming. I'll see you there, Simon."

Connor was on his feet when she went back to the living room. "I should probably be leaving. It's after nine o'clock."

On a Saturday night. She knew the real reason: he

didn't like the reminder of the way he'd stepped into her life. He wanted to forget Simon existed.

But she couldn't, because he was Zofie's father. He would be part of her reality forever, because they were linked through their child. If Connor couldn't accept that...

She was jumping ahead again. Way ahead. They'd just had a first date. They weren't in love, weren't thinking forever.

''Oh? Fine,'' she said pleasantly. ''I'll be seeing you Monday, I assume.''

''I gather Simon's coming to the game tomorrow?''

She nodded.

''I'd thought about...'' He stopped, the muscles in his jaw knotting. ''Never mind. None of us is ready for that.''

''No.'' She was proud of how calm she made that sound, when the very idea had her heart drumming. ''I know I'm not.''

He nodded, his gaze shuttered, and went to the door.

Following him, she felt a sickening sense of disappointment. Was this it? What should she say?

He reached for the knob, then turned abruptly. ''When can I see you again, Mariah?''

''Monday...''

''No. Really see you. Talk to you.'' He reached out and gripped her hands, his warm and powerful. ''Kiss you.''

If she'd thought her heart was beating fast before, now it was deafening her. ''Would you like to come for dinner Monday night? Zofie will be here, too, but...''

His smile was slow and crooked. ''Yeah. I'd like that a lot. I'd like to get to know her.''

''I'm glad,'' she whispered.

He kissed her with stunning intent, his hands staying on her lower back and nape, but she felt the rawness of his need in the teeth that closed on her lower lip and the rigid bar that pressed her belly when she melted against him.

I'm not in love, she told herself again, as he set her away from him, gave her a last smoldering look and left with a curt order to lock up behind him. *Not yet.*

But she didn't believe herself.

CHAPTER ELEVEN

SUNDAY WAS ONE OF THOSE days when Mariah was reminded of why she'd been drawn to Simon in the first place. He was waiting at the parking lot when she pulled in, ready to hoist Zofie into the air with a flash of white teeth.

"You going to score today?" he demanded.

"Two goals," the first-grader claimed, as he lowered her to the ground.

"That's my girl."

They walked as a family to the field, Mariah carrying her lawn chair and umbrella, Simon trying to steal Zofie's soccer ball, her dribbling it away from him and giggling. The wet grass squelched underfoot. Wet maple leaves, fallen from the trees ringing the parking lot, stuck to the white-and-black soccer ball. A steady but gentle rain fell. Simon, typically, wore only a sweatshirt. He was too macho to admit to needing rain gear. Looking around, Mariah saw that he wasn't the only father who insisted on coming without the slicker and umbrella every mother carried.

He had always loved his daughter. Knowing that was why from the beginning she had felt so conflicted when she tried to imagine him touching Zofie sexually. Did the fathers who abused their daughters love them, too? Or did they see them only through the filter of their own needs and wants? If so, did any of them put on as good a front as Simon had?

After she'd asked Simon to leave, Mariah had gone through a brief stretch of educating herself. She'd checked out every book the library had about child sexual abuse and the juvenile justice system. Somehow her questions were never answered. She never *saw* any of those fathers, or the way they interacted with their children.

Simon and she had had a decent love life. He wanted her almost nightly, with urgency that hadn't flagged. The fact that she rarely became very aroused wasn't his fault, but hers—it was one of the reasons she doubted her ability to love a man forever. Why had she gone from finding Simon incredibly sexy to hoping he'd fall asleep without turning to her, all in the space of a year or two of marriage?

One of the many things she'd never learned was whether a man could do that—make love to his wife as if she satisfied him—and then stalk a child the very next day.

Now, mostly, she didn't let herself think about what hideous wants Simon might be disguising. Three years had passed, long enough, surely, for him to have given himself away.

Zofie had no reservations about her dad. There was never any hesitation when he held out his arms. She loved him in an uncomplicated way Mariah preserved. He couldn't be a pedophile and resist abusing his daughter, could he? The fact that he clearly hadn't must mean he had been innocent, that Mariah didn't have anything to worry about when Zofie was with him.

Zofie's trust in her dad left Mariah feeling more guilty, of course, because why else had she left him?

Today Simon stayed beside her when Zofie raced off to join her teammates in warm-ups.

"She's a great kid, isn't she?" he said, watching her dribbling around cones in a line with the other girls.

"Yeah." Momentarily linked in harmony, they were relaxed enough to let their shoulders brush. "She is. She's doing well in school, too. I'll make sure she takes some books when you pick her up Saturday, so you can see how well she reads. She's already at least a grade level ahead."

He nodded. "I was never that good in school. She takes after you."

"Well, *I* wasn't much of an athlete, but look at her." It was easy to be generous. "She gets that from you."

He looked at her, his dark eyes puppy-dog puzzled. "How did we go wrong, Mariah?"

She must have stiffened.

Simon shook his head. "Scratch that. I shouldn't have asked. I don't want to get into it with you today, Mariah. Let's just enjoy watching Zofie play."

She nodded and avoided his gaze as she unfolded her lawn chair and sat, glad of the distance it gave her from him.

Once the game started with the referee's blown whistle, she was engrossed. Zofie played without the timidity of many girls this age, throwing herself into the fray. She scored right before half-time, darting past the goalie who had come out to intercept her and gently tapping the ball into the net. She'd managed to get muddy as well as wet, but her grin shone from a dirt-streaked face as she paused for congratulations before going for her snack and to huddle with the coach.

Second half she played goalie, as she often did, her petite body swathed in the extralong, colorful top and her face in the mask. She made heroic saves, throwing herself atop the ball, getting kicked hard once and still rolling away to protect the ball. She came swaggering off to pats on the back from her teammates, giving them in return.

"Great goal!" she called to one, the mask pushed up, as she arrived at her parents' side.

"Thanks!" the friend called. "See you Tuesday!"

"Practice?" Simon asked.

"Mmm-hmm. The coach has cut back to two afternoons a week, with the weather so miserable and it getting dark so early," Mariah told him.

He laid a hand on Zofie's shoulder. "Have you two had lunch? How about we go out to McDonald's?"

"Yeah!" she exclaimed, her pleading eyes turning to Mom. "Can we?"

She forced a smile. "Why not?"

Simon followed Mariah in his own car. She was glad to see a teammate of Zofie's and her family had arrived ahead of them.

Carrie and Zofie hugged, bounced up and down and talked about the game and school.

"Why don't we sit together?" the other mother suggested.

Mariah had to introduce Simon. She did so simply, as Zofie's dad, not knowing whether the others even knew she was divorced. Conversation was general, the girls had a great time and Mariah was saved from an intimate threesome.

The real trouble, she had to admit, was that she was afraid Zofie would mention Connor. If she kept dating him, it would happen, she knew it would, but she wasn't ready. Panic fluttered every time she imagined Simon's fury.

As they walked out to the cars, Simon asked easily, "What'd you guys do the rest of this weekend?"

Zofie, of course, piped right up, "Mommy went somewhere with…"

"A friend," Mariah finished, squeezing her daughter's shoulder. "Zofie had a horrible time staying home with her favorite baby-sitter, who let her stay up until ten-o'clock and eat *two* helpings of ice cream and watch *The Little Mermaid.*"

"And *Beauty,* too," Zofie said smugly.

"And then Saturday we went shopping. Zofie keeps shooting up like a weed, and half the clothes we bought for school in August don't fit anymore. She got two new pairs of shoes…"

"My soccer shoes are really tight," Zofie informed her mother. "My toes are squished."

"But the soccer season, thank goodness, is almost over. Two more games. We'll buy new ones next year."

"Coach says they're having spring soccer. We should all play, if we want to be the best."

"If you want to," Mariah agreed.

"But I want to play volleyball, too. Can I do both?"

Both parents gazed at their daughter's pleading dark eyes, looked at each other and laughed, the earlier harmony restored.

Danger averted.

"We'll see," Mariah temporized.

They'd paused under the overhang of the building, since the downpour had increased. Simon bent for a hug, said, "Great game, kiddo. I'll see you Saturday," and ran for his car.

Mother and daughter watched him go, a tall, dark man, hair soaked and clinging to his head, his last smile friendly.

Zofie said, "You didn't want Daddy to know about Decktiv McLean, did you?"

Startled, Mariah looked down at the precocious six-year-old. "What do you mean?"

Her daughter gazed gravely up at her. "I just thought you didn't."

Giving herself time to think, Mariah said, "Let's get in the car, out of the rain, okay?"

Zofie was so wet and muddy, Mariah had been embarrassed to take her even into a fast-food restaurant. She'd left her mud-caked cleats in the car, wearing a pair of rubber flip-flops over the soccer socks. Mariah had left her rain slicker in the car, but she still wasn't as wet as her daughter when she started the engine to get the heat going.

"About Connor," she said, trying not to sound as uncomfortable as she felt. "I think when moms and dads are divorced, it takes a long time before they quit feeling married. I never ask you if your dad is dating, either, you know."

Zofie's forehead wrinkled. "I think he does sometimes." Then her eyes widened. "Oh! You didn't want to know."

"No, that's okay. I just don't want to hear the details, that's all. I doubt your dad would be bothered to know that I've been on a date, but he won't want

to hear all about the guy.'' She took a breath. ''And
I'd rather you don't tell him if he does ask.''

''Why?''

''Because we aren't married anymore, and it isn't
any of his business. He *shouldn't* ask you. What if I
go out to dinner with someone he knows, and that
bothers him? If he asks, just pretend you don't know
or can't remember Connor's name.''

Her daughter nodded solemnly, her forehead puckered again. ''I'll try.'' She sounded doubtful. ''But I
like to talk. And sometimes things come out I promised someone I wouldn't tell.''

Mariah gave a choke of laughter. ''If that happens,
it's okay. Don't worry. Six-year-olds aren't expected
to be discreet.''

She spent the drive home attempting to explain
''discreet'' to her inquiring daughter.

Who, she was terribly afraid, wouldn't really understand the meaning of the word no matter how carefully she explained.

But she'd vowed she would never ask Zofie to keep
secrets, just as she'd made her daughter promise she
wouldn't keep any from Mom. If Zofie spilled the
beans, so be it.

The day the divorce was final, Mariah had felt
enormous relief along with paralyzing guilt and a
sense of failure. She would no longer have to fear
Simon's wrath.

So what was she afraid of now?

ON MONDAY, TRACY SAT IN THE chair in front of
Mrs. Patterson's desk and made her confession to the
principal and Mariah, who sat quietly to one side.

''What if Detective McLean had believed you right

away?'' the principal asked, voice even and unsympathetic. ''Would you have let Mr. Tanner be arrested? Would you have lied in court?''

Tracy mumbled from behind the curtain of hair that partially hid her face, ''I didn't know he'd be arrested. I just thought…''

''He'd be fired,'' the principal finished, her expression hard. ''I understand your anger at him, Tracy. I will certainly be discussing with him his brand of teasing. But does losing his job in a way that guarantees he'll never get a comparable one seem a fair punishment for unkind teasing?''

Tracy stole a look up, her face soaked with tears. ''I felt bad when I saw what was happening. I didn't know…''

''I can tell you that I'm very glad you thought better of going through with this.'' At last Noreen's voice softened. ''You know you have one more step to take. Nobody should get away with raping you, Tracy. Whoever it was, whoever was involved, all of us—Detective McLean, Ms. Stavig—'' she gestured toward Mariah ''—and myself are committed to protecting you and making sure you're in a home and school environment where nothing like this can ever happen again. Please think, Tracy. I'm not going to ask you to tell me right now, or ever, but if you're more comfortable talking to me, Ms. Stavig or a counselor than you are to a police officer, please come to one of us.''

Still silently crying, Tracy blew her nose and nodded.

''I feel that I have to give you some consequences for having falsely accused Mr. Tanner. That's something I need to think about.''

The thirteen-year-old nodded again, meekly.

"In the meantime, you won't be going to Computers second period. We'll worry next year about you completing the requirement. For now, I'm going to have you work here in the office second period. Is that okay?"

A damp, muffled, "Yes, Mrs. Patterson."

Sounding more kindly, the principal said, "You may go use the rest room and wash your face, Tracy, then go back to class as soon as you feel presentable."

Tracy fled.

Once the door shut behind her, Noreen shoved a hand into her curly hair. "That poor kid."

"I don't envy you, having to decide how to deal with her," Mariah said frankly.

"I don't see how it can be more than a slap on the wrist, given that she *was* raped. And that, if she's to be believed, Gerald treated her with a real lack of sensitivity."

Mariah nodded. Tentatively she said, "I'm afraid he's not alone. I've overheard kids talk about other teachers teasing in a way they resent."

The principal gave a frustrated sigh. "It's an unsolvable issue. We don't want to get to a point where teachers have to be so careful all the time, they can't relate naturally to kids. Here we are saying, Don't touch. Don't hug. Hide your anger. Phrase everything as an 'I' statement. 'I felt hurt when you deliberately smashed my favorite mug.' Oh, and don't laugh at them. Don't tease." She gave another puff of air that stirred her now wild hair. "We'll end up with automatons at the head of the classroom, droning on and not interacting on a personal level with the kids at all.''

Knowing she was just venting, Mariah only waited.

Noreen made a face. ''Thanks for being here, Mariah. I'm going to write a 'Dear Parent' letter explaining, in a terribly veiled way, why their kids' computer teacher was suspended for a few weeks and is now back. I don't want to leave any doubt that he's innocent, but I also don't want Tracy's identity or other problems compromised. Can I run it by you?''

Mariah smiled wryly. ''Sure.'' Hey, she was an expert, wasn't she?

Noreen had picked up a pencil and was fiddling with it. ''If Tracy talks to anybody, it may well be you.''

''I hope she chooses to. My guess is, the last time she talked to me had such horrible consequences, she won't try again.''

Her suspicion was reinforced by the way Tracy acted in class later, not volunteering and keeping her gaze downcast. Afterward, Mariah stopped her on the way out. Tracy waited, her stare fixed on her sneakers and her face sullen.

Mariah made sure the last student was out in the hall before she said quietly, ''I just wanted to say that I know how tough all this is, but you'll get through it.'' She straightened from where she'd been half sitting on the desk and violated her own rule by giving Tracy a quick hug. ''You're a good kid. You'll make the right choices.''

Tracy's face crumpled, her eyes filled with tears, and she backed away. ''I... Thank you,'' she mumbled, and fled.

Mariah spent the rest of the day trying to put Tracy

Mitchell's problems out of her mind. It helped to be anticipating having Connor over for dinner tonight. She made mental additions to her grocery list—she'd stop at the store before she picked up Zofie. It was easier to do a big shop then than on the weekend, when she had to drag the six-year-old along. This way she could avoid the "Mom, why can't I have *this* kind of cereal?" battles.

Stir-fry? she debated, the one with cashews that Zofie loved? She gazed at the bent heads of her last period class, who were taking a quiz on *To Kill a Mockingbird*. Somehow a quick stir-fry didn't seem very substantial for a big man; Simon had liked his meat and potatoes. Maybe she should stick with something as simple as spaghetti? Only, what if she found out Connor was a vegetarian, or hated tomatoes, or...

"Ms. Stavig." One of her students waved his hand in the air. "Can I go to the bathroom?"

She glanced at the clock. "You only have five more minutes to work on the quiz. Can't you wait?"

He looked disconsolately down at his paper. "I guess."

Watching out of the corner of her eye, she noticed that he didn't write another word. He hadn't seemed enthusiastic lately. She struggled to remember his academic record coming into her class. Was he having problems? She'd have to check her grade book...

The bell rang overhead. A flurry of quizzes rained onto her desk, some floating over the edge to the floor, as the students stampeded out.

They couldn't be any gladder to be gone than she was to have them depart. Briefly ashamed of her ignoble relief, Mariah wrinkled her nose and decided to forgive herself. She loved to teach, but today had been stressful. Scooping up papers from the floor, she thought, Thank goodness it was over.

"Mariah?"

She started and banged her elbow on the desk. "Gerald!"

The lanky, raw-boned man took a tentative step into the classroom. "Got a minute?"

What could she do but smile and say, "Of course?"

He closed her classroom door. "I just wanted to apologize for lashing out at you that day." He sounded awkward. "You were right—you had to report what Tracy told you."

"I could have warned you," she said, standing and putting the quizzes in her hand onto the pile of others, more to give herself something to do than because it mattered right that minute. "I just didn't know how."

"It wouldn't have made any difference." He grimaced. "It was just that…I felt blindsided."

She nodded. "I really didn't blame you for being angry."

He hesitated. "I'm back to work tomorrow."

"I'm glad." Mariah meant it. "I know Tracy has retracted her story."

He shook his head, his face haggard. "I still can't believe it happened. I can't believe how *easily* it happened, and how little I could do to prove my innocence."

"I've read that some people think kids never make false accusations, and that others think they do all the time."

"Thank God it's over!"

Mariah bit her lip. "You know," she said quietly,

"there'll still be rumors. You need to be prepared. Some people are going to think Tracy was telling the truth then, and has somehow been railroaded into lying now. Or they'll figure authorities couldn't prove her story, but there must have been some basis to it."

He stared at her. "You sound like you know. Has something like this happened to you?"

"To my ex-husband," she admitted. "He ended up changing jobs and then, after our divorce, moving. He hated the whispers."

Gerald said nothing for a long moment. Then he muttered a profanity and sank into a student chair, bowing his head and tugging at his short hair. "I wanted to think it was over," he said in agony.

Mariah felt helpless, useless, sitting behind her desk with her hands clasped on the blotter. Should she be hugging him? But they had never been that close.

She had to say something, at the very least. "Maybe I'm being pessimistic. Noreen is writing a letter of explanation. There wasn't anyone who could do that for Simon." Or who would, she didn't add. Even his wife couldn't quiet her doubts.

His head lifted and from behind his glasses his wild eyes sought hers. "You believe I never touched her, don't you?"

"Yes." She was glad to be able to answer honestly. "I never believed it. I urged Detective McLean to look into other possibilities."

"Thank you," Gerald said hoarsely.

She moistened her lips. "I hope you can forgive Tracy."

Pain and anger and shame flashed on his face, flushing it with red. "Apparently I ticked her off."

He gave an angry laugh. "What a way to pay me back."

"She's a troubled girl."

"Oh, yeah. She's that. I can even see why. Have you met the mother?"

The mother. Mariah had been guilty herself of putting it that way, as if Sandy Mitchell were not quite the right *kind* of mother, the one you'd say warmly was "Tracy's mother."

"Yes," she said slowly. "I think she dresses the way she does because she works in a bar. She seems genuinely concerned about Tracy."

Squeezed into the student-size desk, his knees poking up, his elbows akimbo, Gerald said, "And irritated with her for being an inconvenience."

"Wouldn't you be irritated if you were called to conferences every few weeks?" Mariah said, in all fairness.

He shrugged.

He hadn't said whether he'd forgive his accuser.

"Tracy looks more brazen than she is," Mariah tried to explain, knowing it might not be what he wanted to hear right now, but hoping he would understand. "Sometimes she wears her mother's clothes. I think she knows, though, that her mother looks different than the other kids'. She wants to be proud of her and even to be like her, but then she doesn't, too. It's a hard spot to be in at her age, when a girl is trying to find her identity."

"That excuses her trying to ruin me?" he said incredulously.

"No. No, of course not." Would she feel the same, in his situation? Think how she'd hated Connor and the now faceless woman who had come at his side to accuse Simon! She had been too selfish then, too absorbed in her own family's crisis, to feel the compassion or pity she should have for Lily, the girl who had set it in motion. She had tried very hard not even to think about her or what she had suffered or why she had chosen to name Simon. Would she have wanted explanations, justification?

But, remembering, Tracy's small, tear-clogged voice that morning, Mariah had to try.

"I just want you to remember that she's a kid. She had no idea what she was setting in motion. She was scared, and hurting..."

"You know, I'm just damn glad I don't have to face her." Gerald Tanner fought free of the desk, shoving it clattering to one side. His eyes were angry. "Give me time, and maybe I'll cool off. Right now, frankly, I'd like to see her expelled."

"I understand..."

"Do you?" He fairly bristled, pain radiating from his pores like the sweat that beaded his forehead. He blinked, shook his head like a baffled bull, and said in a choked voice, "Maybe you do. Or you're trying. Remember—it can happen to any of us. Just like that." He snapped his fingers.

Goose bumps stirred on her skin; he was right, as she'd known the day Tracy first came to her. If Tracy had denied talking to her, or claimed they'd talked about something else entirely, or that she'd touched inappropriately, she would have had no defense.

But there was something else they had to remember, too. "Rape happens just like that, too," she said.

He didn't hear her, didn't care. He was looking inward. "Why me?" he asked. "I can't be the first teacher who made a student mad."

"Will you keep teaching here at the middle school after this year?"

"I guess," he said bitterly, "that depends on how loud the whispers are."

She nodded. Knowing it was inadequate, still she repeated, "I'm sorry."

"I am, too," he said, and opened the classroom door. "See you," he threw over his shoulder, and left.

Mariah stared after him, all her vulnerabilities stirred. *Why did this happen?* she had asked, and never gotten an answer.

She never would, and that scared her.

Why was she dating the one man who reminded her most of the frailty of her family and her inadequate ability to foresee with confidence the path of her life?

But even shaken as she was, Mariah knew she wouldn't call Connor to make an excuse.

CHAPTER TWELVE

"REMEMBER THE POLICE LADY who came to talk to our class?" Zofie told Connor. "She showed us all the stuff she had hanging from her belt." She leaped up, puffed out her belly and put her hands at her waist, looking stern, then plopped back onto the couch. "Do you have a belt like that?"

"Yeah, but I never wear it," Connor said. "I used to. I drove one of those marked cars you see with the lights on top and I gave tickets for speeding and arrested bad guys for stealing and I even talked to classes like yours. But now I drive a car you can't tell is a police car, and I don't wear a uniform anymore except for dress-up."

"Oh." Her brow furrowed. "How come?"

He glanced for guidance at Mariah, who had stuck her head out of the kitchen and was eavesdropping. She gave an almost imperceptible shrug indicating— he hoped—a "why not."

Connor answered, "I'm what's called plainclothes. Some people aren't very comfortable talking to a uniformed officer, and they're more comfortable with me in my sweatshirt and jeans. Also, they can't look out their window and think, Oh, no, a policeman is coming! I won't answer the door."

"That's sneaky," she marveled.

He grinned. "Yeah. It is."

Zofie was as easy to like as he'd expected. The kid was a wonder, not shy at all with adults, her gaze sometimes disconcertingly direct, her choked giggle infectious. He could tell she was smart from the kind of questions she asked, and from what Mariah said she was an athlete, too.

He admired Mariah even more as he got to know Zofie. Kids were supposed to struggle after divorce in a single parent household. There had to be hard feelings between Simon and Mariah; she'd hinted as much. Yet none of that had tarnished this pretty, energetic girl's bright smile or made her inquiring mind hesitate.

When Mariah called them to dinner, he stood and stretched, thinking how much he liked her apartment, too. Hers was rented, just like his, with the same bland carpet, countertops and kitchen and bathroom vinyl. White walls—her rental agreement probably said she couldn't paint or paper them, just as his did. God forbid a tenant put any permanent stamp on one of these apartments.

But while his still, after four years, looked as if he'd just moved in, hers looked like a home. Her books didn't sit unpacked in boxes, they crammed bookcases. Her couch overflowed with batik pillows in South Sea Island hues of blue and green and teal, colors she'd picked up in a hand-loomed wall hanging and a colored pencil drawing of a child playing in a dreamlike jungle setting. The refrigerator was covered with Zofie-artwork, her kid-size easel was squeezed into the corner of the dining nook, and big baskets of Lego and Barbie dolls fit comfortably under a coffee table that had once been a crate, he guessed.

His unrequited desire for a home was intensified by settling even for an evening into hers.

"You've given this place character," he said, nodding at the plants on a rack in front of the window, the pretty place mats and woven runner on the table, the colorful, casual bouquet in a celadon-green pitcher that sat on the bar dividing kitchen from eating area.

Zofie had a damn cute smile. Her mother's was beautiful.

"Thank you. Why don't you sit over here?" She set a basket of warm rolls on the table. "After Simon and I divided what we had... Well, I had to start over. Zofie and I like to shop, don't we, punkin?"

"Mommy likes 'tique stores. With old stuff," her daughter agreed. Her hand snaked toward the basket and snagged a roll.

Reappearing from the kitchen, Mariah placed a huge, stoneware bowl filled with a great-looking stir-fry on the round table and sat down, her movements contained and graceful. "Connor, help yourself."

"This looks wonderful," he said. "I eat out too often."

"You're not a cook?"

As he spooned cashews and chicken and a medley of vegetables onto his plate, he said, "Actually I kind of like to cook. I just don't do it often. Sometimes for my family. When you live alone, it's easier to nuke a frozen dinner or grab a burger on the way home."

"What's nuke?" Zofie asked, predictably.

"Microwave." Mariah's gaze was as direct and friendly as her first-grader's. "Where do you live?"

He told her about his apartment in a complex with a garden courtyard and wrought-iron balconies and a peekaboo view of the strait. "I'd shared before with other cops—with my brother Hugh for a year, until we decided we had to go our own ways before we killed each other." He bent his head and lowered his voice conspiratorially for Zofie's benefit. "Sometimes it's great having a brother or sister, but you don't want to share a room."

She nodded solemnly, her eyes wide.

"Anyway, I decided it was time I had my own place. I like the privacy but not the loneliness. I bought the basics of furniture, but I've never completely unpacked. I don't spend a lot of time there." Despite his matter-of-fact tone, he knew how sad that sounded.

"You need an interior designer," Mariah said briskly. "The right chair, the right lamp, a rug underfoot, colors that soothe..."

"Maybe you and Zofie could help me."

"We could shop for Decktiv McLean," Zoe said around a mouthful of biscuit.

Amused at the way she mangled "detective," he suggested, "Why don't you just call me Connor. If that's okay with your mom."

She smiled, bringing that quiet radiance to her face. "Why not?"

"I can call you Connor?" her daughter asked happily. "Like we're friends an' everything?"

He had the strangely pleasant sensation of his chest being squeezed. This kid could get to him. "I call you Zofie, don't I?"

"I call my friend Laura's mommy Shari," she told him. "But I don't know her daddy that good. All the grown-up men that I know are Mr. something. You're the only decktiv."

''Yeah, there aren't so many of us.'' He met Mariah's merry eyes and felt his heart lurch. Oh, he was falling in love, all right.

Sure you are. The sardonic comment seemed to be in Hugh's voice. *You're in love with mother, daughter, apartment and the simple, delicious dinner in front of you. Just think. A ready-made family and home. Exactly what you've been craving. Hey, bro. Snap it up.*

Ready-made, since he'd singlehandedly gotten rid of Mariah's hubby and Zofie's daddy.

He swore silently. Way to give himself credit. He was the cop who'd come to her house. That was all. He hadn't named Simon Stavig himself, and he'd investigated fairly.

The fact that he'd been stirred by Mariah's glorious hazel eyes from the first moment she opened the door and looked at him with friendly, puzzled inquiry had never influenced him.

He wanted to believe that.

''Would you like more?'' Mariah asked, jolting him from his submersion in dark self-doubts. ''There's plenty.''

''Thanks. Sure.''

Zofie, he noted, had neatly separated the stir-fry into piles of carrot, onion, green bean, celery and chicken. The cashews on her plate were gone. She was presently working on the chicken. The onion and celery had been squished by her fork into unappealing blobs that he expected would not be eaten. Mariah stole an occasional glance at her daughter's plate, but said nothing.

When she saw him looking, they shared a smile with their eyes more than their mouths, the kind of communication he'd seen and envied between John and Natalie.

The kind he'd never had, except perhaps for a crude form with his brothers, useful mainly when they were closing in on a perp or trying to score a touchdown in a pickup flag football game.

Mariah had baked an apple pie, too, that was still warm from the oven. She served it *à la mode,* and Connor thought he'd died and gone to heaven. Zofie ate only the ice cream.

Her mom excused her to take her ice cream out to watch TV.

"She won't eat pie?" he said incredulously.

Mariah sighed. "She thinks cooking makes the apples mushy."

"More for the rest of us." He gave her a hopeful look.

Her chuckle was as infectious as her daughter's. "Gosh, is there any chance you'd care for seconds?"

"How kind of you to ask. Why...yes. I do think I might be able to squeeze a second piece in."

They both laughed, quietly, as she served him and watched him dig in.

"You really like antiques, huh?"

"Oh, I wouldn't know a genuine Chippendale if it reached out and tripped me. I just like to look for pieces that please me. I can't afford them new," she added simply.

"Want to go shopping with me on Saturday?" he asked. "Help me pick out some bookcases?"

"You're serious." She studied him. "Why now, when you've been okay the way you are for four years?"

"I turned thirty—heck, thirty-one is threatening.

Maybe it's that.'' He scraped the plate for the last half a forkful. ''I don't know. I'm just tired of living like a twenty-year-old who still has a bedroom waiting at home.''

''Do you?''

''Do I what?''

''Have a bedroom at home?''

He gave a grunt of laughter. ''Hell, no! My mother lives in a studio apartment. Which, she announced baldly, she chose so no one would expect to sleep over.''

Her voice and expression went soft, concerned. ''You're kidding.''

''No, but you have to understand that Mom is also willing to stay over at John's anytime to take care of his kids, or help any of us in any way. She's just…brusque.'' That was one way to put it. He tried again, ''No nonsense. Values her private space. Which might be natural, if you'd raised three boys by yourself.''

''She lives here in Port Dare, then?''

''Mmm-hmm.'' He set down his fork and reached for her hand. ''I'd like you to meet her. And my brothers.''

Was it his imagination that she stiffened slightly?

''That would be nice someday.'' She gently withdrew her hand and stood. ''More coffee?''

''Thanks.'' He watched her retreat.

Okay. Too much, too fast. What the hell was wrong with him? Why this urgent need to push her? He'd never before felt this anxiety, this dissatisfaction with a casual dating relationship. They'd had dinner together twice, and he was ready for more.

Much more. The whole enchilada, he was beginning to think. The diamond ring in his pocket, the wait at the altar for the beautiful bride, his own child growing in his wife's womb.

He just knew they were right for each other, however illogical that certainty was considering she'd hated his guts as of a few weeks ago, and maybe for good reason.

Unfortunately she obviously *didn't* know.

He had to give her time, and motivation to fall in love.

If a man *could* make a woman fall in love, just because he desperately wanted her to. Nice trick, if he could pull it off.

"Zofie have a game Sunday?" Connor asked casually, after she had refilled their cups.

She set the pot down on a hot pad. "Yes, but Simon is taking her. We did a switch, and now this is his weekend. Sometimes I go to the game anyway, but this one is in Port Angeles, and..." She made a wry face. "I try to be noble sometimes. I figure he should sometimes get to be the real parent. You know? Once I'm there, she turns to me for comfort and answers. I wish I could see the game, but heaven knows there are plenty of them to go around."

"How about that shopping trip Saturday, then?" he asked. "And dinner?"

Her smile seemed entirely natural, if more reserved than some. "That sounds like fun."

Yes.

"You and Simon seem to get along pretty well where Zofie is concerned," he commented, lifting his coffee cup.

"Actually we do." She almost sounded surprised, and gave a small laugh at her own tone. "Well, in a

weird way. Believe me, I've worked at it, and I think
he has, too. We still have…hard feelings, and we do
fight, but out of her hearing. We've managed, miracle
of miracles, to leave Zofie out of it. I worry, but…''

From the scarred perspective of a cop, he said, ''If
only all divorced couples could do the same. You
wouldn't believe how little thought people give to
their traumatized children when they're battling. I remember one call where…'' He stopped and made a
rough sound in his throat. ''Never mind. You don't
want to hear ugly war stories.''

She looked at him with clear eyes. ''That depends
on whether it helps you to tell them.''

He half stood, kissed her cheek and sat back down.
''Thank you. Sometimes it does help, but not tonight.
My mouth was just running away with me.''

''I'm really not that sensitive.'' She held his gaze,
determination in hers. ''I don't want you feeling you
have to watch what you say with me.''

He held up his hand in a salute. ''Word of honor.''

She nibbled on her lower lip. ''I want to feel the
same way with you.''

Jolted, he set down the coffee cup he'd reached for.
''And you don't right now?''

He sensed how carefully she was holding herself,
her chin high. ''Saturday night, I had the impression
you left just because Simon called.''

Connor would have liked to deny her accusation,
but dishonesty wasn't his way.

''His call was the catalyst,'' he said carefully. ''It
reminded me of how much I fouled up your life, and
made me think what a bastard I am for taking advantage of that.''

Her forehead crinkled. ''Advantage?''

"You might still be married if I hadn't come to your door that night."

"If you hadn't, another police officer would have," she reminded him.

He made an impatient gesture. "Has it ever occurred to you that another police officer might have gone about the investigation differently and proved Simon innocent?"

She looked away briefly. "Of course it's occurred to me," she said in a stifled voice. "How could it not? But after watching you with Tracy, I don't believe it anymore."

He cleared his throat. "Thank you."

"That's all it was? You weren't bothered because Simon and I are friendly?"

"Of course not!" he said in astonishment. "He's her father. Three years ago, I'd have told you not to trust him alone with Zofie. Now..." Connor shrugged. "After all this time, it's hard to imagine him starting something. Maybe he draws the line at his own kid. Maybe he was innocent. I don't know. But he's her father, and you can't keep him from seeing her. I know you'll be talking to him, and he'll be here. I wish all divorced parents could handle it as well as you have."

"Now it's my turn to say thank you." She made a face, trying to smile. "I want to trust him now. But sometimes I'm still scared when..." She pressed her lips together, swallowed. In a low voice, she said, "I want to be creeping around his house, peeking in his windows when Zofie is there."

Connor nodded toward the living room. "You talk to her?"

"Are you kidding? She's the best prepared kid in

the state of Washington. Every time she comes home, I have to restrain myself from asking every word Daddy said, everything they did, where she slept, how Daddy touched her. Especially how Daddy touched her.'' Mariah looked at him, her eyes shimmering with the despair and fear of those lonely weekends. ''But I can't. Somehow I have to find a happy medium between leaving her unprotected and making her fearful.''

Again he took her hand. This time, she returned his clasp, her fingers achingly tight.

''It looks to me like you've done just that,'' he said, voice gruff.

''I don't know. Will I ever know?'' she begged.

''About how she comes out? Sure you will. You can already see the promise.''

''And what about him? Do I have to wonder forever?''

''He might reoffend.''

''Why hasn't he?'' Frustration and anger filled her voice. ''If he did it, if he needs to do things like that with little girls, how can he go years without?''

''I wish I could tell you.'' He shook his head. ''Maybe he has. Has he found friends for Zofie to play with when she's there?'' Seeing the appalled look on her face, Connor regretted mentioning the possibility. ''There might be neighborhood kids Zofie hasn't even met. Is he doing some volunteer work?''

Her mouth opened and closed. ''I don't know.''

''Maybe Lily was…an experiment. Maybe he horrified himself, and he's managed to suppress those kinds of impulses. There must be men out there who feel some sexual response to children but who don't act on it, or don't even acknowledge the feelings because they're so taboo. Simon could be basically a decent man who, just once, gave in to curiosity.''

''Is that possible?'' she asked.

''Sure it is.'' He sighed. ''I honestly don't know, Mariah. Does anybody totally understand a pedophile? Tell me this—was he ever sexually abused as a child, that you know of?''

''I don't... No. Wait.'' She frowned, thinking. ''There was a grandfather. He never said that he'd been a victim. Just that his paternal grandfather was the kind of dirty old man the kids in the family avoided whenever they could.''

''Would he have admitted it if he had been abused?''

Slowly she shook her head. ''I doubt it. He was—is—too macho.''

''The one common thread in the story of pedophiles is that they were abused themselves as children.''

''Yes, I know. I even told myself Simon couldn't be one because he wasn't...'' She gave a crooked, unhappy smile. ''But I'd forgotten. Maybe I didn't want to remember.''

''Is there a family member of his you could ask?''

She thought. ''Maybe. But does it matter now?''

''Probably not. It just might help settle the issue.'' He moved his shoulders. ''I don't know. Maybe what we need to do is quit flogging a dead horse, as long as Zofie is okay.''

Mariah gave a theatrical shudder. ''What an unpleasant metaphor.''

''Was it a metaphor?''

''Shall I give a lecture on similes, metaphors and analogies?''

"If it pleases you. I won't remember."

"Nobody ever does," she said gloomily.

"Now come on. Don't lie." He let a grin tug at his mouth. "You have to think about which is which, don't you?"

Her chin went up. "Certainly not!" The corners of her mouth crinkled. "Almost never." A full-blown smile was born. "Okay. Sometimes."

"Atta girl," Connor congratulated her.

"Which leads us from the point," she said severely.

"Yeah." His own smile died. "I'm thinking that you'd quit flogging this particular horse until I popped up in your life again."

She let out a small sigh. "I wish I could say yes. The truth is…sometimes. For days at a time, I might not think about what happened, or why Simon and I were divorced, or what he might do to—" she lowered her voice "—um, Zofie when he had her alone. But then, I'd wave goodbye to her, smiling like everything was just grand—" she demonstrated, this smile as bright and artificial as a theater marquee "—and then I'd shut the front door and have this massive panic attack. Did he? Would he? Why would he? I have wondered every wonder, thought every thought, ten million times. I can't stop. I want to. But I can't."

Pity grabbed at his throat, roughened his voice. "Sweetheart, she'll grow up. She'll be a feisty kid who'll look with grave astonishment at anyone who tries to take advantage of her. And before you know it, she'll be a self-confident teenager who won't take any crap. And then she'll be all grown-up, and you can—almost—quit worrying about her safety."

Although he'd seen the quick flare of astonishment when he called her "sweetheart," Mariah chose to let it pass. She gave him a smile that was a little better than her last attempts. "It's happening fast, isn't it?"

"That's the way it goes. One night, you tuck her into a crib, the next she's taking a driver's test."

"Now you *are* scaring me."

From the doorway to the living room, Zofie said, "You don't look scared."

"Actually I was kidding." Mariah held out an arm and her daughter naturally walked into the curve of her embrace. "Connor was telling me how you're going to be a teenager ready to be driving a car before I know it."

"I wish I could drive *now*," Zofie said, perfectly seriously. "'Cept I'm too short. I can't see where I'm going."

"You could sit on pillows," Connor suggested, straight-faced.

She wrinkled her small, impish nose at him. "But then I couldn't reach the pedal to make the car go."

"Or stop," her mother said. "Remember, you can stop, too."

Connor pretended to frown. "You're not going to make me give you a speeding ticket someday, are you?"

"I'll be a good driver," she declared.

"Uh-huh," her mother said. "You, kiddo, are reckless on your bike. *And* on the soccer field. Why should I trust you behind the wheel of a car?"

"'Cause you have to. Once I'm growed up, I have to know how to drive," she said logically. "'Sides, Daddy can teach me."

"Oh, don't play your father against me!" Mariah

tickled her daughter. *"Besides—"* she put emphasis on the first syllable "—he's scared, too. All parents are scared when their children are first learning to drive."

"Oh." Zofie considered it. "But you'll teach me anyway, right?"

"Probably," Mariah conceded, with another big hug. Her cheek was against her daughter's head, and only Connor saw her blink away tears.

The evening wound down after that. Mariah started Zofie getting ready for bed, while Connor insisted on clearing the table and loading the dishwasher. He said good-night to Zofie when she reappeared in the cutest damn pair of pajamas, flannel and oversize, decorated with comical chickens. Her face was pink from being scrubbed, her hair newly braided, and her manners excellent.

"Good night, Connor." She blushed a little more at having said his name. "Thank you for coming to dinner."

"Thank you for having me." He smiled. "Sleep tight."

"Mommy says that, too. 'Sleep tight, and don't let the bedbugs bite.'" Her brow furrowed. "My bed doesn't have any bugs."

"No bugs!" He pretended dismay. "Hey, when's your birthday? Not until April? Hmm. Wait, wait. Christmas is coming." He grinned. "I promise. Bugs for Christmas."

She went off to bed, cackling happily at his wit.

When Mariah returned, she was shaking her head and smiling. "My daughter says she likes my 'Decktiv.' You should be flattered."

"I *am* flattered." He smiled, slow and warm. "Your daughter is a total charmer."

"She is, isn't she? And smart, and sweet, and kind to everyone. And, oh, just being her mother scares me every day."

He snagged her into his arms. "I've heard John say the same thing about his two. It's the curse of loving someone so much."

"I know you're right." Her eyes sparkled with unshed tears. "Sometimes it just...gets to me."

His thumb caught the first tear to fall. "Hey," he said softly. "You're doing fine. You're doing great. It appears Simon is, too. I wish I hadn't scared you all over again."

"You didn't." She smiled through her tears. "Okay, that's a fib. But it wasn't just you. It's Tracy, too."

Connor nodded, one of his hands easing over her back, gently massaging, while the other cupped her cheek. "As a teacher, you're going to encounter this again, you know. It happens."

"It shouldn't."

"No, it shouldn't," he said flatly. "But it will."

Mariah blinked hard, sniffed and said, "We're doing it again. Talking about nothing but. Why don't you come and cuddle on the couch with me, and we'll talk about something completely trivial?"

Cuddling on the couch sounded good to him.

"Deal," he said. "As long as I can kiss you, too."

Her lashes swept down shyly and pink blossomed on her cheeks, but she also nodded. "That sounds nice."

"Nice," he said, "is only the beginning."

CHAPTER THIRTEEN

MOM WASN'T WORKING TONIGHT and hadn't said anything about going out. She was even making dinner, a tuna casserole Tracy hated. The smell drifted down the hall to Tracy's bedroom and made her nose wrinkle. But still, she liked it when she and Mom had dinner together, just the two of them.

They could talk. Tracy lay on her back on the bed, staring up at the ceiling decorated with glow-in-the-dark stars.

Maybe she'd even ask Mom about *him.* Tracy kept thinking about what the police officer had said, about how she'd never feel safe—never *be* safe—if she didn't do something. The whole idea of just looking across the table at her mother and saying, "Did you tell that guy he could have me?" scared her so bad, though. She didn't know if she could do it.

And what if the answer was, "Sure, why not? I figured you were old enough." What would she do then?

Even worse would be if Mom looked shocked and hurt and said, "What are you talking about?" Things would never be the same if she accused her own mother of something like that and was wrong. She felt hot one minute and then icy cold the next, even thinking about it.

No. She couldn't do it.

They could just have an evening like…like when Tracy was little and Mom made dinner more often. Mom would tell her about people who came into the bar and make her laugh. Tracy hadn't told her mother about the dumb requests kids had when they came to the school office, either. Picturing them laughing like they used to, Tracy hopped off her bed and headed for the kitchen where Mom was singing along with Madonna on *MTV*.

"What's for dinner?" Tracy asked, as if she didn't know.

Mom turned from the oven. "Tuna casserole. Don't make a face. I know you don't like it, but it's my best recipe, and I asked a friend from work to dinner."

Tracy's hopeful mood went bang! like a balloon that met a sharp fingernail.

"You mean, a guy," she said flatly.

She should have known. Mom hardly ever cooked anymore, instead of doing the microwave or order-in thing. Besides, just looking at her, Tracy could tell. Mom was all made-up, and her hair was bundled on her head in a way that looked casual but Tracy knew had taken her forever. She wore her favorite tight jeans, and heels instead of the fluffy pink scuffs she would have had on if no man was around.

"You don't have to say it like that." Mom was bustling, this cute ruffled apron tied around her waist. "Norm is nice. I know you'll like him."

Mom always said that when she was bringing a guy home. Every single time. Tracy didn't know if even she believed herself.

She was going on about how *Norm* was sensitive about this little bald spot he had on his head, like *that* made him nice, and how he'd been hanging around the bar every evening for weeks because he liked Mom.

Fear swelled in Tracy's chest from a first tiny nub to a huge, crushing thing.

"We're just friends…" Mom said.

"Sure," Tracy said rudely. Lashing out seemed to quiet the fear. "Like Jason was 'just a friend.' Two days before he moved in. *Friends* don't sleep in your bed. Do they?"

Mom faced her, eyes flashing. "What's so bad about my having a boyfriend? Why should I have to be a nun just because I'm a mother?"

"Because I hate all your *friends!*" Tracy yelled. Her hands knotted into fists. "Either I'm invisible, or else I have to hide from them!"

"What do you mean, 'hide from them'? Because they're trying to be friendly?" Mom came toward her, one hand out.

Tracy backed up so violently the table shuddered when she bumped it.

Her mother stopped, her nostrils flaring. "I don't know what they're teaching you at school to make you think every man who hugs you is trying something, but I've told you and told you that you're wrong. You hurt Jason's feelings. He and I might still be together if you'd just tried to be nice."

The hurt was a quick knife thrust. Tracy let all her pain sound in her voice. "You mean, let him feel me up? Walk into the bathroom even when he knew I was in the shower?"

"It was an accident!" Mom yelled back.

"It was not! He did it over and over! You just didn't want to admit it because you were jealous!"

Mom slapped her.

Tracy stood very still, feeling the sting.

"Oh God!" Mom clapped a hand to her mouth and then reached out for Tracy. "I'm so sorry!"

Tracy shook off her touch and shoved a chair so she could back away. "It's true."

"Honey, you're a pretty girl. If he…maybe flirted a little…" Mom was begging. She wanted an excuse.

"He grabbed my breasts."

Her mother pinched her mouth together. "I asked him to leave."

Tracy heard herself as if someone else was talking, a long way away. "I heard him. He's the one who got bored. You wanted him to stay. You never listened to me."

"You weren't scared of him, were you?" Mom was pleading, but almost immediately her voice changed, as she talked herself into believing what she'd wanted to believe all along. "You never said that. All you did was complain that he brushed your breast with his hand when he was reaching for a cereal bowl in the cupboard. That kind of thing happens all the time! I thought you were imagining things!"

Tracy started to shake. "What about that other guy you brought home? What about Eddie?"

Mom looked startled and mad at the same time. "What about him? He didn't even spend the night, for Pete's sake!"

"You mean, he didn't spend it with *you*."

In the silence that followed, Tracy couldn't breathe. She saw the expressions leapfrog across her mother's face: shock, guilt, anger, and then a stunning kind of pain.

"What do you mean?" Mom said quietly.

"You know what I mean!" she screamed, and ran past her mother and out of the kitchen.

"Tracy!" her mother yelled.

Just as she reached her bedroom, the doorbell rang. Tracy threw herself facedown on her bed and buried her sobs in her pillow. She heard the murmur of voices, and then her mother's footsteps and the sound of the bedroom door opening.

"Honey..."

She stiffened and clutched her pillow. "Go away!"

"We need to talk about this."

She drew a shuddering breath. "I don't want to talk about it."

Mom was quiet for a long time, but she didn't go away. At last she asked, in a low voice, "Why did you never say?"

Tracy shook her head violently.

"It wasn't that teacher at all, was it?"

Tracy's face convulsed in a silent wail she hid in her pillow.

"I didn't hear Eddie leave. I should have walked him out. I'd had a few drinks, and—" She stopped. "Honey..."

"Go have dinner with your *friend*." Tracy's voice was thick with tears. "He's out there, isn't he?"

"I can ask him to leave." Mom sounded defensive.

"I don't want to talk now."

She was silent for a minute. "All right," she agreed finally. "But we have to, you know."

Tracy didn't say anything.

The door hinges squeaked. Mom asked, "Can I bring you some dinner?"

Tracy only shook her head. Her stomach hurt so

much, she would only throw up if she ate. Especially if she ate her mother's gross casserole.

"Honey, I wish..." Mom's voice died away. She stood there for a moment without saying what she wished. Then she closed the door and went away.

Tracy thought about running away. She could take all the money out of Mom's purse tomorrow right before she left for work. Mom didn't usually look in Tracy's bedroom when she got home; she wouldn't even notice Tracy was gone. She could hitchhike to Seattle. Maybe look for her dad. Mom had said that's where he lived.

Her huge racking sobs slowed, as if her body was too exhausted to keep them up. Tracy began to feel almost numb, listening to first voices from the kitchen and finally laughter.

It was the sound of her mother laughing that made Tracy think dully about killing herself. Mom would find her slumped in the bathtub, blood everywhere. She'd be sorry then.

Tracy played with the pictures in her mind: with Mom finding her, the announcement at school, the funeral. Reluctantly, at last, she turned to the practicalities. Could she get her hands on a gun? That would be the fastest. You wouldn't even have to think. Just pull the trigger, and it would all be over in a booming second. Or she could just get a knife out of the kitchen drawer. But doing it that way would be harder. Wondering if she was brave enough to cut her own wrists, Tracy dropped into a heavy sleep.

ON WEDNESDAY, the long-lost Jason Haworth was pulled in on a warrant for a missed court appearance on an assault charge. Galvanized, Connor went straight to the jail.

A guard brought a sullen Haworth to an interrogation room. Lanky hair pulled into a ponytail, he wore the jail's white T-shirt and denim pants. Trouble on the hoof.

A resentful gaze swept Connor. "I don't know you," he said in faint surprise.

From his place behind the table, Connor said evenly, "No, I'm not interested in your drunk driving or bar fights."

Haworth pulled out a chair. "I was trying to get into treatment."

Uh-huh. His attorney was trying to get him into treatment. "Your honor," he would say, "my client realizes he has a drinking problem. Prison isn't the answer. Give him a chance to clean up his life in a thirty-day program." He'd have a treatment center prepared to accept Haworth. Chances were all too good that the judge, unhappily aware of the overcrowding at the jail and prisons, would say, "Fine."

Not Connor's problem. Not today.

"I'm here to talk about Tracy Mitchell." He watched Haworth carefully.

A blank stare was his reward. "Who?"

"Until a month ago, you lived with Sandy Mitchell. Tracy is her thirteen-year-old daughter."

"Oh." He slouched in his chair. "Tracy. Yeah, sure. That was her name. The kid. I remember her."

Big of you, Connor thought.

"Pretty girl." Connor made his tone musing.

The bastard shrugged. "Yeah, nice tits. So?"

"Mom didn't mind you getting a little on the side with her daughter, huh?"

He shoved his chair back and half rose in a quick, violent motion. "What are you talking about?"

"Tracy says she was raped."

Alarm exploded on his face. "I never touched that little bitch!"

"But you looked."

"Sure I looked!" He sat again, but on the edge of the chair, his hands braced on the table. "I mean, the kid is parading around in tank tops without a bra and shortie pajamas. Who wouldn't look? But that's all I did. Shit, she isn't even in high school!"

Connor couldn't shake him. Okay, Tracy had whined to her mother a few times that he'd bumped her or walked into the bathroom when she was naked, but he swore to God those were accidents.

"I may drink too much, but I don't screw little girls," was his final word.

To his regret, Connor believed Haworth. He would have enjoyed putting this son of a bitch behind bars, the only cure for a drinking problem like his.

"Will you agree to a DNA test?" he bluffed.

Haworth looked him in the eye without flinching. "Sure I will. I never touched her."

Connor nodded to the guard, who steered a still protesting prisoner back to his cell.

Tapping a pencil on the table, Connor gazed blindly at the scarred wall. So Tracy wasn't raped by her mother's last boyfriend, the one who'd left after a big fight. So who the hell had raped her?

And who was she protecting?

In a call to Mariah that evening, he asked again.

"I don't know," she said, "but I wish you'd find out. Tracy wasn't in school today. Why would she skip, when she'd already faced the worst of the talk?"

"She could just be sick," he suggested.

"Or have bad cramps. I know." She was silent for a moment. "Tracy has just been so...subdued since she came back. She seems to be quieter and quieter. As if she's fading away." Mariah sighed. "That sounds melodramatic. I'm sorry."

"Don't be." He stood in front of the window in his living room looking out at the courtyard. Wet leaves plastered the cobblestones and the bare branches of the trees dripped. His own frustration and discouragement sounded in his voice. "The last time I talked to her, I thought she was scared. But I got to tell you, Mariah, I'm running out of ideas. About all I can do is keep stopping by, make myself available in case she changes her mind."

Mariah was quiet for a moment. "Do you think it would be all right if *I* called tonight, just to be sure she's okay?"

"I don't know why not. You must contact students and parents at home sometimes."

"Yes, but not usually to find out why a kid has missed one whole day of school."

He said what he'd been thinking. "Tracy is a pow- derkeg."

"I think I have all the students' numbers here." Paper rustled. "Yes...no. Wait." More rustling, and then a triumphant, "Here it is."

"I could have given you her number," he said mildly.

"Is that ethical?" she asked, in a doubtful tone.

"Is it ethical for me to discuss her with you?" He rubbed the back of his neck. "I don't know. You tell me."

She apparently gave it some consideration, because after a pause she said stoutly, "I think it must be okay, as long as all of us only want to help her."

One corner of his mouth lifted in a crooked smile. "Keep our eye on the goal, huh?"

"Shouldn't we?" She sounded tart, as if he had criticized.

His smile deepened. "Yeah. That's my philosophy."

"Well, then…"

"Call. Just… Let me know if you reach her, okay?" His own uneasiness made him add, "Or if you can't."

She phoned back ten minutes later. "I talked to Tracy's mother. She said Tracy has a bug, that she's been throwing up all day."

Reading her tone, Connor said, "But you don't believe her."

"I don't know. For starters, why's Mrs. Mitchell home?"

"It's Tuesday. This can't be a big night at the bar."

Her voice lightened. "You think Monday and Tuesday are her regular days off?"

He hated to tell her. "Actually, Sunday and Monday are. But she's probably entitled to extras, just like anyone else."

Mariah sighed, her mind already having moved on. "She just sounded…too perky. You know? 'Oh, no, everything's fine. Poor Tracy just caught a bug.'" Dropping the mimicry, she continued, "I stumbled through some explanation of how I was just concerned because Tracy has missed a lot this semester and how I hope I'll see her tomorrow in class."

"Better to stumble than not take the step in the first place."

"The philosopher again."

"That's me."

"You must be working on ten other cases."

Involuntarily he turned to glance at the sheaf of notes he'd dropped on the breakfast bar. "Five active, a dozen others on the back burner."

"This isn't that big a town!"

"I handle a variety of crimes, remember, from child sexual abuse to rape, indecent exposure—unfortunately I have a goody right now, a fellow who strolls up to school bus stops and whips open his raincoat. Classic. I'm even checking out a stalker right now, because there's an implied sexual threat. I'm an all-around guy," he mocked himself.

"How will you catch the, um, exhibitionist?"

"Loiter around school bus stops in a raincoat, I guess." He grunted. "Sorry. Black humor. Only half-true. I have loitered in a discreetly parked car near bus stops every morning for the past week and a half. No cigar."

Her voice softened. "You don't often see people at their best, do you?" She giggled, then stifled it. "Oh, dear. I just realized…"

He had to grin. "That I might yet get to? When he opens his raincoat?"

She gave another choked giggle. "I'm so sorry!"

"Nah. If we can't laugh…"

He heard a voice in the background. Mariah briefly covered the phone and answered, whatever she said muffled. Then she came back. "Time to tuck Zofie into bed. Let me know if…well…"

"Yeah," he agreed laconically. "Mariah?"

Instead of sounding wary, she answered with warmth. "What?"

"When does Simon take Zofie?"

"Right after work on Friday."

"Any chance we could have dinner Friday night, too?" He held his breath. Damn it, he just had to push.

"You're not going to get sick of me?"

"I think about you all day," he said quietly. "Whenever something happens, I think, I can tell Mariah. Or I see a mom and child and start to turn, thinking, Mariah. I want to know what you'd say about an idea. I want to know why you clam up sometimes, why you became a teacher, why you so rarely mention your parents."

In the silence that followed, Connor thought, *Way to go. Tell her you've got it bad.*

"Because we're not that close. But mainly, because they didn't like Simon," she said unexpectedly. "I told you that. It made me mad. I never told them why we're divorced. I refuse to admit they were right."

"What?"

"That's why I don't often mention my parents."

"Ah."

"As for why I became a teacher, I guess I can tell you Friday night. If you really care."

He heard the roughness in his voice. "I care."

"Why me?" she asked. "I don't want it to be because you feel... I don't know. Responsible, maybe. The fact that I left Simon was not your fault."

Wasn't it? He gritted his teeth against the uncomfortable reminder. He had thought Simon Stavig was guilty as hell, and he'd tried to impress that on her. He'd wanted her to leave her husband. And she was trying to tell him he hadn't influenced her decision.

"Nice try," he said.

From her tone, it was clear that her chin had shot up. "What's that mean?"

"Different cop, you might have made different decisions."

"So that's it?" She sounded stunned, hurt. "That's why you're interested in me? Because—what? You owe me?"

"No." Now his voice grated. "My...sense of responsibility is why I *shouldn't* be seeing you."

"Then why are you?" she challenged.

Because I'm falling in love with you. I am in love with you.

"Let me count the ways," he said, almost lightly. "The way your forehead crinkles when you think, and your chin comes up belligerently when you're feeling defensive. Your expression when you look at Zofie. Your eyes, green with little flecks of gold. The pink that touches your cheeks when I embarrass you. Which, by the way, is easy to do," he added. "Your intelligence, your kindness, your sense of responsibility, your laugh. Your passion, and I mean both kinds. The sway of your hips and the swell of your breasts and the way your hair smells. Should I go on?"

"No." She swallowed. "That was...very romantic."

Damn. He couldn't tell whether she was genuinely moved, made uncomfortable by him coming on so strong, or amused at his idiocy.

''Thank you,'' he said, still in a tone that suggested he wasn't altogether serious.

Coward, he accused himself.

''So, what do you say to dinner?'' He gripped the cordless phone so hard the plastic creaked.

''Dinner will be nice,'' she said primly. ''I'll probably blush when I see you now, but then, apparently I do often.''

''It's cute,'' he assured her.

She chose to ignore the less than staggering compliment. ''Simon usually picks up Zofie about six. Shall we say seven?''

''Deal,'' he said. ''In the meantime, maybe I can catch Tracy when she gets home from school tomorrow.''

''I wish you would.'' This hesitation had a different quality. ''I just feel as if she's...fragile.''

He knew exactly what she meant. Fragile in an almost literal sense, as if the teenager would shatter at the wrong word.

Teenagers, unfortunately, had more options when they cracked emotionally than they did a hundred years ago. Despite the Port Dare PD's best efforts, a cornucopia of drugs were all too readily available. Teenage runaways no older than Tracy sold themselves to sailors on the streets of Bremerton and shot up heroin in derelict buildings in Seattle. Locally a fifteen-year-old high school freshman had killed herself with her daddy's gun just last spring.

Tracy had some powerful inner conflicts and no way acceptable to her to resolve them. That put her at serious risk.

"I'll see her tomorrow," he promised. "I hope you will, too."

"Okay. Good night, Connor."

"Good night," he murmured, and ended the call.

Tracy, he thought grimly, wasn't the only one having to deal with inner conflict.

The fact that I left Simon was not your fault.

Wasn't it? he asked himself again, and didn't like the answer.

CHAPTER FOURTEEN

SHE *WAS* CHICKEN. SHE WAS.

Tracy hated knowing she was too scared to kill herself or run away or do anything but sit here in class like a good little girl and then go home and lock the door and huddle inside, praying Mom didn't ask creepy Norm to move in.

Today, she'd already done her stint in the school office, writing late passes and calling on the intercom for students to come to the office when their parents arrived to pick them up. Now she was in Integrated Math 1, not listening to Mrs. Caproni drone on about graphing. But she *pretended* she was, too much a chicken to be open like Renee in the back row who slouched in her seat twirling strands of her hair and reading a comic book, the pages turning with an audible whisper every minute or so. No, Tracy held a pencil poised above the paper and followed the teacher with her gaze, even though her dark thoughts were about a million miles away.

She'd looked in Mom's medicine cabinet yester-day, knowing she took sleeping pills sometimes. The amber bottle sat there, half-full. Tracy counted the pills. Thirteen. Would she die if she took only thirteen? Or would she just puke them up? Or—worst of all—wake up some kind of…of vegetable? She could wait until Mom refilled the prescription, but that might be *months*. Mom didn't take them every night.

Tracy had actually gotten into the tub one night with the butcher knife from the kitchen and drawn the edge gently across the delicate blue vein in her wrist. But she was just...practicing, not really doing it. She didn't press, and the knife wasn't that sharp anyway. She felt the cold blade slip across her skin and imagined pushing harder, until blood trickled and then poured. But she could not do it. Her hand had been shaking when she set down the knife on the bath mat. She'd buried her face in her knees and cried.

She didn't want to die.

She just couldn't stand going on like this.

Lying to the policeman when he stopped by, which he kept doing. Avoiding Ms. Stavig's eyes, rushing out of her class so she couldn't stop Tracy and say something so kind she crumpled and admitted everything.

Every day Tracy went home more scared than the day before. The past two days, she'd made excuses or slipped away so she didn't have to walk with her friends and put on this big show of laughing and gossiping like nothing was wrong. Alone, she could walk fast, with her head down, and think about running away and how she'd find her dad, and he'd be so glad to see her and he'd tell her that he had been writing and calling all these years, but her mother never told her.

She'd almost made up her mind she *would* run away when last night she and Mom got into this screaming thing, and she yelled, "I hate you! I'm going to go find Dad!"

Mom yelled back, "Have fun visiting his grave, then!"

Tracy stared in shock.

Mom's expression changed. "I'm sorry. I found out just last week that your dad died six years ago. I should have told you..."

"You thought I wouldn't care?"

"No, I..." Mom closed her eyes for a moment. "I wanted to find out more. I hoped he might have some life insurance or have left something..."

Hurt and anger blinded Tracy. "He probably divorced you. Maybe I wasn't his kid at all. How do you know I am? You like having a man around, right? There were probably *lots* of men."

Mom slapped her.

"I hate you!" she screamed again, and ran to her bedroom.

Mom didn't follow her.

Usually, since Mom didn't go to bed until three in the morning, she didn't get up with Tracy. But this morning, she'd shuffled out of her bedroom in her bathrobe, her mascara smudged black around her eyes and foundation she hadn't washed off cracked and blotchy. Her hair was a rat's nest.

"Tracy," she said wearily. "I'm sorry I slapped you. You're just...pushing all my buttons these days. What's wrong with you?"

This great dark howl rose in her: *I'm scared. I'm so scared, Mommy.* She had to turn her face away so her mother couldn't see her expression.

She shrugged.

"Tracy, you are so hard to live with right now. I shouldn't lose my temper like that, but honest to God..."

Tracy set her cereal bowl in the sink and gave her mother an insolent glance. "You should have washed your makeup off last night. You look really bad."

Mom's hand involuntarily went to her face before she made a frustrated sound, like steam shooting from a vent, turned and stalked back to her bedroom.

Tracy hurried and gathered her books into her pack and left for school.

She did not want to go home. But she was ashamed to know that she did, too. Every time she thought about running away, she felt terror and this great wash of loneliness. Her mother loved her. Tracy knew she did. No one else in the world loved her. Mom was just drunk that night. She hadn't meant it. They were a team, the two of them, like Mom used to say.

But they weren't, because Mom always had to have some man there, too. And they were all awful. Tracy hated them. She'd been getting more and more scared these past years, as her body changed and they looked at her differently. She couldn't stand it anymore. The accidental brushes against her, the lingering leers, the sly insinuations, all leading up to the footsteps that paused for the longest time outside her bedroom door at night when Mom was at work.

If Mom brought Norm home now... The point of Tracy's pencil snapped off, as her hand tightened.

She could not stand it.

She had to do something. Dying should be the easiest, but it didn't seem to be.

The bell rang, and she stood with all the other students, shoving her binder and calculator back in her pack, her mind circling like a trapped animal revisiting every corner of a cage.

Kill myself... How? Run away... But where? How

to survive without doing…it. She wouldn't! No matter what. Talk to someone. Tell on Mom. No. Just go on… No! I can't, I can't! Maybe some friend's mom or dad would have a drug in the cabinet… But I don't know what will work. Aren't there shelters for teenagers? But somebody would send me home, I know they would. Talk to Ms. Stavig. No! Survive another night. Pray something, anything, happens. Pray Mom says, "I know what you feel. I'll keep you safe."

Tracy swiped at tears and went to her next class, like a good little girl.

FRIDAY NIGHT THEY LAUGHED, talked and ate pizza with a thick, yeasty crust, a rich sauce and piquant mix of cheese that stretched in rubbery strands and tasted divine. Then they went to a comical British movie where they whispered translations of the dense Yorkshire accents in each others' ears.

It felt natural to walk out of the theater hand in hand. Mariah momentarily panicked when Connor suggested going to his brother John's for dessert and coffee, but then decided defiantly that she had nothing to be nervous about.

"Why not?" she said. "If they really invited us this late."

"They're grown-ups," he assured her. "Sometimes they tuck the kids into bed and stay up until midnight."

Mariah laughed. "Okay. You can tell how often *I* stay up until midnight."

John McLean, the oldest brother and another member of the Port Dare Police Department, owned a shingled cottage in Old Town. Dwarfed by the Victorian on the corner, it was more charming because it was cosy.

Connor parked in the driveway and led her via a brick courtyard covered with an arbor to the back door, where he knocked.

The man who opened the door was instantly recognizable as Connor's brother, although his eyes were vivid blue instead of gray and his face plainer, more blunt-featured.

"Connor. Hey." He slapped his brother on the shoulder in greeting before turning an exceptionally sweet smile on Mariah. "You must be the famous Mariah Stavig. Come in."

"Famous?" she queried under her breath.

Connor pretended not to hear.

The moment she stepped into the back hall and saw the dining room and living room opening ahead, the ceilings gracefully high, the beautifully refinished woodwork and floors gleaming, she sighed with pleasure. "I've always wanted a house like this."

"A woman with taste," Connor's brother said with satisfaction.

The pretty, dark-haired woman who accepted the circle of his arm smiled. "I married him for his house. Can't you tell?"

Mariah laughed. "I'd certainly understand! Hi. I'm Mariah." She held out a hand, shaken all around.

Natalie McLean had baked an exquisite blueberry pie that she offered with coffee. They ended up in the living room, settled on deep couches and broad-armed chairs, the men's feet on the coffee table, eating and talking. The two women hit it off from the first, finding common ground in their jobs, friends, soccer and books.

"Why have we never met?" Natalie wondered. "It sounds like we know so many of the same people."

"Chance." Beginning to feel a little drowsy, but too contented to suggest leaving, Mariah found herself comfortably curled beneath Connor's arm, casually outstretched on the back of the couch. "Everything is chance."

John pounced on her half-frivolous explanation of life's vagaries. "Now, you don't really believe that, do you?"

They ended up having an amiable argument about how much a person could affect her fate, one Connor refereed with lazy amusement.

It was one o'clock before Connor and Mariah reluctantly left. "I had a wonderful time. Thank you," she said at the door.

Natalie kissed her on the cheek. "I'm so glad you came." She gave a sly glance at her brother-in-law. "Now we know why Connor has been mooning over you."

"I haven't been that bad," he protested halfheartedly.

"No, it's been very sweet," she told him.

He groaned and steered Mariah away from the doorstep. "With family like that..."

"Who needs enemies?" she suggested.

Laughter followed them into the night.

He tugged her close to his side. "Something like that."

How long had it been since she had walked hip-to-hip with a man? Tucked under his arm, she felt petite and feminine, conscious of his hard hip and thigh bumping her, of the scent of his aftershave, of his sheer size.

"You are very lucky," she told him, just a little breathlessly. "I'm green with envy."

"Do you have brothers or sisters?" He opened the passenger side door for her.

She regretted the moment when his arm dropped from her shoulders and he stepped back. "One brother, ten years older," Mariah said. "We were just too far apart in age, I think. He's an attorney in Portland. We see each other every couple of years, maybe."

"That's too bad." Connor closed the door after she was in. Getting in behind the wheel, he continued, "We did our share of fighting as kids, and Hugh and I sure as hell didn't like living together as adults, but we're all close. Hugh and John are my best friends."

"I can tell," Mariah said. "You *are* lucky."

His teeth flashed with a grin as he started the engine. "There you go. Chance again. If your mom had just gotten pregnant with you sooner, you and your brother could have been best buds."

"If Mom had gotten pregnant, it would have been with a different egg, and I wouldn't be me." She thought about that one. "Or something. If I *was* me, I'd be ten years older than you, and we probably wouldn't be here together now."

He hummed a few bars of mysterious music. "Chance again," he intoned in a deep, Hitchcockian voice.

"And you didn't even take my side in there," Mariah complained, then gave a broad yawn. "Oh! I'm sorry."

"Don't be." Connor reached out and squeezed her hand. "You've been up a lot of hours."

"Mmm," she agreed, sleepiness hitting her now,

in the dark car, as if the caffeine in the coffee had quit working from one second to the next. "I worked today. *You* worked today," she remembered. "Did you catch your flasher? You never said."

"No, but a mom called 911 to report me hanging around near a bus stop watching the kids. A squad car rolled up behind me to check me out."

"Oh, no!" Mariah pressed fingers to her mouth to try to stifle her giggle. "How embarrassing!"

"Yup. I had to explain myself. Fortunately our guy wasn't watching. He was busy exposing himself at a bus stop four blocks away."

"Oh, dear. But so close? Is he sticking to a neighborhood?"

"Yeah, he apparently is on foot. His, um, startled audience reports that he dashes off and disappears up someone's driveway or down an alley."

She couldn't help giggling again. "He's a walker."

With the help of a streetlight, she saw the wryness of his glance. "Thank you."

"You're welcome."

"Home sweet home," he observed a minute later, slowing to ease over a speed bump at the entrance to her condominium parking lot.

"Your brother's house looks a whole lot homier."

"Yeah, his place has spoiled me," Connor agreed. "Every time I spend the evening there, I wonder why I don't buy a house."

"Money?"

"I could afford it." He pulled into an empty slot in front of her building. "Just haven't acted yet. Maybe buying a house just for yourself isn't as much fun." Turning off the engine, he reached for his seat belt catch. "I'll walk you up. Make sure there are no bad guys lurking."

"In raincoats."

"Yeah, wouldn't want you shocked."

On her doorstep he waited while she unlocked, then kissed her gently, sensuously, a taste more than a demand. She had agonized over the eternal questions: *What if he wants to come in? Am I ready?* Mariah had shocked herself with the knowledge that she was. But tonight he didn't ask, and she was too sleepy to do more than stand passively, clutching the lapels of his coat and enjoy being kissed.

Her eyes were still closed when he lifted his head, turned her with a firm hand and gave her a nudge over the doorstep.

"Lock up. Sleep tight." He sounded rueful and faintly amused. "Noon tomorrow?"

"If you're not tired of me yet."

He might have said, "Never." Mariah wasn't sure, because he spoke so quietly at the same time as he was pulling the door shut, leaving him on one side and her on the other.

She went straight to bed and fell asleep reliving the kiss and smiling.

Never.

Ten o'clock was the latest she remembered sleeping since she was in college. She raced through breakfast, a shower and some housekeeping—just so Zofie, and perhaps Simon, wouldn't wonder what she'd done all weekend. At noon, she was ready, her heart lifting in anticipation when Connor rang the doorbell.

In faded jeans that fit his lean hips snugly and a sweatshirt that emphasized the bulk of his shoulders, he was incredibly sexy. Even his short-cut hair was rumpled today, as if it were taking a day off from the regimen of a cop.

"Good morning," she said shyly. "Or is it afternoon?"

"We'll split the difference." His gaze seemed to devour her. He kissed her briefly but thoroughly, sending her pulse racing. "You're bright-eyed today."

"In contrast to last night?"

"You looked like you needed tucking in," he said in a low rumble.

She wasn't quite confident enough to say, "Weren't you tempted to do it?" But something knowing in his eyes made her suspect he knew quite well what she was thinking.

A guide to antique stores listed twenty-three in Port Dare. Over a dozen were within a three-block radius in Old Town, where turn-of-the-century homes and carriage houses had been converted into retail space, their small-paned windows the perfect showplace for rows of bottles in pale purple and green and gold, their high-ceilinged rooms splendid for displaying huge armoires and long, heavy mahogany tables and cupboards full of old linens. Mariah loved prowling these stores, fingering beautifully refinished woods and holding glass up to the light and coveting antique quilts with thousands of tiny stitches.

"Will you be bored in half an hour?" she asked Connor, when they entered the first store, their footsteps loud on the painted boards of the front porch.

"I don't know. I've never been in one of these places," he admitted. "No, that's a lie. There was an antique store down on Fourth—I don't know if it's still there. Stacks of wrought-iron gates leaning against the stone wall in front?''

''It's still there,'' she assured him.

''They were robbed some years ago. My case.''

''Were antiques stolen? Or money?''

''Both, as I recall. Not the iron gates. Small stuff. I remember some carved ivory figures that we did find in a pawnshop. Worth a hell of a lot more than the thief ever guessed, I gathered.'' Inside the cluttered first room, he stopped at an elegant cherry tea table with spooled legs. ''Hey. Now that's pretty.''

''Mmm-hmm.'' Mariah winced at the price tag. ''Are we seriously looking for furniture for you?''

''Damn straight. I like this.'' He crouched to study the legs and underside of the dainty table.

''Do you have a place for one this small? It's not quite end-table size, too tall for a coffee table.''

''It's the perfect height to go under one of my windows.'' He straightened reluctantly. ''I suppose I shouldn't buy the first thing I see.''

''No, just remember what you really liked. The odds are, it'll still be here at the end of the day.''

They had a wonderful time discussing the purpose of peculiar objects, imagining life when women would have spent hours a day in front of the spinning wheel or on their feet feeding the enormous, elaborately decorated cast-iron cooking stoves. Connor studied old tools with interest, thumbed through books and expressed a preference for simple American furniture with clean lines, versus the more elaborate European imports.

He bought two glass-fronted bookcases for obscene amounts of money that Mariah enjoyed vicariously spending. They went back for the pretty little tea table and a gorgeous maple dresser with an attached beveled mirror. The store owners all promised to deliver.

"I didn't buy anything," she realized at the end of the day. They strolled up the sidewalk toward their starting point, where they'd left the car. Closed signs were starting to appear in windows, and the sidewalks were emptier than they'd been earlier. The gray sky was deepening into dusk.

"I think I bought enough for both of us," Connor said.

Mariah took his arm. "It was fun," she decided. "I got all the satisfaction and none of the pain. After all, it's not my checkbook."

"Hey, thanks." Connor poked her with his elbow. "You egged me on."

"Did not!"

"Did, too."

She poked him back. "Did not. I'm too cowardly to spend that much money, even if it's *not* mine."

Tacitly admitting defeat, he said with satisfaction, "Now I can unpack my books."

"Mmm-hmm," she agreed contentedly, slowing to look into a toy shop window at a wonderful train set, the tracks laid to wind through a cotton-batting wonderland of fir trees and tiny villages sparkling with Christmas lights.

"I always wanted one of those," Connor said, first going stock-still, then crowding close to the window to take in every detail, like a child with his nose pressed to the glass.

"If you have a son..." she suggested gently, watching the wonder on his face rather than the chugging train.

"Yeah." Clearly reluctant, he turned away from

the display, then stopped. "Hey! Maybe Evan would like one for Christmas."

"What kid wouldn't?" She trailed him into the toy shop and offered consultation when asked as he chose a beginning set.

"Once you get started," the clerk told him, "you can add a car or more tracks or accessories for a birthday or another holiday."

Connor and Mariah made it back to the car, both lugging heavy bagfuls of boxes containing railroad cars and tracks.

"An early start on Christmas shopping," Connor declared, as he opened the trunk and unloaded them both.

"I've been buying all fall."

"Yeah, but you're a woman. That's different."

"We plan ahead?" she said in amusement.

He grinned at her, making her heart skip a beat. "Something like that."

"Exactly why women should be running the world."

"What shall we do for dinner?" he asked as they got into the car. "You in the mood to gussy up and go out on the town? Or shall we stick to jeans and go for burgers or Chinese?"

Mariah grabbed for a little bit of courage and suggested, almost casually, "We could cook."

Hand outstretched to turn the key, Connor suddenly went very still, his narrowed gaze pinning her. "Are you sure you'd rather? I figure you have to cook every day."

Her smile was meant to be flirtatious and came closer to tremulous. "I thought *we'd* cook."

"Are you sure?" he asked again, voice husky.

Her minute amount of courage deserted her. "If you'd rather eat out…"

"No," he said. "I'd love to cook with you."

The rough moment was past. She could almost pretend they'd only been talking about dinner. As they drove to the grocery store, they discussed what to make, settling on chicken in an incredible—he claimed—orange sauce with her wild rice cooked in chicken stock with herbs. Asparagus looked good, they decided, browsing the produce section. Connor chose a white wine.

"Zofie and I baked cookies Thursday night. Two kinds," she told him, when he asked, "oatmeal raisin and peanut butter. Will that do for dessert?"

"Milk and cookies?" He nuzzled her cheek, brushing a kiss below her ear. "Are you kidding?"

He insisted on paying the total, but they companionably carried the groceries into her apartment and prepared their feast, pausing only a dozen times or so for slow kisses that made her guess dizzily that Connor already expected to stay.

Mariah dug in the back of her buffet for her good crystal, candlestick holders and a pair of elegant white tapers she'd saved for a rainy—or romantic—day. She lit them and then turned off the dining-room lights.

In the golden light of the candles she could almost imagine this wasn't really the table where she and Zofie ate every night, the six-year-old separating all her food into color categories.

When Mariah said so, Connor laughed. "I didn't like foods mixed together when I was a kid, either. Especially unfamiliar ones. Mom was always ripping out recipes for casseroles from the newspaper or the

back of a box and presenting it without warning. I'd
sit there wondering what that evil bit of green was.
'Eat,' she'd order.''

"I'm too tolerant," Mariah admitted. "Your
mother's way is probably best. You aren't picky anymore, are you?"

"I still like to know what's going in a dish."

She took a first bite of tender chicken. "This is
divine."

"And perfect with the rice." He smiled at her, the
flickering light accenting cheekbones and the strength
of his jaw, casting shadows that made him mysterious.

Mariah wondered if she looked any more exotic
without bare electric lighting.

As if he'd read her mind, he suddenly set down his
fork. "Do you know how beautiful you are?" he
asked, voice thickened. "You have the sexiest mouth
I've ever seen, and the most glorious eyes. Your eyes
were the first thing I noticed about you."

"They're just…hazel." She swallowed. "I always
wanted dark eyes, like Zofie's."

"Yours look like a forest floor with shafts of sunlight touching it." He took her hand, his thumb drawing patterns on the back. "Have you ever hiked up
in the Olympics? Back to places where moss creeps
across the ground and up the trunks of ancient trees?
Where the silence is so profound, you barely dare
breathe?"

She shook her head wordlessly.

"I'll take you and Zofie. This summer. I want to
see you there, with a band of sunshine lighting the
fire in your hair and bringing out the gold in your
eyes."

"That...would be fun," she whispered. "I've never hiked. I didn't know where to go."

He lifted her hand to his mouth, pressed a soft kiss on the back, and gently returned it to her. Taking a sip of wine, he seemed to make a deliberate effort to become a good guest again, rather than an ardent lover. His voice was only a little husky when he resumed talking, this time meditatively. "I grew up in the mountains. Hiking, climbing—I was sixteen when John and I went up Mount Olympus. Hugh was plenty steamed at being told he was too young to go."

"I'll bet."

"He talked someone into taking him the very next summer, when he was fifteen. Never let us forget he was the youngest to climb Olympus."

They both ate, but not as much as the dinner deserved. Conversation began and trailed off sporadically. Mariah was conscious only of his shadowed eyes, the curve of his mouth, the strength of his big hand fingering the delicate wineglass. She had never been so very aware of anyone before, had never made a decision like this—*I will make love with this man.* Simon had been her only lover, and their first time had just...happened. This was far more difficult, and yet she had no doubts.

Connor suddenly looked directly at her. His voice roughened. "Am I staying tonight, Mariah? Is it too soon for me to ask?"

"No...I mean, yes. I mean..." She gave up. Took a deep breath. "Please stay."

"Then," he pushed back his chair and stood, "I'm done eating. All I can think about is you."

Her heart leaped and tumbled, her pulse bouncing

in her ears and making her own voice sound far away to her. "I'm…not hungry, either."

He held out a hand; she took it and let him pull her to her feet. Then he framed her face with his hands and looked for a long time, his mouth curving. "Ah, Mariah," he murmured huskily, just before he kissed her.

CHAPTER FIFTEEN

HE STARTED GENTLE, seeking, his lips soft, touching her nowhere but here, with his mouth on hers and his hands lifting her face. She shivered and swayed, and abruptly the kiss deepened. His tongue probed her mouth, sliding over hers, and his hands dropped to her shoulders, then her back and hip as he pulled her tight against him.

Mariah had thought she might feel many things: pleasure in the closeness to another person, perhaps, or acute nervousness or a sweet unfurling of passion. What she had never expected was this sudden raw urgency, ignited by powerful thighs hard against hers, by the evidence of his arousal, by the skill of his touch. She wanted closer, she was desperate to feel his bare skin beneath her hands, his mouth on her breast, his weight pressing her down.

Connor nipped her neck. "I have wanted you," he said hoarsely, "from the minute you walked into the principal's office. I thought, It's her."

Her voice wasn't her own. "And all I could think about was your eyes on me. I could never forget your eyes." She kissed the hollow at the base of his throat.

A sound vibrated beneath her lips. "Sometimes I feel so damned guilty…"

"Don't!" She pressed a hand over his mouth. Her

breath came in small gasps. ''Not now. Please. Not now.''

He groaned and took her mouth in a long, drugging kiss. ''Not now,'' he whispered. ''You're right. Anytime but now.''

He blew out the candles. Then, without warning, he bent and lifted her into his arms. Letting out a cry, she wrapped her arms around his neck and held on as he maneuvered her through the doorway and started down the hall.

''Which room?''

''At the end.'' His neck was strong, the skin smooth and she loved the smell of sweat and aftershave and Connor. Mariah kissed his throat, felt him swallow, kissed him again.

Her bedroom was plainer than the rest of the apartment; Zofie's needs came first. Mariah had a moment of wanting to explain, forgotten when Connor lowered her to the bed. He hadn't even looked at her room. His eyes hadn't left hers. He knelt beside the bed and untied her sneakers, tossing them aside, the socks after them. Just his hands on her feet sent heat crashing though her. Then his fingers wrapped her ankles and gently massaged.

She moaned.

Connor rose to kick off his own shoes and socks before he joined her on the bed. Instead of kissing her, he began unbuttoning her blouse, taking his time, running a fingertip down the bare skin from one button to the next. Mariah held her breath and watched his face. She saw much the same wonder as when he looked at the magical train set, but more was there, too: tenderness and desire that made the silver-gray of his eyes molten.

After he spread her blouse wide, he flicked open the front catch of her bra. Murmuring his pleasure, he filled his hands with her breasts. The river of heat pouring through Mariah's veins pooled in her belly. She shivered and arched, pushing her hands under his sweatshirt to stroke bare skin. He groaned in turn and bent to take her breast in his mouth.

They said everything and nothing as they explored each other, shedding one article of clothing at a time. It was lovely and slow and infuriating, so that she was glad when he cracked first, suddenly pressing her back on the mattress, his mouth hot and demanding, his knee urging her thighs apart. She opened herself to him willingly, with no trepidation, no *thoughts* at all, only an intense waterfall of feelings.

There was a pause during which he swore under his breath and she heard the tearing of a package. He had come prepared, thank goodness. For all her vaunted ability to plan, she hadn't. Not about this.

One more kiss, a glimpse of his face, taut with wanting, eyes glittering, and he was pressing into her. The effort to go slowly cost him; he was shaking, his teeth gritted. But, oh, it felt exquisite, as unfamiliar as if it were her first time, and yet not so frightening. Her body adjusted, tightening when he tried to pull back.

The next time he filled her felt just as good. He moved faster, harder, deeper, until she was clutching on to him for dear life, meeting his every thrust, crying out for the completion that was a breath away.

It came in stunning waves that brought his name to her lips, a whisper, a paean. "Connor!"

He groaned, shuddered and joined her. "Mariah," he said against her neck. "Sweet Mariah."

Eventually he rolled off her, drawing her to his side. With her head pillowed on his shoulder, hearing the powerful beat of his heart, comforted by the steadiness of his breathing and the warmth of his body, she wondered briefly whether he would stay or decide soon that he should leave. But her eyelids were leaden, her relaxation so complete she couldn't have formed a sentence if fire had leaped through the bedroom door. She slept.

When she awakened it was dark and she had a jolting moment of disorientation because there was a heavy arm lying across her waist. Her nose was burrowed against his side. A man...

Remembering, she smiled against his skin. So as not to wake him, she carefully disentangled herself and slipped out of bed to go to the bathroom. Every light in the apartment was blazing. She turned them all off, pausing for barely a moment to look at the wasted food and dirty dishes spread over the dining-room table. Then she turned out that light, too, and made her way back to the bedroom.

Faint illumination from a street lamp outside fell through the cracks in the blinds. It wasn't enough to keep her from stumbling over a shoe and giving a muffled gasp on the way. Whether she'd woken him, or he had already been awake, she didn't know, only that his hands reached for her when she slipped into the bed. His mouth found hers as unerringly as if he could see her clearly.

Her body responded without hesitation. There was something deliciously intimate about making love in near-complete darkness, saying nothing, touch taking the place of other senses. They didn't play so long this time; instead, he entered her gently, and passion built in slow, pleasurable stages.

The words, *I love you*, rose to her lips, but she bit them back. Not love. A fling.

Wasn't it?

They climaxed together, Connor murmuring words that didn't include *I love you*. Irrationally, she wanted them.

The next time she awoke, morning-sunshine filtered through the blinds. Connor still slept beside her, the covers down around his waist, one forearm across his eyes as if he were resisting the intrusion of light.

She lay there looking her fill, savoring all the little details she hadn't seen last night in the first urgency, or in the dark. Even relaxed as he was, powerful muscles in his chest and arms and shoulders were well defined. He had dark, ridiculously long lashes that any girl would envy. His mouth was softer when he wasn't guarding his expression. Sexier, she thought, tempted to touch it.

The pronounced auburn to the fine hairs curling on his chest made her guess that, if he grew a beard, it would be a deep red. If he had children, would one of them be a carrot head? She pictured a small defiant Connor with freckles, clear gray eyes and flame-bright hair. Smiling, at last she stole from bed and went to take a shower.

He joined her, with predictable, if wickedly erotic, results. It was nearly eleven o'clock before they reached the kitchen to make breakfast.

"Let's clean up first," Connor suggested. "I can't leave you with this." He saw her glance at the clock and asked, "When does Zofie get home?"

She checked the schedule on the refrigerator and

relaxed. "Her game is at noon in Port Angeles, so there's no way they'll be here until one-thirty or so, later if they stop for lunch like they usually do."

The cleanup went fast. They sat at the breakfast bar afterward and ate toasted raisin-cinnamon bagels, talking languidly about very little. Around noon, Connor said reluctantly, "I should get going. I have laundry to do, and the usual weekend chores."

"I should do the same," she admitted. "This was a lovely weekend, Connor."

Eyes intent even if his mouth was smiling, he said, "It was just the beginning."

She actually felt the sting of tears. "I hope so."

"Count on it." He tugged her against him for a hard kiss. "Walk me out?"

"Of course." Mariah put on slippers and a sweater against the chill and stepped over the Sunday paper on her doorstep to stroll out to his car with him.

Connor pulled her into his arms again and growled, "Damn it, I don't want to go," before he kissed her with regret and sudden frustration and sensual promise. When she started to pull back at the sound of a car turning in behind them, his arms briefly tightened before he let her go.

"Mariah, I..." He looked past her, and his mouth clamped shut.

On a rush of fear, she turned, just in time to see Zofie, in her soccer clothes, tumble out of Simon's car and fling herself at her mother.

"I don't feel good, Mommy!" she wailed.

Simon, who had gotten out on the other side, stood frozen, staring over the car roof at Connor. It was the longest time before his anguished gaze swung to Mariah.

Whatever she had expected and feared, it was not this. *Please,* she thought, unable to look away from his wounded eyes. *Please let him be angry. Let me see anything but this terrible pain and bewilderment at my betrayal.*

CONNOR LOOKED AT THE MAN whose ex-wife he wanted and felt the greatest shame of his life.

He couldn't lie to himself. He was at least partially responsible for the breakup of their marriage, and see what a prize he was winning now for his role. What did that make him? he wondered in disgust.

What if he had been wrong about Simon? What if Simon Stavig had never touched little Lily? Connor hadn't been able to prove a damn thing; he hadn't been able to make an arrest. But Simon had been irrevocably damaged by the mere allegation. He'd lost his wife, his hometown, his job. His child, in a meaningful way.

What if I didn't try hard enough to find alternative explanations for Lily's abuse, just because I didn't like Simon Stavig? Connor asked himself, appalled.

Mariah turned her head and gazed blindly at him. "Just go," she said.

"I can't leave you," he argued in a low voice.

"Go!" she repeated fiercely. "We'll be fine."

Stavig still hadn't moved. He looked stunned and defeated.

Connor clenched his jaw and nodded. "I'll call," he told Mariah.

She didn't acknowledge him, maybe didn't hear him.

"Let's get your stuff out of the car," she was telling Zofie. "I'm so sorry you're sick. And you had to miss the game, didn't you?"

Connor went only as far as the entrance to the parking lot, where he pulled over. He watched the tableau in his driver's side mirror as Mariah opened the car door and took out a small pink suitcase. She and Stavig spoke briefly, tensely, and then he got in the car and backed out with screeching tires. He didn't even see Connor as his car passed, bursting out of the parking lot on two tires.

Connor watched until Mariah and Zofie went into the apartment. Then, feeling sick, he started home.

His beeper vibrated before he got that far. He returned the call irritably.

"I'm sorry to bother you on your day off, Detective McLean," a young officer told him. "I'm told you are working on a case involving a Tracy Mitchell."

"Yeah." The light turned green ahead of him. He didn't notice until the car behind him honked. Accelerating, he said, "Yeah, I am. What's up?"

"She apparently ran away yesterday. Her mother didn't notice until today. She says she thought Tracy was at a friend's when she went to work at four o'clock, and she didn't look in her daughter's bedroom when she got home in the middle of the night." His carefully dispassionate tone suggested what he thought of such carelessness. "This morning, the mother thought Tracy was sleeping in. When she did finally discover her missing, she called around to Tracy's friends before reporting her gone. Just an hour ago, a state patrolman picked her up on Highway 101 near Silverdale."

Connor cut to the chase. "Where is Tracy now?"

"She's at a receiving home. Um—" papers shuf-

JANICE KAY JOHNSON 263

fled in the background ''—the Farrells', 1936 Nis-
qually.''

"Got it," Connor said. "Thank you."

This might be the break he'd been waiting for. He
wished it had come at any other time.

Rachel Farrell was a woman in her fifties who had
been running a receiving home for teenagers since her
youngest had left for college ten years ago. She was
a gem, caring for troubled teens briefly until social
workers, family or the court decided where long term
placement would be. Her common sense, structure
and comforting hugs had been just what a hell of a
lot of kids had needed.

"Tracy?" she said, when she answered the door.
"She's sobbing in her room. One minute she wants
her mom. The next she screams, 'Don't call her!
Please don't call her!''' She shook her head. "I don't
know if she's ashamed or scared."

"Can I talk to her?"

"She knows you?"

"Yeah." He grimaced. "She probably ran away
because she's tired of evading my questions."

He knocked hard on the door. "Tracy? It's Detective McLean."

"Go away!" she yelled.

He winced. This wasn't his day.

"Tracy, we need to talk. We might as well start
now."

"I don't want to!" she wailed.

He paused, head bowed. How could he give her a
lecture about facing the unpalatable when he'd been
doing his damnedest to avoid personal responsibility?
But he knew what had to be right for her—just as he

knew what he had to do to settle the demands of his own conscience.

"Tracy," he said quietly, "you need to help us decide where you should go now. Will you do that? Or would you rather we decide for you, without understanding who hurt you or why?"

The silence stretched so long he was about to give up for now when he heard her say, in a small voice, "You can come in."

She was sitting up on one of two twin beds, a pillow clutched to her middle. Her face was a mess, wet and puffy, and her hair was wind-whipped and dirty. Nobody would have guessed her to be a pretty girl.

He nodded at the foot of the bed. "Can I sit down?"

She pressed her lips together and nodded.

He sat and then waited.

She squeezed the pillow and said explosively, "I have to go home!"

"Why?"

Tracy looked at him as if he were crazy. "Because Mom'll be freaked. I can't just…just not go home!"

"But you ran away," he pointed out logically.

"But that doesn't mean…" She stopped, apparently snared in her own confusion.

"It suggests something is wrong at home."

She stared defiantly at him from puffy eyes. "Maybe I just, like, wanted an adventure."

He waited patiently.

Her chin trembled first, then her mouth. Fat tears rolled down her cheeks. Suddenly she hunched and buried her face in the pillow. Her shoulders shook.

"Ah, Tracy." Damn it, he shouldn't touch her, but

he couldn't sit here and watch her shatter. He moved over and tentatively touched her shoulder.

She rolled toward him, burying her pillow and her head under the circle of his arm. He sat, awkwardly patting her back, while she cried out her sadness against his side.

HER GRIEF SANK INTO MISERY, and finally faded altogether into a kind of numbness. Still Tracy didn't move for the longest time. She felt...safe, as if she were a baby, swaddled in a blanket, conscious only of the heartbeat and warm encircling arm that were her security.

Weirdly, when she finally sniffed, wiped her face on the pillowcase and pushed herself upright, what she felt instead was old. Old and tired.

He was waiting, his face kind. Tracy wished suddenly, passionately, that he was her father.

"It was this guy my mother brought home." Somehow it wasn't so hard to say after all. "Eddie. I don't know his last name. She brought him home one night after work. They were both drunk. I think Mom, like, passed out."

The police officer nodded, his gaze steady. He seemed to know she wasn't done, because he waited some more. He was good at that.

"Mom always has boyfriends living with us. She won't listen when I tell her they're staring at me or barging into the bathroom when I'm in the shower or even...touching me. She says I'm imagining it."

"Are they all like that?" He asked carefully; she could tell what he was thinking. That she just didn't like her mother having boyfriends at all.

"No." She clutched the pillow again, even though

it was wet and probably snotty. It helped to hold something. "Not when I was little. And this guy who lived with her for a couple of months when I was in sixth grade was okay. But Jason was a creep! And the guy before him, too."

"And you told your mother."

"She thinks I'm just trying to get rid of them!" Even as wrung-out as Tracy was, it hurt to think about how her own mother wouldn't listen to her. Wouldn't defend her. Having a boyfriend was more important to her than her own daughter.

"Tell me about Eddie. Had you ever seen him before?"

She shook her head.

"Did you get a good look at his face? Will you be able to identify him?"

She nodded. "He turned on the light." That was almost the worst part, that he'd wanted to look, that he'd made *her* look. It would have been bad enough in the dark, but then at least she could have pretended he didn't have permission to be in her bedroom.

"Tracy." Detective McLean's voice and eyes both held a command. "Where was your mother while you were being raped?"

Tracy had to bite her lip savagely to dull the other kind of pain. "In her bedroom. Like I said, she passed out."

"Before that. Did you hear them arguing? Talking?"

The light wasn't the worst part. This was.

She didn't know if she could tell him until she actually heard herself speaking, her voice a small, dry husk of itself. "They yelled. She said she wasn't in the mood. And…and he said she'd asked him home, she owed him. She…she said he could have anything else he wanted. To…to go find Tracy. She said, '*She's* not sleepy.'"

"Had he seen you?"

She gave a tiny nod. "I had a movie on in the living room. I just had on some pajamas. Like, shortie ones. He…he kind of leered. You know?" She shuddered at the memory. "And so I said good night really fast and went into my bedroom and turned out the light and pretended I was asleep."

"So you think your mother offered you to him." It wasn't a question.

Her face crumpled. She hadn't thought she had any more tears in her, but she did. He held her again, while her body shook.

Eventually he had her tell him everything that had happened. She went through every word she'd overheard, then made herself put into words what that creep had done to her. The anger she saw on the policeman's face helped. Instead of making her feel worse, talking about it seemed to ease some tightness inside her.

"Tracy," Detective McLean said finally, "have you talked to your mother about this? Did you ask her whether she was suggesting this Eddie take you in her place?"

"She says she doesn't know what I'm talking about," Tracy said in a low voice. "She says she would never do anything like that. She tried to make me feel bad for even thinking it. But I heard her!"

"You know, I doubt very much that she actually meant any such thing," he said.

A tiny spark of hope she had never let die brightened.

"I suspect she thought he'd ask you for a drink or something to eat. It wasn't smart of her, but somebody drunk enough to pass out—and black out—isn't what you'd call smart."

She swallowed. "Then...can I go home?"

He shook his head, his brow furrowed regretfully. "The decision isn't totally mine, but I'm going to recommend you go into foster care for a little while, at least. Your mom has some problems she needs to work out before she can really take care of you. She's been putting you at risk by inviting men she didn't know that well to live in your home and then being gone at night, leaving you alone with them. Her drinking seems to be a problem. You should have been in counseling to help you deal with some of the feelings left by a rape. She needs to make changes so that you can feel safe at home."

Mostly what Tracy felt was this huge *relief*. She loved her mom. The idea of going to live with strangers was scary. But she'd told somebody, and other people would be helping her now. She didn't have to bottle it all up until she thought she might explode into a million tiny shreds of herself.

Her eyes damp with tears, she sniffed. "Okay."

After a short silence, he asked, "Was telling me so bad?"

Tracy shook her head. "I wanted to. You're really easy to talk to. It was hard not to tell you. But..."

"You love your mom. You didn't want anyone else to think bad things about her."

She gave a small nod.

"You know," he said, in an odd voice, as if he weren't totally sure of himself, "I'm thinking about not being a police officer anymore. I may go back to college for a master's degree so I can be a counselor for kids like you.''

"Really?" she said on a rising note. "Could I see you?''

Detective McLean shook his head. "It'll be too late for you. We'll find somebody great for you to see. No, I just wanted you to know that you helped me make up my mind.''

"I didn't know…''

"Yeah." He tapped her lightly on the arm with his knuckles. "It's a good thing, Tracy. Thank you.''

Totally confused now, she said, "You're welcome.''

He laughed in a friendly way and stood up. "I've got to write a report about you and contact DSHS. A social worker will come to talk to you, and she'll be the one to find you a foster home. But, listen—you call me if you're ever scared or need to talk or hate the decisions that are being made for you. Okay?''

She bit her lip and nodded. She thought maybe she really *could* call him. In fact, she wished…

"You don't take foster kids, do you?''

"Not right now. And since I'm not married and you're a young woman, I wouldn't be the best choice anyway.''

"But I trust you." She flushed. "You don't look at me like…you know.''

"Most men won't, Tracy." He was frowning again, but not as if he was mad at her. "Your mother doesn't have very good taste in boyfriends, I'm afraid. I guess you already knew that, huh?''

"I don't think she really likes them, either. I think

those jerks are, like, the only kind of guy she ever meets.''

"That may be. It also may be that they're the only kind of guy she thinks she deserves.'' He let that sink in. ''Some counseling might help your mom realize she's worth more. She's a pretty woman. She can do better.''

Tracy nodded and took a deep breath. ''Will you arrest him?''

"Oh, yeah.'' Something hard glinted in his eyes.

It made her fiercely glad. ''Thank you,'' she said. ''I mean...for everything.''

"You're welcome, too.'' His smile was *so* cool— sweet and gentle and friendly, as if he liked her. Looking at the closed door once he was gone, Tracy made a vow. She wouldn't fall in love, no matter what, until she met a guy like Detective McLean. He'd be, like, her *standard.*

A knock came on the door, and Mrs. Farrell came in. She had kind eyes, too. ''How are you, Tracy?''

Tracy gave her a twisted smile that kind of hurt and kind of felt good. ''I'm okay,'' she said. ''I will be.'' And she knew it was true.

ZOFIE SLEPT HEAVILY, her face flushed and damp tendrils of hair clinging to her sweaty forehead. Mariah sat by her bedside in the dim bedroom, too spent emotionally to slip out and do housework or read or watch TV or even seek her own bed to doze until Zofie woke, miserable again.

She dreaded the ringing of the telephone. Connor would call, but she didn't know what to tell him.

She'd known from the beginning that she shouldn't

date him, shouldn't fall in love with him. How had she thought it would end? she asked herself with a silent moan. She'd kidded herself that she was having a fling, that Simon need never know.

A woman having a fling didn't bring the man home to meet her daughter. Zofie was six years old; she had a big mouth. Sooner or later, she would have told her dad that Mommy was seeing this policeman named "Decktiv McLean, only he said I could call him Connor." Mariah could see now that she'd been *asking* for Simon to find out.

That horrified her most. Had she wanted to hurt Simon that badly? Subconsciously, was that part of Connor's attraction?

But she couldn't believe herself to be so cruel. No, she'd fallen in love with Connor despite their past, not because of it. She had to believe that if she were to salvage any self-esteem.

The question was, what did she do now?

She knew the answer and hated it.

She could not keep hurting Simon by rubbing Connor in his face. What she'd done to him was bad enough without this final insult.

It was best, anyway, she tried to tell herself. Look how she'd failed Simon, her love dying in the short course of their marriage. What was to say she'd be any more constant if she married Connor? Assuming, she thought with a wrench, he wanted any such thing.

Mariah buried her face in her hands. After this weekend, how could she tell Connor, *Sorry, made a mistake?*

How could she not?

Zofie liked him.

But Zofie loved her dad.

The little girl stirred, and Mariah straightened, hastily wiping her tears with her sleeve. But after a whimper, Zofie settled back into slumber. Very gently, Mariah smoothed the hair back from her small daughter's hot forehead.

Hadn't she told herself that she'd be content raising her daughter and working? That she wasn't meant to share her life with a man?

Apparently that, too, had been a lie.

Finally, stiffly, she stood and tiptoed out of the bedroom. It was only seven-thirty, but maybe she'd clean up the kitchen quickly and take a book to bed. The way she ached all over, it could be that she was coming down with a bug, too.

Sure, her inner voice jeered. *It's called a broken heart. Or was it an inflamed conscience?*

She was wiping the counter in the kitchen when the telephone rang. For a moment she hesitated, wanting badly to let it ring, to go shut herself in the bathroom so she didn't hear the message. She had a fleeting image of herself as a turtle, pulling into her shell. And then she thought, *Zofie.* The phone would wake her. Mariah snatched it up before it could ring again.

"Hello, Mariah," Connor said, in that calm, deep voice. "How's Zofie?"

"Not feeling very well." She kept her voice down and one eye on Zofie's bedroom door down the hall, left a few inches ajar. "She has a 101.6 fever."

"And couldn't play her game."

"They lost. One of her teammates called. They missed her in goal."

"I'm sorry," he said quietly.

She bit her lip. "Connor…"

"I'm sorry about more than Zofie. I shouldn't have…lingered this morning. I knew you weren't ready for Simon to find out."

"I don't think I was ever going to be ready," she admitted. "I should never have dated you, Connor. It was cruel of me."

Anger edged his voice. "I investigated your ex-husband over three years ago. I didn't arrest him. I wasn't the one to accuse him. He and I were not mortal enemies."

"He doesn't see it that way," she said wearily. "It wasn't a job for him, like it was for you. It was personal. Of course he hated you."

"If anybody here should have a problem, it's me. I have to bear some responsibility for your marriage breaking up." Sudden intensity crackled through the phone wires. "What if, with my attitude, I made you afraid Simon had molested that girl, and *he didn't do it?* Would you still be married?" He made a harsh sound. "I'm in love with a woman who might still be married if I hadn't taken a dislike to her husband. What does that make me?"

Shocked, she said, "Connor, I'm the one who made a marriage vow. I'm the one who left my husband. I did it after you were gone from our lives. Yes, you scared me. But I should have had faith in him, and I didn't. That's my fault."

"Is it?" he asked.

She sat still for a moment, replaying the conversation. "You love me?" she whispered.

"You hadn't noticed?"

"Maybe," she swallowed, "I was trying not to."

"Because you don't love me?"

"Because I don't want to," she said starkly.

He was silent for a long time, but she knew he was still there. "What are you trying to tell me?" he asked finally.

Every word scraped her throat. "I should never have started this."

"And now you're going to end it?" He sounded disbelieving.

Whatever she did, she hurt someone. Everyone. She deserved the pain. But Simon didn't, and Connor didn't.

"I don't know," she said softly. "I need to think."

Voice raw, Connor said, "I'm going to find out whether Simon did it. You need to know. I need to know."

She opened her mouth to say… *No.* Shocked, she sat slack jawed. *No?* she asked herself in utter incredulity.

No, I don't need to know. No, it isn't the point. Maybe it never was.

"I…" she whispered. Of course she wanted to know, because of Zofie. But not to understand her own choices.

"When I have answers," he said with quiet force, "we'll talk."

"I…" was all she could manage.

"I love you. I don't think you could have made love with me the way you did last night if you didn't feel the same. Don't throw what we have away because you doubt yourself."

"Yes," she said, shaken. "I'll think. You don't need to prove anything about Simon."

"Yeah," he said. "I think I do." His voice gentled. "Go take a hot bath. Get to bed yourself. You know Zofie will be up during the night. You take care of yourself, okay?" A quiet click ended the conversation.

She was left with hot tears pouring down her face and the terrible conviction that she had never really faced what had been wrong with her marriage.

CHAPTER SIXTEEN

"THANK YOU FOR SEEING ME, Mrs. Thalberg." Connor gingerly chose a dainty chintz-covered chair not scaled for him. Nothing in the living room was—the furniture was all feminine and upholstered in pastel colors. It suited the petite blond woman, elegantly dressed, who had let him in.

"I don't quite understand *why* you wanted to talk to me now," she said, sitting on the edge of the chair, her hands folded tensely in her lap.

"I don't like unresolved cases like your daughter's," Connor explained. "Sometimes when I'm able to look at them with a fresh eye, I find answers I didn't at the time." He paused. "Is your husband unable to join us?"

Her gaze shied from his. "I didn't tell you on the phone, but...we're divorced."

Connor's interest sharpened. "I'm sorry. I hope your problems had nothing to do with the stresses brought about by Lily's molestation."

"Oh, it's..." Her hands fluttered. "It's hard to say."

"Does he see Lily often? Would he be willing to speak to me, do you think?"

She still didn't quite want to look at him. "He's actually in California now. The Bay Area. It's been a year, and he hasn't seen Lily yet. He does pay child support, but… Well, she's very young to get shipped off like a parcel. He recognizes that.''

''Yes, that would be difficult.''

She met his eyes again, her chin lifting. ''What is it you want to know?''

''Will you tell me the story again to the best of your recollection?'' He forestalled her. ''I do have notes and my reports, but it's possible some memory has come back to you since then. I'm hoping to hear your perspective as if I never have before.''

She agreed, although the telling obviously distressed her.

Lily had squealed in pain when she stepped into a soapy bath. ''Down there hurts,'' she said. Ellen Thalberg's first thought was of a yeast infection, but Lily did go to day care, so of course her mother worried about hidden abuse. She asked questions. Lily was terrified, but she was too young to keep a secret for long. *He* said they were playing a game and did things to her, and had her touch him. She didn't want to say who, but finally she did: Zofie's daddy. That's when they called the police.

Connor led her through memories of where Lily had gone the week previous to her accusation. Mrs. Thalberg mentioned one other friend's house that wasn't in his report. He made a note to check it out.

He asked how Lily was doing, and was glad at least when her face brightened. ''You know, I think she's completely forgotten. She's doing wonderfully in school and has lots of friends. I'm…undoubtedly overprotective, but you can see why. I don't let her spend the night at other people's houses, and I like to know them before she goes over, and…'' She stopped with a sheepish smile. ''I'll probably be trying to guard her when she's eighteen. Maybe I'll become her dorm mother. Except I'm afraid they use students for resident hall advisors now, don't they?''

He smiled back at her. ''Yes, but you'll relax as the years go by. Trust me. She'll make you.''

She half laughed. ''Yes, I suppose she will.''

Seizing the moment when her defenses were lowered, Connor said straight out, ''Mrs. Thalberg, I'm going to ask you now to be honest with me. Have you, in the years since that incident, had any reason to suspect that her father might have touched Lily inappropriately?''

She stared at him openmouthed. ''Her father? Why…why…of course not!'' The last sounded forced. ''Don't be ridiculous! Would I let Lily visit him if I thought anything so…so horrible?''

''But in fact Lily hasn't visited him,'' Connor reminded her. ''Which did make me wonder.''

''I explained!''

''Yes, and very reasonably.'' He waited.

She clasped and unclasped her hands, moving restlessly, at last saying, ''What a terrible thing to suggest. No. The answer is *no*. I have never suspected Tom. I would never.''

''I'm sorry to have to ask,'' he said quietly. ''Unfortunately fathers do sometimes abuse their own children.''

Her nostrils flared. ''Zofie is the one you should worry about!''

''That has certainly been a concern of her mother's. But in fact, Mr. Stavig seems never to have reoffended, if he did molest Lily.''

''Of course he did! Lily said so.'' Her agitation increased to the point where she shot to her feet.

"Why would she name him if he didn't do it? Children don't make up things like that!"

"They do only if the truth is something too awful to face. They can reason, 'It couldn't have been my daddy. It had to be somebody else's.'"

"I'm going to ask you to leave now," she said frigidly. "Tom certainly has his flaws, but he would never, never do something like that to his own child. Please go."

He rose slowly, careful not to alarm her. "I'm sorry I upset you, Mrs. Thalberg. I'm very glad that Lily has made such a wonderful recovery. I'll be in touch if I learn anything you should know."

She quivered, torn between shame and indignation. "I know you didn't mean anything by your suggestion. I appreciate what you did for us."

His mouth twisted. "Not enough, I'm afraid."

"We couldn't have Lily testify in court."

"As I said at the time, a videotape would probably have been acceptable. But, given her age, her word alone would not have been enough to convict Mr. Stavig."

"No. I understand." She saw him out and shut the door very firmly behind him.

He heard the click of the lock and understood that he was not welcome to come back.

As Connor made the long drive back to Port Dare, he reviewed his week's activities without much satisfaction. The only good part had been arresting Eddie Page. The son of a bitch hadn't been cocky enough to continue as a regular at the Customs House where Tracy's mom worked, but he hadn't been hard to find. Connor didn't know when he'd enjoyed slapping cuffs on someone so much. Tracy was gaining in confidence by the day. He thought she was going to make a hell of a witness on the stand.

The rest of his week, though, had consisted of spinning his wheels. He'd interviewed Lily's preschool teacher, the parents in the other homes she'd visited in the couple of weeks before her mother's hysterical call to 911, and the Thalberg's pastor. None had painted a different picture than he'd seen at the time: the Thalbergs were upright, likable people, genuinely concerned about their daughter's welfare. During her other play dates, Lily had not been alone with any man, that Connor could determine. Other parents from the preschool had not liked Simon Stavig. He was abrupt, often unfriendly, pushy about getting what he wanted for Zofie, uninterested in casual friendships.

And yet he had been willing to stay home from a planned golf game to watch over Zofie and her cute friend. Such uncharacteristic cooperation had bothered Connor then, and bothered him now.

As did Ellen Thalberg's discomfiture at every mention of her husband and Lily in the same breath. Maybe she didn't want to think anything so horrible about him, but he'd had the distinct impression that she had done so anyway.

Traffic was sparse this Thursday afternoon once he broke free of Bremerton and Silverdale. It left him free to brood about other avenues he could pursue.

Talk to Tom Thalberg—he'd get his address from DMV records. Track down this other family and find out—if it wasn't far too late—whether Lily had actually played there. He'd have liked to talk to Simon, but couldn't.

He felt an uncomfortable sense of urgency. Panic

crowded close behind him. He had trouble not looking over his shoulder constantly.

What if he found no answers? Could he live with
himself? Would Mariah give him a chance?

Could he blame her if she didn't?

He'd called twice this week. Both times they had
talked guardedly. Zofie was feeling better. Mariah had
only had to miss one day of school herself. He'd remembered to tell her about Tracy, who was back in
class by Tuesday, seeming freer, Mariah reported, as
if a nightmarish burden had been lifted from her. Mariah hadn't talked to Simon; he hadn't called, and she
hadn't known what to say so she hadn't phoned him.
Connor didn't suggest they get together, didn't ask
what she was thinking. She wasn't objecting to his
phone calls. That had to be enough for now.

Until he could settle the doubts that had clouded
both of their lives for the past three years.

Damn it, the truth was out there, he thought with
intense frustration. He just had to find it.

EXCEPT FOR MONDAY, MARIAH managed to appear
in front of her students every day that week with her
lessons planned, her eyes sharp and her hair well
groomed. She picked up Zofie from after-school care
on time, they were never out of milk in the morning,
and she stayed on top of the laundry so that Zofie
could wear her favorite jeans on Friday.

She amazed herself.

Inside, she was a mass of painful recollections and
raging arguments. She would be strolling through the
classroom, watching students bent over an assignment, her expression deliberately watchful but pleasant, while in her head she was reliving year two of

her marriage, or the fifth summer, or Zofie's birth, or the fights with her parents before the wedding.

She began to see that, childishly, she had gone through with the wedding in part *because* of their objections. In her fierce resentment at their opposition, she had drowned her own doubts.

That understanding took her further back yet, to see how hard she had worked for her parents' sakes to be a ''good girl,'' and how wistful she had sometimes been when others broke the rules or even their hearts. But her parents were different than her friends', older. Their expectations were so high, she had never quite felt loved just for herself. She had spent her childhood scrambling to measure up to the standard set by her brother, who seemed another adult to her.

She'd met Simon in college. Although she dated in high school, he was her first real love, Heathcliff and Darcy and Benedick all rolled up in one. Simon was dark and handsome and moody, a romantic hero, and he loved *her*.

So what if he was angry sometimes without her quite understanding why, or if he wouldn't explain himself when he missed a date or snubbed one of her friends or stalked out of her parents' house when her father questioned him about his ability to support a wife and family? He had been wounded at some time in his life. Literary heroes did brood and even sulk. He just wasn't the kind of man her parents wanted her to marry. *They* valued insincere charm over depth. She would follow her heart, she had told herself grandiloquently.

He made love to her with careless passion. He was always intense, and seldom patient. Now, after the one night with Connor, she could see that she had needed more tenderness, more seduction and less demand. Her body never responded quickly enough. After a while, it had quit responding at all.

The first year, she had still seen him as the wounded hero. By the second she had become frustrated with his moodiness. But she was pregnant with Zofie, and they were both excited, and she couldn't admit her parents had been right. He didn't abuse her; if he cut her off curtly, refused to talk about something important to her, or was inexplicably, even frighteningly angry when he walked in the door after work sometimes, she walled off her unease, her anger, her resentment. She was good at that, she realized. She'd spent a lifetime doing the same.

And he did love Zofie. Sometimes he hurt her with his moods, but mostly he tried for her sake as he didn't for Mariah's. By the time Detective Connor McLean knocked on her door that long-ago night, Mariah knew now, her marriage was a pretense. The sad part was, she had pretended not just to others, but to herself. She hadn't wanted to fail at marriage.

Good girls didn't. They had nice families.

It was Thursday night, when she was making dinner, that Mariah came to a conclusion of the sad story of her marriage. Her hands stilled over the cutting board, the knife suspended above the deep green broccoli, glistening with droplets.

Lily Thalberg's accusation had given Mariah an excuse. Yes, she'd feared for Zofie. But most of all, finally she had a reason she could accept to leave him.

She looked down blindly at the broccoli, seeing the past instead of her kitchen, her present.

Oh, how fiercely she had clung to that reason, refusing to admit to herself that she had chosen poorly, endured rudeness if not emotional abuse, *failed*. She'd rather think that she had a lack than that she had been wrong. And, of course, she could always fall back on her belief that she had left Simon for Zofie's sake.

Perhaps she even had, she thought, slowly setting down the knife. What she hadn't recognized was her enormous relief.

"Mommy? Is dinner ready?" Zofie asked, coming into the kitchen. She still wore her soccer shorts and practice jersey, but had shed the muddy socks, shin guards and cleated shoes at Mariah's insistence.

Mariah glanced back at the broccoli. "I still have to cook the vegetable."

"But I'm hungry!"

Another glance at the stove told her the noodles were ready to be drained and the stroganoff was done. "Oh, heck," she said. "Forget the broccoli. We can have some baby carrots."

Zofie, who only grudgingly ate anything green, brightened. "I'll set the table."

As Mariah put the broccoli away in the refrigerator and got out the bag of carrots, she felt…lighter. More at peace. Not sure yet what was right or wrong, but better for understanding what had never been.

TRACY TENTATIVELY APPROACHED Ms. Stavig the next day, after her class. Students were still brushing by when she paused in front of the teacher's desk.

"Um… Can I talk to you for a minute?"

Ms. Stavig smiled warmly. "Of course you can."

"I'm not living at home anymore." She took a deep breath. "The man who raped me was this guy my mother brought home. He's in jail now. My mom says she'll never bring any man home again, but Detective McLean and my social worker and my foster mom think we both need some time in counseling before I go home.''

''Yes, I'd heard.'' Ms. Stavig's eyes were as nice as the police officer's. ''Are you all right, Tracy? Is your foster mom good to you?''

Tracy hadn't wanted to cry, but her eyes felt wet when she pressed her lips together and nodded. She took a deep, steady breath. Rushing, she got out, ''I just wanted to say I'm sorry for lying to you.''

''I understand why you did,'' Ms. Stavig said simply. ''Just...don't do it again, okay?''

''Okay.'' Beginning to feel awkward, Tracy fidgeted. ''I guess that's all. I just... Well, I'm sorry.''

''Will you stop and talk to me every week or two?'' the teacher asked, sounding as if she meant it. ''So I know how things are going?''

Tears threatened again. Tracy nodded hard. ''Sure,'' she said, as she backed away. ''I promise.''

''And will you try out for the spring play?''

Tracy stopped, hope blooming. ''Do you think I might get a part?''

Her teacher's smile was a little mischievous. ''I think you have great dramatic potential.''

Amazed at being teased, she began to dream as she left the classroom. Maybe she'd get a lead role. Her mom would be in the audience—without *any* guy. It would be just the two of them, like it used to be. Only maybe Detective McLean would come, and of course Ms. Stavig would be in the wings.

Tracy did a dance step and bumped into a senior guy, who frowned.

''Hey, watch it!''

"Sorry!" she said, but she was still smiling when she whirled away.

CALLING SIMON WAS THE second hardest thing Mariah had ever done, right behind telling him she wanted a divorce.

"I suppose you're going to justify necking with my worst enemy right where you knew I'd see," he said bitterly.

It had hurt him. *She* had hurt him. Mariah bit her lip and said, "I didn't expect you for hours. You know that. I have never been cruel, Simon."

"Haven't you?" His tone raked her.

She let it pass, because he had some right to be angry.

"There are things I should have said to you years ago," she began. "Because I'm a mother, I've been afraid. But I don't think in my heart I ever really believed you molested Lily."

He gave a harsh laugh. "I can't believe I'm hearing this. It's a little goddamn late, Mariah. Do you expect me to be touched by the way you backed me?"

She didn't let his fury do more than shake her briefly. "I'm sorry." Her voice quavered, but she kept on. "I wasn't honest back then with either of us. I didn't want to admit that our marriage was over, that I didn't love you anymore."

"You didn't love me." His incredulity blistered the phone line. "It was that easy? You fell out of love, so you ditched me at the worst possible moment?"

Because she felt guilty, she reined in her hot response. "Easy? No, it wasn't easy," Mariah said quietly. "I worked at our marriage more than you did." She told him some home truths, then, which he didn't want to hear. He was no more ready now to admit that he was moody, angry, domineering, than he had been then.

Perhaps the worst part was when his voice became quieter and he said, "Why didn't you suggest counseling? Why didn't you confront me?"

"You always brushed me off. I think," she admitted, "I was afraid of you."

"I never hurt you! Not once!"

"You didn't hit me," she corrected him. "You hurt me in small ways every day, when you didn't think my opinion was worth hearing, when what I wanted or needed didn't matter, when you didn't care about my day or my mood or my beliefs. I think to you women are second-class citizens, and I refuse to live as one."

His string of obscenities didn't shock her; they made it easier to finish.

"The way I met Connor McLean had nothing to do with our past, and our relationship has nothing to do with you. I'll try to keep the two of you from coming face-to-face if it's important to you, but I am not responsible for how you react to his presence in my life. I will not let your moods dictate my choices." She was shaking, sick to her stomach, but exhilarated, too. "That's all I have to say, Simon."

When he began to rant, she quietly hung up the telephone. It was done.

SATURDAY NIGHT, when Connor called, Mariah asked if he might like to come to Zofie's final soccer game on Sunday.

There was a brief silence. Finally, sounding cautious, he said, "Simon isn't coming?"

"No." She thought about saying more, but she wanted to see his face when she told him about her confrontation with Simon.

"I'll be there," he said. "What time?"

Miraculously for a final game in November, the day was clear if very cold. Following a stream of others, she and Zofie crunched across frozen grass to their field, where girls a year older were just finishing a game. Mariah couldn't help noticing how much more aggressive they already were than the younger girls.

They chose an empty place along the sideline, and Zofie started to shrug out of her coat.

Mariah stopped her. "Leave it on while you warm up."

"But I'm not cold. Besides, no one else is wearing one." Zofie tossed the coat at her mother and trotted off with her ball under her arm. In a reluctant concession, she did wear leggings and a turtleneck under her team shorts and jersey.

"Damn, it's cold," Connor said from just beside her.

Mariah jumped six inches. "You scared me!"

"I'm sorry." He looked genuinely surprised. "I didn't sneak up."

"I just didn't expect you so early," she defended herself.

"I was looking forward to seeing you."

Her cheeks might have turned pink if they weren't so cold. Her nose, of course, already *was* pink, she felt sure. So much for her careful makeup and the time she'd spent on her hair, tucked under a fleece hat.

He looked formidably masculine in a parka over

jeans and boots. He did wear gloves but not a hat; none of the fathers had, she saw in an automatic glance along the sidelines. Hats, like umbrellas, were sissy-wear.

She smiled a little at the idea that this big, tough cop harbored some vanity. To hide her amusement, she asked, "How was your week? Did you catch your flasher?"

"Actually I did. I'd mapped his, uh, appearances, as well as the directions he took in his escapes. One block was clearly central. I checked out residents and found a few likely candidates—men who lived alone, and one in his forties who lived with his elderly mom. We staked out those houses, and he presented himself in a raincoat at eight-fifteen on the nose Friday morning. Not a pretty sight when we cuffed him." Connor gave a sly grin, "I think the cold got to him."

She gave a choked giggle. It shouldn't be funny, but was anyway. "Oh, dear."

On the field, the referee's whistle blasted, one team leaped up and down in triumph, and after a brief lineup where the two teams slapped hands, everyone streamed off the field. Parents closed lawn chairs, held out coats to their daughters and departed in visible relief.

The parents of Zofie's teammates took their places, calling greetings to each other and last-minute reminders to the girls running onto the field. Mariah returned a few greetings, but she'd chosen a spot well down the field in hopes she and Connor would be alone.

"Oh, Zofie's playing goalie first half. She's going to freeze since she's not running around," Mariah said, worried.

"That depends on how good her team's defense is. She may be busy."

"It'll be easy to slip with the ground frozen."

"And land in very cold slush," he agreed, eyeing the areas in front of each goal where the ground had been torn up over the season, turning into mud holes that had frozen last night and were partially thawed by trampling feet today.

Mariah sighed. "Zofie loves mud."

He laughed. "A true athlete."

They watched the brief warm-up in silence, Mariah hugging herself against the cold and wriggling her toes inside her athletic shoes and thick socks. She hadn't expected to feel so…awkward. So unsure how to start. Somehow, in her imagination it had seemed easy. She would cast herself into Connor's arms and declare, "I'm free!" and he would say, "Marry me."

Instead, not looking at her, Connor asked, "How was your week?"

"Actually, not bad," she said in surprise. "Better than I expected."

Now he did turn his head, his expression wary. "Why is that?"

"I did a lot of thinking," Mariah confessed. "And I nerved myself to talk to Simon yesterday."

The two teams lined up for the kickoff, the substitutes running off. Zofie was doing jumping jacks under her goal. The ref blew his whistle, and the action headed toward the opposite goal.

Connor watched her. "Did he succeed in making you feel guilty? Or was he gentleman enough not to try?"

"Are you kidding? His anger just made it easier for me to get out what I had to say."

Connor's eyes had narrowed, which didn't disguise his intense curiosity. "Which was? Or isn't it any of my business?"

"It's your business." She automatically followed the action as an opposing player broke away with the ball and raced toward Zofie. When a defender kicked the ball out of bounds, Mariah stole a shy glance at Connor. "At least, I think it's your business," she added. "Do you want it to be?"

"I want," he said succinctly.

"Oh."

The other team threw the ball in, and a player kicked it high toward the goal. Zofie leaped and caught it. Along with the entire sideline, Mariah and Connor cheered.

Once Zofie had cleared the ball, Mariah said, "I told Simon things I should have said years ago." Her voice didn't tremble this time, as she told Connor what she'd said.

Connor came as close to gaping as she'd ever seen this very self-possessed man do. "What if he wasn't guilty? What if I *am* responsible for breaking the two of you up?"

"But you see," she said with quiet composure, "that's what I spent the week discovering. You didn't. I was relieved when you presented me with an excuse to leave him." She told him some of what she'd thought that week and understood about herself. "I'm ashamed," she said, "to have been so stupid. Everybody always told me I was so mature. Then what do I do but marry a guy because my parents don't want me to!"

Connor watched her with a furrow between his eyebrows. "Was it really that simple?"

"No." She smiled wryly. "Of course not. He was handsome, passionate, charming when he wanted to be. He seemed exciting in a way the boy-next-door types I'd always dated weren't. I just didn't let myself see his darker side."

Connor made a sound in his throat. "I expected...I don't know what. Anything but you announcing cheerfully that you told your ex-husband off."

"Do I sound cheerful?"

He gave a grunt of laughter. "Perky as a cheerleader."

"How repulsive." She made a face, then had to laugh herself. "I guess I *feel* cheerful. I'm sad, too, and I'll always feel guilty for leaving him the way I did, but I'm also proud of myself for facing the truth and finally being honest with him."

Expression achingly tender, he lifted his hands to run his knuckles down her cheek. "I'm proud of you, too."

"Thank you," she whispered.

A burst of cheering from the other sidelines and groans from hers made her swing around guiltily. Zofie had somehow let a ball go by.

"Oh, no!" Mariah said. "I didn't even see it."

"Good try!" the coach called.

Zofie kicked the ball out to the referee and her teammates circled by to pat her on the back.

Once the game was underway again, Connor said meditatively, "I've spent the week reopening my investigation."

"Of Simon?" So he'd meant it. Their surroundings blurred, the yells fading, until all that existed was the two of them. Mariah was surprised by the clutch of apprehension she felt. "Did you...learn anything?"

He swung to face her, his shoulders hunched, his hands shoved in his pockets. Under a wooden expression, a cauldron of emotions simmered. "Not a damn thing. I promised you and myself I'd find an answer, and I haven't."

"How could you, so long after the fact?" she asked quietly.

"Cold cases can be cracked. People remember things, let secrets slip."

"But not this time."

He shook his head. "I know why I was so convinced Simon was guilty. I've got to tell you, Mariah, I still think he did it. But I have some doubts I didn't have then, too."

He told her about the divorce of Lily's parents and the refusal of each to talk about the reasons for it. "I only talked to him on the phone, since he lives in San Jose, but he was evasive about why he isn't seeing his daughter, and Mrs. Thalberg was damn uncomfortable at the idea of Lily visiting him. I didn't pick up those vibes, then. I have to wonder if something happened."

"So it might not have been Simon at all." She couldn't understand her lack of reaction. Shouldn't she be...relieved? Hopeful? Angry? *Something?* "It might have been Lily's dad."

"It's a possibility." He was frowning. "Oh, hell, call a spade a spade. It's a wild guess. I'm reading between the lines." His hunch deepened. "Damn it, Mariah, my best guess is still Simon."

"Oh." She bit her lip. "Then why..."

"Hasn't he gone for Zofie? I don't know. Like I said before, maybe Lily was an experiment. Maybe he horrified himself. For all we know, he's in counseling to deal with the urges. Maybe coming so close to getting arrested scared him.''

"What you're telling me,'' she said, staring blindly at the bunched girls on the field, "is that we'll never know.''

He drew a harsh breath. "I made you a promise I can't keep.''

Mariah faced him. "I told you not to make it. That I didn't need those answers.''

His eyes searched hers. "The questions are going to hang over us.''

"Not if we don't let them.'' She vaguely heard the whistle blow, knew the girls were running off the field. "You are not responsible for the end of my marriage.''

He swore softly, the muscles in his jaw knotting. "I want to believe that.''

She sought desperately for a way to convince him, for words she hadn't said before, and failed. "Whether you and I…see each other or not, I am divorced. No matter what you learned about Simon, he and I would not have gotten back together. You did your job. That's all. Now you've done more than your job.''

His gloved hands gripped hers. "Trying to prove him guilty.''

"But if he'd been innocent, you would have told me that, too.'' She felt the gentle smile curve her mouth. "You're an honest man, Connor McLean.''

Zofie rushed up. "Where's my coat, Mom? I'm cold!''

Connor released Mariah's hands. Flustered, she turned and found where she'd set the jacket. "Hurry. Put it on.''

"I let them score!" Zofie said unhappily.

"Goalies can't stop every kick," Connor told her. "That's why you have teammates. How many did you stop?"

"I don't know." Her face cleared some. "A bunch. But I *could* have gotten that one."

"Then next time you will." He cuffed her lightly on the shoulder. "You're six years old, kiddo. Give yourself a learning curve."

She studied him. "You were holding Mommy's hands."

"Yeah. I was."

"You aren't going to get married or something, are you?"

"Maybe." He contemplated her, although his gaze flicked to Mariah to catch her reaction. "Would you mind?"

Her forehead puckered as she thought. "No, I guess not," she decided. "You're nice."

"Thank you," he said gravely.

"I gotta eat my snack. I'm playing forward second half," she announced. "I bet *I* can score."

"I know you can." He grinned at her. "You go get 'em, Zofie."

"Okay." She sounded matter-of-fact until she gave a cheeky grin. "You watch me."

He laughed, Mariah hugged her, and Zofie hurried off to join her teammates.

She was barely gone when Mariah felt Connor's gaze.

"Are we going to see each other?" he asked. "Is that what you have in mind?"

She turned uncertainly. "Isn't that what you wanted?"

He gave a crooked smile in which she read vulnerability that stunned her.

"It's a start," he said. "But…no. That's not what I had in mind."

"Then…then what?" Her voice had sank to a whisper.

He took her hands again, and she wished desperately that they weren't wearing gloves, that she could feel his heat and strength.

"I have in mind marrying you," he said simply. "If—when—you'll have me."

"We haven't known each other that long." It had to be the prissy "good girl" speaking.

"I told you." He still smiled, with tenderness and aching vulnerability. "I knew right away, that day in Mrs. Patterson's office. I took me a while to recognize what I felt, but somewhere inside I knew. From that day forth."

Her fingers tightened on his. "Me, too. Maybe not from that day. I think it was when you came to see me in my classroom."

His eyes darkened. "You love me?"

She gave a small nod.

"Is it too soon to give me an answer?"

"Can you live with our past?" She watched him carefully. "Simon will be around, you know. He's Zofie's father. We can't…pretend he doesn't exist."

"If you don't blame me, I can live with it." His voice was low, rough. "God, I love you."

Drowning in his gaze, she whispered, "I wish we were somewhere else."

"Me, too." He cleared his throat. "I think they're playing again."

"Are they?" She didn't look away.

"Zofie might score."

"Mmm-hmm."

"Sweetheart..." A muscle jumped in his cheek. "There's something else you need to know."

Mariah drew back slightly. "What's that?"

"I've decided to quit my job. I'd like to try counseling kids and teenagers. It'll mean going to graduate school at UW. Money might be tight for a couple of years."

"Oh, Connor." Tears stung her eyes and despite their surroundings she hugged him. "I think that's a wonderful idea."

"I can commute. Come home weekends."

"Better yet, I can get a job in Seattle," she said firmly. "Maybe get a leave of absence from the school district, if we think we'll want to come home to Port Dare when you're done."

"You're really going to marry me." He sounded dazed.

She smiled up at him, letting him see the sparkle of tears in her eyes. "If you'll have me."

"Oh, yeah," he said, his laconic tone belied by the potent emotions in his eyes. "I'll have you."

She tried to sound casual and failed. "I've arranged for my daughter to go home with a friend after the game. Did I mention that?"

"No. You didn't."

"Just in case we wanted some time to ourselves."

"Which we do," he said in the gritty voice that told her what he felt. And wanted.

Happiness filled her chest, making her buoyant. "I had better watch *some* of the game first."

He laid a heavy arm over her shoulders and turned her to face the field. "I can be patient."

They looked just in time to see Zofie break away from a defender and kick a powerful line drive that shot past the goalie and into a corner of the goal. Arms in the air, screaming in delight, she grinned at her mom and Connor, who both laughed and waved back.

"Zofie makes it easy to be patient." Eyes smiling, Connor watched Mariah's daughter run down the field. "I'm a lucky man."

"Yes, you are." Mariah leaned contentedly against him. "But I'm feeling pretty lucky myself right now."

Welcome to Montana

BIG SKY COUNTRY

Home of the Rocky Mountains,
Yellowstone National Park,
slow-moving glaciers and
the spectacular Going
to the Sun Highway.

Set against this unforgettable background,
Harlequin Superromance introduces the
Maxwells of Montana—a family that's
lived and ranched here for generations.

You won't want to miss this brand-new trilogy—
three exciting romances by three of
your favorite authors.

MARRIED IN MONTANA
by Lynnette Kent on sale August 2001

A MONTANA FAMILY
by Roxanne Rustand on sale September 2001

MY MONTANA HOME
by Ellen James on sale October 2001

Available wherever Harlequin books are sold.

HARLEQUIN®
Makes any time special ®

Visit us at www.eHarlequin.com   HSRBSC

Harlequin truly does make any time special. . . . This year we are celebrating weddings in style!

A Walk Down the Aisle WEDDING CELEBRATION

To help us celebrate, we want you to tell us how wearing the Harlequin wedding gown will make your wedding day special. As the grand prize, Harlequin will offer one lucky bride the chance to **"Walk Down the Aisle"** in the Harlequin wedding gown!

There's more...

For her honeymoon, she and her groom will spend five nights at the **Hyatt Regency Maui.** As part of this five-night honeymoon at the hotel renowned for its romantic attractions, the couple will enjoy a candlelit dinner for two in Swan Court, a sunset sail on the hotel's catamaran, and duet spa treatments.

Maui • Molokai • Lanai

To enter, please write, in, 250 words or less, how wearing the Harlequin wedding gown will make your wedding day special. The entry will be judged based on its emotionally compelling nature, its originality and creativity, and its sincerity. This contest is open to Canadian and U.S. residents only and to those who are 18 years of age and older. There is no purchase necessary to enter. Void where prohibited. See further contest rules attached. Please send your entry to:

Walk Down the Aisle Contest

In Canada	In U.S.A.
P.O. Box 637	P.O. Box 9076
Fort Erie, Ontario	3010 Walden Ave.
L2A 5X3	Buffalo, NY 14269-9076

You can also enter by visiting www.eHarlequin.com
Win the Harlequin wedding gown and the vacation of a lifetime!
The deadline for entries is October 1, 2001.

HARLEQUIN®
Makes any time special ®

PHWDACONT

HARLEQUIN WALK DOWN THE AISLE TO MAUI CONTEST 1197
OFFICIAL RULES
NO PURCHASE NECESSARY TO ENTER

To enter, follow directions published in the offer to which you are responding. Contest begins April 2, 2001, and ends on October 1, 2001. Method of entry may vary. Mailed entries must be postmarked by October 1, 2001, and received by October 8, 2001.

Contest entry may be, at times, presented via the Internet, but will be restricted solely to residents of certain geographic areas that are disclosed on the Web site. To enter via the Internet, if permissible, access the Harlequin Web site (www.eHarlequin.com) and follow the directions displayed online. Online entries must be received by 11:59 p.m. E.S.T. on October 1, 2001.

In lieu of submitting an entry online, enter by mail by hand-printing (or typing) on an 8½" x 11" plain piece of paper, your name, address (including zip code), Contest number/name and in 250 words or fewer, why winning a Harlequin wedding dress would make your wedding day special. Mail via first-class mail to: Harlequin Walk Down the Aisle Contest 1197, (in the U.S.) P.O. Box 9076, 3010 Walden Avenue, Buffalo, NY 14269-9076, (in Canada) P.O. Box 637, Fort Erie, Ontario L2A 5X3, Canada.

Limit one entry per person, household address and e-mail address. Online and/or mailed entries received from persons residing in geographic areas in which Internet entry is not permissible will be disqualified.

Contests will be judged by a panel of members of the Harlequin editorial, marketing and public relations staff based on the following criteria:

- Originality and Creativity—50%
- Emotionally Compelling—25%
- Sincerity—25%

In the event of a tie, duplicate prizes will be awarded. Decisions of the judges are final.

All entries become the property of Torstar Corp. and will not be returned. No responsibility is assumed for lost, late, illegible, incomplete, inaccurate, nondelivered or misdirected mail, for technical, hardware or software failures of any kind, lost or unavailable network connections, or failed, incomplete, garbled or delayed computer transmission or any human error which may occur in the receipt or processing of the entries in this Contest.

Contest open only to residents of the U.S. (except Puerto Rico) and Canada, who are 18 years of age or older, and is void wherever prohibited by law; all applicable laws and regulations apply. Any litigation within the Province of Quebec respecting the conduct or organization of a publicity contest may be submitted to the Régie des alcools, des courses et des jeux for a ruling. Any litigation respecting the awarding of a prize may be submitted to the Régie des alcools, des courses et des jeux only for the purpose of helping the parties reach a settlement. Employees and immediate family members of Torstar Corp. and D. L. Blair, Inc., their affiliates, subsidiaries and all other agencies, entities and persons connected with the use, marketing or conduct of this Contest are not eligible to enter. Taxes on prizes are the sole responsibility of winners. Acceptance of any prize offered constitutes permission to use winner's name, photograph or other likeness for the purposes of advertising, trade and promotion on behalf of Torstar Corp., its affiliates and subsidiaries without further compensation to the winner, unless prohibited by law.

Winners will be determined no later than November 15, 2001, and will be notified by mail. Winners will be required to sign and return an Affidavit of Eligibility form within 15 days after winner notification. Noncompliance within that time period may result in disqualification and an alternative winner may be selected. Winners of trip must execute a Release of Liability prior to ticketing and must possess required travel documents (e.g. passport, photo ID) where applicable. Trip must be completed by November 2002. No substitution of prize permitted by winner. Torstar Corp. and D. L. Blair, Inc., their parents, affiliates, and subsidiaries are not responsible for errors in printing or electronic presentation of Contest, entries and/or game pieces. In the event of printing or other errors which may result in unintended prize values or duplication of prizes, all affected game pieces or entries shall be null and void. If for any reason the Internet portion of the Contest is not capable of running as planned, including infection by computer virus, bugs, tampering, unauthorized intervention, fraud, technical failures, or any other causes beyond the control of Torstar Corp. which corrupt or affect the administration, secrecy, fairness, integrity or proper conduct of the Contest, Torstar Corp. reserves the right, at its sole discretion, to disqualify any individual who tampers with the entry process and to cancel, terminate, modify or suspend the Contest or the Internet portion thereof. In the event of a dispute regarding an online entry, the entry will be deemed submitted by the authorized holder of the e-mail account submitted at the time of entry. Authorized account holder is defined as the natural person who is assigned to an e-mail address by an Internet access provider, online service provider or other organization that is responsible for arranging e-mail address for the domain associated with the submitted e-mail address. **Purchase or acceptance of a product offer does not improve your chances of winning.**

Prizes: (1) Grand Prize—A Harlequin wedding dress (approximate retail value: $3,500) and a 5-night/6-day honeymoon trip to Maui, HI, including round-trip air transportation provided by Maui Visitors Bureau from Los Angeles International Airport (winner is responsible for transportation to and from Los Angeles International Airport) and a Harlequin Romance Package, including hotel accomodations (double occupancy) at the Hyatt Regency Maui Resort and Spa, dinner for (2) two at Swan Court, a sunset sail on Kiele V and a spa treatment for the winner (approximate retail value: $4,000); (5) Five runner-up prizes of a $1000 gift certificate to selected retail outlets to be determined by Sponsor (retail value $1000 ea.). Prizes consist of only those items listed as part of the prize. Limit one prize per person. All prizes are valued in U.S. currency.

For a list of winners (available after December 17, 2001) send a self-addressed, stamped envelope to: Harlequin Walk Down the Aisle Contest 1197 Winners, P.O. Box 4200 Blair, NE 68009-4200 or you may access the www.eHarlequin.com Web site through January 15, 2002.

Contest sponsored by Torstar Corp., P.O. Box 9042, Buffalo, NY 14269-9042, U.S.A.

PHWDACONT2

In October 2001
Look for this
New York Times bestselling author

BARBARA DELINSKY

in

Bronze Mystique

The only men in Sasha's life lived between the covers
of her bestselling romances. She wrote about passionate,
loving heroes, but no such man existed...til Doug Donohue
rescued Sasha the night her motorcycle crashed.

AND award-winning Harlequin Intrigue author

GAYLE WILSON

in

Secrets in Silence

This fantastic 2-in-1 collection will be on sale October 2001.

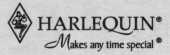

HARLEQUIN®

Makes any time special ®

COMING SOON...

AN EXCITING
OPPORTUNITY TO SAVE
ON THE PURCHASE OF
HARLEQUIN AND
SILHOUETTE BOOKS!

*DETAILS TO FOLLOW
IN OCTOBER 2001!*

YOU WON'T WANT TO MISS IT!

PHQ401